W9-BKN-103

Praise for Jessica Clare

Titles by Jessica Clare

Wyoming Cowboys

ALL I WANT FOR CHRISTMAS IS A COWBOY
THE COWBOY AND HIS BABY
A COWBOY UNDER THE MISTLETOE
THE COWBOY MEETS HIS MATCH
HER CHRISTMAS COWBOY

Roughneck Billionaires

DIRTY MONEY
DIRTY SCOUNDREL
DIRTY BASTARD

The Billionaire Boys Club

STRANDED WITH A BILLIONAIRE
BEAUTY AND THE BILLIONAIRE
THE WRONG BILLIONAIRE'S BED
ONCE UPON A BILLIONAIRE
ROMANCING THE BILLIONAIRE
ONE NIGHT WITH A BILLIONAIRE
HIS ROYAL PRINCESS
BEAUTY AND THE BILLIONAIRE: THE WEDDING

Billionaires and Bridesmaids

THE BILLIONAIRE AND THE VIRGIN
THE TAMING OF THE BILLIONAIRE
THE BILLIONAIRE TAKES A BRIDE
THE BILLIONAIRE'S FAVORITE MISTAKE
BILLIONAIRE ON THE LOOSE

The Bluebonnet Novels

THE GIRL'S GUIDE TO (MAN)HUNTING
THE CARE AND FEEDING OF AN ALPHA MALE
THE EXPERT'S GUIDE TO DRIVING A MAN WILD
THE VIRGIN'S GUIDE TO MISBEHAVING
THE BILLIONAIRE OF BLUEBONNET

Her *Christmas* Cowboy

JESSICA CLARE

JOVE
New York

A JOVE BOOK
Published by Berkley
An imprint of Penguin Random House LLC
penguinrandomhouse.com

Copyright © 2020 by Jessica Clare
Excerpt from *The Bachelor Cowboy* copyright © 2020 by Jessica Clare
Penguin Random House supports copyright. Copyright fuels creativity, encourages
diverse voices, promotes free speech, and creates a vibrant culture. Thank you for buying
an authorized edition of this book and for complying with copyright laws by not
reproducing, scanning, or distributing any part of it in any form without permission.
You are supporting writers and allowing Penguin Random House to continue to
publish books for every reader.

A JOVE BOOK, BERKLEY, and the BERKLEY & B colophon
are registered trademarks of Penguin Random House LLC.

ISBN: 9780593102008

First Edition: October 2020

Printed in the United States of America
1 3 5 7 9 10 8 6 4 2

Cover art: cowboy image © Tony Demin / Getty Images;
barn image © Stephen Simpson / Getty Images
Cover design by Sarah Oberrender
Book design by George Towne

*For LaDonna, Michele, Alicia, and Caye,
who keep me sane on a daily basis,
even when there are deadlines!*

CHAPTER ONE

Caleb Watson had skills. Or so he told himself. He could rope a runaway heifer from horseback. He could keep even the most ornery herd of cattle together. He could ease a breech calf out of its mother without blinking an eye. He could saddle a horse faster than anyone he knew.

And that was just ranching skills. Back when he lived in Alaska, he could track anything, fix a snowmobile out in the field, survive on his own for weeks. Heck, he could even build a log cabin and have it fully functioning within a short time frame.

He was strong. Capable. Self-sufficient.

He stared at the front doors to the elementary school and wished he could stop sweating.

Because Caleb had to acknowledge that when it came to skills in the field or in ranching? He could handle himself with the best.

When it came to talking to people?

He was the worst.

The absolute worst.

His younger brother, Jack, was smooth. He could talk the pants off anyone and always managed to get his way with a smile and a wink. His older brother, Hank, wasn't much of a talker, but he was still better than Caleb.

It wasn't just that Caleb clammed up around people. His mind went blank and nothing would come forward. It was like the moment he was required to give a response, he forgot what words were.

Most of the time he didn't care. He was a cowboy; the cattle didn't mind if he was silent. His brothers didn't mind if he wasn't chatty.

But around women, it was a problem.

Caleb had never had a girlfriend, which was fine when you were a kid, or when you lived in the remote wilds of interior Alaska and you might not see a single woman for months on end. Here in the town of Painted Barrel, Wyoming, though, he felt his lack of social skills acutely.

Very, very acutely.

Because Caleb was in love.

Just thinking about love made him reach into his pocket and pull out his bandanna, then mop the sweat on his brow. Love was difficult even in the best of times, but when you had trouble speaking to women, it was pure torture. Every time he got up the nerve to talk to a woman, it ended up badly.

There was that time he had a crush on a cute bar waitress back in Alaska, who he'd blushed and stammered over until she thought he was mentally disabled.

There was a girl who had worked at her uncle's game-processing shop one summer. He'd gone there often all summer, just to try to speak to her. He'd paid other hunters through the nose for their kills so he'd have some excuse to go into the shop. When he did finally get up the nerve to talk to the object of his affection, she thought he was creepy because he was "killing so many animals" and wanted nothing to do with him. There were a few other passing women he'd managed to somehow insult without meaning to.

And now there was Ms. Amy Mckinney, an elementary school teacher in Painted Barrel.

The moment he'd looked at her, he'd been in love. Amy had a gorgeous face and a smoking-hot body, but what he liked most about her was that she was kind. Or she seemed to be. He hadn't quite got the nerve up to talk to her himself. He'd been around when she was talking to other people, though.

He might have showed up at several PTA volunteer meetings just to hear her talk. Not that he had kids. He didn't usually volunteer, either. But he showed up anyhow, because he'd get to watch her from afar, see her smile at others as she talked easily, and wish he wasn't such a damned idiot the moment he talked to a pretty woman.

Today, though, he had a reason to talk to her. His brother Hank was out in one of the distant pastures, and Caleb had been cleaning out the barn when Hank had texted and said his horse was limping and he was going to walk it in, but that meant he'd be a few hours, and Hank's daughter, Libby, needed to be picked up from school.

Caleb had immediately volunteered to go pick her up. It was the perfect opportunity. Ms. Mckinney was Libby's teacher, so he'd stroll into class, tip his hat at her, announce he was there to pick up Libby, and strike up a conversation.

His mind went blank. A conversation about . . . what? What did one talk about to a schoolteacher? The weather? Everyone was going to talk about the weather to her. He needed to say something different. Maybe something about school? But he didn't have children that went to the school . . . Maybe Christmas?

Surely he'd think of something. He wiped his brow, sucked in a deep breath, and got out of the truck.

Most of the parents at Painted Barrel Elementary knew the drill for picking up their children. Amy took the ones who rode the bus out to the bus driver's line in front of the principal's office. She quickly counted heads and then went back to her classroom, where the other children waited with their backpacks for their parents to pick them up. Picking up their child in the classroom instead of outside was better all around, Amy figured, since it was cold and snowy in Wyoming in December, and little hands needed gloves, and those were the first things her students tended to lose.

Plus, it gave Amy a good chance to talk to the parents, to pass along notes about behavior, and to make sure everything was going well. With a small class of twelve students, she could do such a thing. It was one of the main reasons she'd moved out to Painted Barrel and accepted the low-paying teaching job instead of taking a far more lucrative one in a big city. She really wanted to connect with her students. She really wanted the opportunity to influence her kids and watch them grow. She wanted to be a teacher they remembered.

Plus, she was starting over—her life, her career, everything. What was better than starting over in all ways? She'd lived in bigger cities all her life. Now Amy just wanted to blend in to a tight-knit community and be part of things. Maybe being part of a community would help choke down that black hole of loneliness inside her that had just gotten bigger and bigger since her divorce.

Maybe.

This wasn't the time to think about her divorce from Blake, though. Right now, she had to focus on her kids. So as the first parents showed up, she went into teacher mode, chirping about how wonderfully this or that kid did in class today, helping put on little jackets, and finding mittens. More parents showed up, and then her classroom was an absolute cluster of people bundling small children in warm outdoor gear, and so she got her clipboard and checked off names and parents while one of the PTA moms chattered in her ear about the upcoming school Christmas Carnival. It was another one of those ways Amy was probably a bit too anal-retentive about her kids, but she was able to get away with it because it was a smaller class. She carefully kept track of who picked up who every day, and then kept a logbook in her desk. Safety was important.

As parents left with their children and the room started to clear out, she tried to focus on the woman talking non-stop in her ear. She kept an eye on the children left in the classroom as Linda talked about Santa's Workshop and the plans to give each child a small present from the teachers.

"Don't you think that's a good idea?" Linda asked as Amy gazed at the empty rows of desks in her classroom.

"Great," Amy enthused, noting that she was down to two students. One was Billy Archer, whose mom worked a bit later on certain days, so it was to be expected. The other was Libby Watson, though, and usually her enormous bear of a father was here right on time. That was unusual. Libby was calmly coloring at her desk, unconcerned.

"So you'll be Mrs. Claus?" Linda asked as Amy headed toward the school hallway. "We really need a volunteer and I think you'd be great."

"I can do that. Would you excuse me for a second? I just

want to make sure I didn't miss someone." Tucking her clipboard under her arm, Amy headed out into the hall and looked around. Occasionally a parent would get distracted by their phone and wander into the wrong classroom, so it was worth checking. She peered down the hall and didn't see anyone, then turned around—

—and nearly ran into a large, bearded man with a cowboy hat in his hands.

Amy bit back a yelp of surprise, hating that she'd jumped up, startled. Her hand went to her chest, where her heart was hammering. "Oh, freaking heck, you startled me."

The man clutching his hat flushed a deep red. "Sorry," he mumbled.

She bit her lip because she'd almost cussed a blue streak—and right in the middle of an elementary school filled with students and parents. Trying to compose herself, she smoothed a hand down her skirt. "Can I help you find a classroom?"

The man opened his mouth. "Libby," he managed to croak out after a moment.

She waited. When he didn't say anything else, she tried to fill in the blanks. "Are you saying you're here to pick up Libby? Mr. Watson didn't leave me a message."

"He's . . . lame."

Amy blinked. "What?"

The man cleared his throat and looked distinctly uncomfortable. "Horse. Lame."

"Oh." She studied him. "And you are . . ."

"Brother. Caleb." He stuck out his hand, then blurted out, "Weather's Christmas, ain't it."

She took his hand gingerly and tried not to notice that it was sweaty. He was nervous, poor man. It was obvious from his actions and the way he stumbled over his words, then closed his eyes after he spoke, as if he were regretting every syllable that came out of his mouth. Her heart squeezed with sympathy.

"Well, Mr. Watson, I appreciate you coming by, but I can't release the students to anyone—even family—without one of the parents' permission. If you'll come inside and wait, I'll call the other Mr. Watson or his wife and make sure it's all right before I send Libby out with you." She gestured at the door, indicating he should go inside her classroom. This was usually a test on its own. If it was a creep of any kind— not that she'd met any in their tiny town—calling the parents would normally make someone run. But this man simply ducked his head in a nod and followed her in, which meant he was likely legit.

She was still calling the parents anyhow.

As he walked inside, Libby jumped up from her seat. "Uncle Caleb," she called, beaming at him. "I drew you a horse! Come see!"

The man's face creased into a broad smile at the sight of the little girl. He glanced at Amy.

"Please, have a seat. This won't take long."

She watched as the big cowboy pulled out a child-size red chair and perched on it, his long legs folded up against his thick, puffy cold-weather vest. Uncle Caleb—Hank's brother. She could see it. Hank was a massive, massive man with a grim face and a thick black beard. He was utterly terrifying-looking at first, but the way he doted on his petite wife and his equally tiny daughter showed he was harmless. Caleb was obviously cut from the same stock—he was as tall as his brother, if not as broad. His face wasn't as hard, but maybe it was because he had dark, dark eyes framed by thick lashes that made him look soulful. He had the same beard and build that his brother did, though.

Handsome, too, not that she was supposed to be looking. Handsome and shy, she decided, when he glanced up at her and immediately turned bright red again. She'd seen him around town and had probably met him before but had never realized he was Libby's uncle. She was bad with faces, which was why she had the clipboard. Both he and Libby looked entirely at ease together, so Amy pulled out her phone and texted Becca Watson—Mr. Watson's recently married bride and Libby's stepmother.

> AMY: Hi Becca, this is Amy. A man named Caleb is here to pick Libby up and says Hank has a lame horse? Does this sound legit to you?

Linda cleared her throat, sidling in next to Amy. "Did you hear what I said?"

"Oh. I'm sorry." Amy looked over at her, forcing an apologetic smile to her face. "I didn't catch it."

"I asked if you had a boyfriend. We need a Santa Claus to go with our Mrs. Claus." Linda's expression was avid.

Amy tried not to flinch. Being that it was a small town, relationship stuff came up a lot. "No. I'm sorry, I'm divorced."

Her phone pinged and Amy quickly glanced down at the text.

> BECCA: Caleb is totally fine. Do you need a description? Big bearded guy, stumbles over his words. Looks like a shy Hank. Or I can come get her. Let me know.

She smiled down at her phone and glanced up at Caleb and Libby. The man was watching her with those dark eyes, his expression unreadable. For some reason, it made her feel a little flustered and shy herself. "You're good to go, Mr. Watson. Thank you for waiting."

He nodded in a jerky way. "Libby's mine . . . ah, my pleasure." He coughed and then slowly closed his eyes again.

She bit the inside of her cheek not to laugh. Stumbling over his words was right.

Amy started to text Becca back when Linda nudged her, continuing to talk about the Christmas Carnival. "Do you know of anyone that can do it? Curtis is running the popcorn machine and Jimmy said he'd be in charge of the midway. Terry dressed up last year but his wife is insisting that we find someone else. She thinks he's flirting with the elves." Linda tittered at her joke, missing Amy's horrified expression.

The last thing she wanted was to cause problems in someone's marriage. She knew how that felt. "Maybe I shouldn't be Mrs. Claus, then—"

"Me."

Both of the women looked up.

The cowboy stood next to Libby's desk, his face flushed. His hat was practically crushed in his big hand as he spoke. "I'll do Mrs. Claus."

"You mean you'll be *Mr.* Claus," Libby called out, giggling.

He looked for a moment as if he wanted the floor to swallow him up but managed to nod. His gaze remained locked on Amy, as if trying to silently communicate something to her.

What it was, she didn't know. But she put on her best teacher smile. "Sounds like you and I are going to make quite the pair."

* * *

Caleb carried his niece out to his truck and tried to walk calmly. Tried. His boots crunched on the snow as he cut across the grounds of the school, not bothering with the cleared sidewalks because he just wanted to get to the safety of his vehicle as soon as possible. Inside the truck, no one would see how red his face was, or how much he was sweating. They wouldn't notice just how uncomfortable he was.

"Your hat is crushed, Uncle Caleb!" Libby called out helpfully as he opened the back door to his truck and pushed the passenger seat forward. "Why is your hat all messed up?"

"I'll tell you later, Libster." He settled her in her car seat and buckled her in with the ease of someone who'd done this a hundred times before. He had, too. Up until a few months ago, his older brother was a single parent, and that meant leaning on his brothers for help. Ever since Libby was born, Caleb had pitched in when needed, changing dirty diapers, doing laundry, and helping with feeding. Now that Hank was married, Caleb wasn't needed as often and his uncle duties were mostly babysitting for the occasional date night and watching *Frozen*, but he didn't mind. Libby was a good kid.

Most of the time. She was a loud kid, too. "Your hat looks so funny, Uncle Caleb! You smooshed it!"

She wasn't going to be quiet about his damned hat, was she? He snatched it off his head and threw it in the back seat, then shut the door and jogged around to the other side of the truck. His boots slid on the icy slush, but he ignored it. He just needed to get away from the school. Needed to get away from Amy Mckinney, who was so pretty that it made his chest ache.

Actually, she was so pretty she made his entire soul ache.

She'd talked to him today. Acted like he was a total stranger even though he'd met her twice before now. Once, he'd gone to the school with Hank and had stood mutely behind his brother like a big, bearded fencepost. Another time he'd run into her in town and they'd nearly collided on the sidewalk. She'd dropped a package in surprise; he'd mumbled an apology and handed her package back to her. Their fingers had brushed.

Caleb remembered every second of that encounter. It was burned into his mind. Her hair had swung over her shoulder as she'd leaned over, and her blue eyes had gone wide. She'd been wearing a gray turtleneck dress that hugged her curves, and tall black boots. She'd laughed and taken the package from him—one she'd gotten in the mail.

He remembered everything.

And she didn't remember he was alive. That stung, just a little, but it was to be expected. No one ever noticed Caleb.

Even so . . . she hadn't remembered his face? He had hers memorized. It was engraved into his brain. He noticed everything about her, right down to the little mole just below her ear.

He drove back to the ranch in silence, listening to Libby chatter about her day. She'd colored pictures and was learning about animals today. "Did you know platypuses lay eggs, Uncle Caleb?" she mentioned in the middle of a constant stream of talking. "Because they do. They have duck noses and they lay eggs. Miss Mckinney says so."

He grunted a response. Miss Mckinney. She had his

phone number now. She'd given him the most curious smile when he'd volunteered to be Santa, as if she weren't entirely certain he was sane. "You sure you want to do this?" He'd nodded mutely, because words always failed him, and then she'd taken down his phone number.

His phone.

Amy Mckinney had his phone number. That made him start sweating all over again. What if she called him to talk about the whole Santa thing and he messed up his words again? He'd wanted to grab Libby and haul her out of the room the moment he said he'd *do* Mrs. Claus. The other woman had tittered and looked at him like he was a creep, but Amy had just given him the most gentle expression, as if she understood how hard it was for him to talk to women.

She couldn't know. Most people didn't have any idea that he and his brothers had grown up in the remote reaches of Alaska and that he'd only seen women when he'd gone into town with his father. He'd never talked to them, either, because he was just a kid. Back then, he could be a quiet type and no one thought anything of it. But at twenty-seven? Living in a town like this? He was sorely missing communication skills that had never been given to him. It was easy to talk to his brothers. Fairly easy to talk to Uncle Ennis.

Impossible to talk to a woman without the words tripping over his tongue and coming out wrong.

It occurred to him that he had no idea how to be Santa if he was going to have to talk to people. Of his brothers, Caleb was the silent one. Hank was quiet, but he didn't have problems talking to most people. Jack, the youngest, wouldn't shut up. He talked about anything and everything—kinda like Libby. Caleb was the middle child, the peacemaker.

The listener. If Amy Mckinney wanted an ear, he could give her one.

If she wanted him to talk, he was in trouble.

He pulled up to the Swinging C Ranch and unloaded Libby, who was still talking about platypuses and clutching a crayon drawing in her hand. He pulled the car seat out of the back of his truck and put it in Hank's truck, then picked up Libby—still talking—and took her inside.

Jack was in the kitchen, grinning as he polished off the last of the Christmas cookies that Hank's wife had sent up with them.

"So did you see her?" He wiggled his eyebrows. "The love of your life?"

Caleb felt his face get hot.

"You love Miss Mckinney?" Libby said, surprised. "Like Mommy and Daddy love?"

Oh hell. He glared at Jack, who just snorted with laughter. Jack wasn't supposed to bring up this sort of thing in front of Libby, because she'd repeat everything. The last thing he needed was his niece blurting out his infatuation to her beautiful teacher. "No. Not her," he said quickly. "Someone . . . else."

"Miss Lindon?"

Caleb shot Jack another angry look. He didn't know who Miss Lindon was, but he suspected it was another teacher. "Someone *else*," he said again, setting her down. "Uncle Jack, where's Libby's dad?"

"He's in the barn with Trixie. Checking her hoof out." Jack poked Libby with a finger. "You want to watch *Rudolph* while we're waiting for him to return?"

Her face lit up, and Caleb set her down, letting her race into the living room while Jack turned on the Christmas movie. Christmas. Right. He was in a heap of trouble now. Jack returned to the kitchen a few moments later and gestured at the living room, where the TV was blaring with jingling bells and Christmas music. "You didn't take her to the salon?"

Caleb waved a hand in the air. "Hank said to bring her here. Becca's busy. Something about a hair emergency for someone. Look, that's not important. I've got a problem."

Jack picked up the plate and ate a few of the stray sprinkles. "What, did you say something stupid to that teacher?" He grinned. "Oh damn, did you call her Tits like you did Tina?"

Caleb clenched his jaw. He was never going to live that down. "No. But I volunteered to be Santa at the Christmas Carnival at the school."

Jack's brow wrinkled. "What? You?"

"Yeah. Me."

Jack stared at him, bewildered. After a moment, it finally sunk in, and he began to laugh. "Are you serious? You? You can't even hold a conversation around that woman. What makes you think you can be Santa?"

He crossed his arms over his chest, feeling like an idiot. "I don't know. She just . . . she said she was going to be Mrs. Claus and they needed a Santa, so I said I'd do it. I wasn't thinking." He didn't tell Jack the part where he said he'd *do* Mrs. Claus. Jack didn't need more ammunition for teasing Caleb. "What do I do?"

"What do you mean, what do you do?" Jack grinned hugely. "You practice your 'ho, ho, ho.' You wouldn't want to disappoint the kids, would you?"

Damn it.

Maybe he could be a silent Santa.

Santa with bronchitis.

Santa that had taken a vow of silence.

A mime Santa.

Something.

He immediately wanted to cancel . . . but he didn't have Amy's phone number. He'd forgotten to get it, and now unless he went back up to that school and told her that he was out, he was going to be Santa. He was stuck.

CHAPTER TWO

When Amy got home that night, the ceiling in her bedroom had caved in.

It had been a long day already. The children were fine—the children were always fine—but she'd had two parent meetings after class and had discovered that Tim Howerton had left his inhaler in his cubby at school, so she'd driven out to the Howertons' house to drop it off just in case. Then she'd gone back to school to clean up her classroom and to take down the fall decorations in preparation for the holiday decor.

Unfortunately, her holiday decor left a lot to be desired, so she'd spent some time shopping local teacher supply shops and clutching at her neckline at the prices. Lord, it was expensive to decorate a classroom. She was on an extremely limited budget, too, which meant she'd be cutting out paper snowflakes and making garlands with construction paper. Maybe some of the thrift places would have sales this weekend? Or she'd find another estate sale to hit up? She made a mental note to check the local paper and watch the local donation lists online, then packed up her laptop and headed home.

It was dark early, thanks to winter, and she slipped twice on the icy sidewalk. That's what happened when you were from the South and didn't know how to handle winter. She got inside all right, though, with only her backside and pride bruised, and discovered the problem with the ceiling.

Really, it was the perfect end to a perfectly awful day.

She put her laptop down on her table in the living room and stepped inside the bedroom gingerly. Water was dripping from upstairs, which was kind of odd, because she hadn't realized she had an upstairs. She peered up at the soggy remnants of her ceiling, determined not to cry. Sure, her bed was soaked and it was ten degrees outside, and she had no ceiling, but she could handle this. She could.

She was strong. Independent.

She didn't need to count on anyone to fix this.

Well, sort of. Amy immediately texted her landlord, Greg.

AMY: Hi there! It's me on Madison Lane. The ceiling in the bedroom collapsed . . . ?

Impatiently, Amy watched her phone as the three dots flashed up, indicating someone was typing, and then disappeared again. No message came through right away, so she grabbed the two towels she had, made a mental note to buy more towels, and did her best to start mopping up the mess. Between the third and fourth wring-out of her towels in the bathroom, her phone buzzed with an incoming text. She raced over and picked it up.

GREG: Hey there! How'd that happen?

GREG: Been meaning to talk to you. I was thinking
about Italian on Friday night and I know this great
little place a few towns over. You interested?

She fought back a scream of frustration. Was he asking
her out? While she was staring down a squishy mattress
and a ceiling that gaped into the attic above? Amy took a
deep breath (or three) and finally composed an answer that
didn't sound rude.

AMY: Hi! I'm busy Friday. My ceiling . . . ?

She snapped a picture and sent it to him. Surely now he'd
do something? Come over and fix this? If nothing else, bring
fresh towels so she could clean up on her own? She stared in
frustration at the mess. There went her plans for just grabbing a glass of wine and relaxing for the evening. She was
going to be cleaning and doing laundry all night.

GREG: It looks like the ceiling got wet and
collapsed. Do you have renter's insurance?

Renter's insurance? That was a thing? If it was, she
didn't have it.

AMY: This is my first rental. I didn't know I needed
renter's insurance. Can't you come and fix this?

GREG: Oh. Well, in the future you might want
renter's insurance. I'll call my guy and see if he can
make it out there this weekend. Did you store
something with water in the ceiling?

Her jaw dropped. She clamped her mouth shut, took a deep breath, and looked up at the hole again. She could see the night sky through the roof, which wasn't a good thing. Given all the snow they'd had lately, the water had probably leaked in from the attic until it destroyed the ceiling above her bed.

Fun.

AMY: I think there's a hole in the roof. I can see the stars. Also, you said you'd fix the leak in the kitchen. And the window in the living room.

He sent her an emoji for a thumbs-up and she knew that was the end of the conversation. When she'd moved here, she'd been told that most people in tiny Painted Barrel didn't move much at all, so housing was at a premium. Her Realtor, Greg, had acquired a property that he was willing to rent to her, and she'd gladly taken it. It was a few blocks from the school, which meant it wouldn't tax her ancient car too much, and the price was reasonable given her tiny teacher's salary.

He'd told her it wasn't posh when she moved in, and she'd said it was fine because she needed affordable, not posh. Unfortunately, she was starting to realize that "posh" was a faucet that didn't leak and doors that shut properly and a window that didn't have a finger-size crack that let in all kinds of cold air. She'd reported it all to her landlord like the articles online said to do.

Greg always texted back that he'd "get his guy" on it. She'd never seen the "guy" and wasn't actually sure he existed. But what other choices did she have? With one last frustrated sigh, she put her phone back down and got back to work.

A while later, her shoulders were aching, her entire house smelled like mildew and water, but the mess in the bedroom was mostly cleaned up. She'd gathered up the waterlogged particleboard of the ceiling and had tossed it into garbage bags that now waited in the mudroom to be taken out to the garbage cans. She was tired, sweaty, and exhausted, but it was done. Oh sure, her bed needed to air out and she had no bedding and no genuine place to sleep other than a love seat, but she'd handled it.

And wasn't this why she'd moved out to Wyoming anyhow? So she could learn how to be self-sufficient? To figure out how to handle things on her own?

All in all, she was going to chalk it up to a good life experience. Maybe not one she'd ever really wanted to have, but a good experience all the same. With that in mind, she closed the door to the bedroom and threw on her jacket to take the bags of rotted ceiling to the garbage cans.

The cans were back behind the house, and she went down the two slippery steps to get to them before she noticed the stars. The view was utterly gorgeous, the vibrant nebulas out in force and the midnight sky lit up with colors she'd never seen in the city. Each time she saw this, it took her breath away.

That was another thing she couldn't get in Houston— stars like these.

Even though it was cold and she was tired, she threw the garbage in the cans and then sat down on the top step to watch the stars for a bit, to stare up at them in wonder and daydream.

It took a minute for her to hear the growling.

Amy clutched at the neck of her jacket, her entire body going stiff at the quiet, low growl. She looked out behind her house, but there was nothing to see. Painted Barrel's "main" part of town was small, and beyond the main street, there wasn't much but a scatter of houses. Her rental was on the edge of things and backed up to a large pasture, which meant there was a lot of open space.

And something was . . . growling.

She remained frozen in place, unsure what to do. She didn't have a weapon of any kind at hand. The garbage can lid was plastic and attached to the can, so she couldn't even use that as a shield. If she turned around and leapt into the house, would it attack her the moment she stood? Amy waited . . .

And waited.

The growling stopped. Did that mean the creature was gone? She got to her feet slowly . . . and it started again the moment her boot scuffed against the wooden step.

Okay, that was odd. It sounded like a dog, but as far as she knew, her neighbors didn't own dogs. Heck, she'd never owned one herself. In her mind, the creature was something fierce and terrible and enormous. She had to see what it was for herself, though. Carefully, she crept up the stairs and grabbed her flashlight, then shone it out the window.

A pair of eyes shone back. It looked like . . . a collie? It wasn't a wolf; that was for sure. The dog lurked at the edge of the fence, near the pasture, and she waited for it to leave. Instead, it just sat there. After a while, it turned around three times and lay down, and when it did, she noticed that it looked impossibly thin.

Her heart squeezed.

"Okay, dogs aren't scary," Amy told herself. "Lots of people have dogs." Except her mother had been terrified of them and Blake had said they were filthy, so she'd never really been around them much. Now, though, she was curious. What was this dog doing behind her house? Was he lost?

Maybe he needed a friend.

That random thought decided her. Maybe it was because Amy desperately needed a friend, too, that rescuing the strange, growly dog was suddenly very important to her. She opened the pantry and looked inside for something that seemed appealing to a dog. There was a lot of ramen noodle— her cheap pantry staple of choice—but she was pretty sure dogs didn't eat that. Did they? She looked through her cans— beans, corn—and found a jar of peanut butter. Dogs liked that, didn't they? She pulled it out and used a spoon to get a huge, sloppy blob and then went back to the back door. With her flashlight in one hand and peanut-butter spoon in the other, she moved out onto the step.

The dog growled again, but when she shone her light, it didn't move from its spot near the fence.

"Hello?" She clicked her tongue, trying to call the dog. "Come here, boy. I have peanut butter." When that didn't entice him, she tried something else. She smacked her lips and made appreciative noises. "Mmm, good."

The growling turned into a whine that broke her heart, but he still didn't get up. Worried, Amy crept off the step and into the snow. She headed toward the dog, even though it was bitterly cold, the wind biting. She couldn't leave the dog outside, not when he was whining like that.

So she crouched over and crept forward, step by step, into the darkness, and held the peanut-butter spoon out like a peace offering. "Come on. Don't you want this? It's yummy."

The closer she got, the better the look she got at him. It was hard to tell, but his face was thin and looked unhealthy.

His coat was ratty and filthy, black on the ears and body and gray everywhere else. His muzzle was gray, too, and his eyes looked to be milky white.

Oh. He was blind.

Her heart squeezed again, because he was sniffing the air, but he didn't get up. He was shivering, too, she noticed. She tried shining the flashlight right in his eyes, but it got no reaction. Only when her feet crunched in the snow did the dog get alert.

Definitely blind.

"I got some yummy peanut butter for you," she told him, vaguely aware she was using a baby voice to talk to him. His tail gave a hopeful thump, though, and so she kept talking in that silly, insipid voice. "It's so tasty good, and I can't possibly eat it all. So I thought, hey, why don't I bring some out to my puppy friend. Can that be you, good boy?"

The tail thumped again.

Feeling encouraged, Amy set down the flashlight, then reached out and touched the dog's head.

He snapped at her, catching her fingers. They both yelped in surprise, and she fell backward in the snow. The peanut-butter spoon fell, and Amy clutched her hand tightly. It stung, but he hadn't broken the skin. Even now, as she watched, the blind dog's head bobbed and he sniffed the snow, looking for the spoon. He was still hungry, just scared. And here she was, the dummy that tried to touch a blind, scared dog. Of course he snapped at her.

"You're coming inside with me," she told him. "I have a plan." Amy gently tossed the spoon closer to him, and when he began to lick it hungrily, she crept back toward the house and grabbed her only blanket. Mental note: she needed more linens. Maybe she'd look for some at estate sales this weekend. For now, her scared dog friend needed it more than she did. She grabbed the jar of peanut butter, too, and took it with her as she went outside. The dog was still there, licking at the spoon, and before she could lose her courage, she marched up to him and set the jar of peanut butter down and opened it under his nose. When it distracted him, she wrapped him in the blanket and picked him up.

He snapped at her. She expected that, because he was scared. And even though he twisted and yelped and scratched at her arms, Amy made soothing sounds and carried him inside despite everything. When she was finally in the house, she set him down and began to rub him with the blanket. "It's okay," she promised him in a soft voice. "It's warm in here and no one will hurt you."

He hunched his shoulders and slunk over to a corner, where he huddled, shivering. She draped the blanket over him, then went outside and retrieved her flashlight and peanut butter. By the time she sat down, she was wiped and smelled like wet dog. Had she eaten? Did she care? She was exhausted, but she might as well put something in her stomach before she figured out what to do with her new friend. Maybe a neighbor was missing his buddy. She'd look online after she had something in her growling stomach.

The moment she got the ramen out of the microwave, though, the dog started sniffing and looking interested, so she made another bowl and then sat near him on the floor while they both ate.

"I don't suppose you know how to fix ceilings, do you?" Amy murmured between forkfuls of noodles. "Because I could use a guy."

The dog ate messily and didn't answer. He was clearly starving, though; that much was obvious. By the time he licked the bowl clean, half the broth was on the floor and he was still hungrily looking for more, so she gave him hers. Under all that matted fur, she'd bet he was pitifully thin. If someone was missing their dog, they'd been missing him for a few days now.

All right, her new buddy would stay with her tonight, and if she couldn't find a missing dog description of him on the neighborhood forums, she'd get him some dog food and some dog shampoo—they made that sort of thing, didn't they? And she'd have herself a new roommate.

Her new town and new life seemed a little less lonely now. Amy looked around the bare house, at the secondhand love seat with the ugliest floral pattern ever and the broken CRT television in the corner that weighed more than she did. Her house was as bare as her social calendar, but she was determined to change that.

"Isn't that right, Donner?" She smiled at the dog. He wasn't a Rudolph or a Vixen, but maybe he could be a Donner. It was just Christmasy enough, she decided.

She and Donner were going to have a great holiday, Amy decided.

CHAPTER THREE

She woke up to Donner licking her face, which made her
sputter and realize that she'd slept on the floor . . . and
she'd overslept for work. After walking and feeding Donner
using rope for a leash, Amy raced out of the house with her
hair in a bun and her blouse unironed—luckily she could
throw a cardigan over it and complain she was cold. The
day breezed past, and it was a Friday, which meant it was
her favorite of all days.

Payday.

At least, she was pretty sure it was payday. Which was
good, because she was broke. She had a neat little app on
her phone that let her check her bank balance—a novelty
for her since Blake had never let her touch their money in
the past—and when she checked her account, it showed a
bright red number and a lot of negatives pending.

Whoops. That was a new experience, too.

Once school was out and her students sent home, she texted
her accountant. Not that she needed an accountant, but she

did need someone she could trust that was good with money, and Layla had helped her get started when she'd arrived in Painted Barrel, clueless about bank accounts and credit lines and anything of that nature.

Also, Layla was about the same age as Amy and into thrifting and estate sales, so she was determined to befriend her.

AMY: Hi Layla! Did I get paid?

LAYLA: You get paid semimonthly.

AMY: What's that mean? It's Friday. I get paid on Friday right? Every other Friday?

LAYLA: No, you get paid on the 15th and the 30th. You don't get paid today. Sorry!

Oh. Well, that sucked. Chewing on her lip, she considered. The fifteenth wasn't for at least a week, and she was broke as a joke. You would think she would have gotten the hang of how her paycheck worked at this point, but nope.

AMY: Did my alimony payment come in from Blake? That's supposed to come in at the beginning of each month, right?

LAYLA: It is and no surprise, it has not. I'm sorry. I know he's supposed to pay. Because he's self-employed it's harder for the state to shake payments out of him.

Amy sighed. She knew all about that. Ever since she'd divorced Blake, she'd learned that he loved to hide his money—

and she knew he had some—in various businesses and pretend like he didn't cut himself a check. Even though he was supposed to send her alimony money every month, it never showed up. Layla was helping her with that, but she could only do so much.

AMY: OK, thank you. Any leads on any estate sales in our area?

LAYLA: No, but there's a huge one in Casper! You should check it out. It was on all week and they're closing everything out later today. That means everything left will be 50% off and I know you like a sale.

Oh, heck, she did. The only things she bought anymore were on sale. Layla texted her the address, and it was close to a consignment shop in Casper, so she rushed home, fed the dog, shoved a bunch of her designer clothing into the back of the car—and some of her jewelry—and drove as fast as she could to Casper, which was more than an hour away with the snowy weather.

Much to her disappointment, the consignment shop didn't pay in advance, so she hocked her delicate Rolex and her pearl earrings with the matching bracelet that Blake had gotten her for their second anniversary. She left the clothes with the consignment shop anyhow, since she'd probably need more than the hundred bucks she had on her now, and drove as quickly as she could to the estate sale. They were packing up as she arrived, but they let her pick through the boxes after she begged prettily.

Fifty dollars later, she had some dishes, some linens, a dog bed, and an entire box of random Christmas decorations that looked pretty dated. She was positive she could repurpose them to be useful, though. After all, the animatronic Santa humping on Mrs. Claus didn't *have* to be humping, did he? She could separate them and then just have . . . two happy, jolly old elves who happened to have weird expressions on their faces.

It'd work. She'd make it work. That was Amy Mckinney's new motto—she was independent, damn it, and she didn't need her ex-husband, Blake Todd, to run her life. With a firm, angry nod at the world, Amy packed her finds into the back of her car and put the key into the ignition.

It didn't start.

Her heart stuttered. She panicked. Took a deep breath. Sure, her car was old, but it wasn't that old, was it? She closed her eyes, said a little prayer, and then tried the key again. This time, the car choked, but the engine turned over.

Triumphant, Amy set off on the road back to Painted Barrel in the darkness. Today was a much better day than yesterday.

A
t least, Amy's day was better for about half an hour. Halfway back to Painted Barrel, with the distance equally far back to Casper, her car sputtered. She coasted to the side of the road as the lights died out and everything just went . . . dead.

She allowed herself to panic. Just a little, as she sat in the darkness. Cars didn't just die like that because it was cold, did they? Something else had to be wrong, and she wasn't close to anything at all. There wasn't a nearby gas station or even a rest stop. There was nothing on this stretch of road and the cars that passed weren't nearly as plentiful as she wanted them to be. This was fine, though. She'd figure this out. With that thought in her head, she closed her eyes and calmly turned the key in the ignition.

Nothing happened. The car didn't respond.

Amy sucked in a shuddering breath, then popped the hood of the car. She got out, wincing at the bitterly cold air, and clutched her jacket closer to her body. She lifted the hood and peered down at the dark engine, because it felt like something she should do, as a capable person. She had no idea what she was looking at, though, and gazing down into the shadows at a bunch of mechanical parts made the bubbling despair she was trying to fight rise to the surface anyhow.

She was . . . stranded.

She had no idea what to do now. What did one do when a car stopped? If she were back in Houston—and still Amy Mckinney Todd, wife of Blake Todd, high-powered entrepreneur—she'd call her husband, knowing full well that he'd chastise her like she was a child. But he'd take care of it. He'd taken care of everything. He'd controlled everything.

Without that rigid, smothering control, she felt free. She also felt completely out of her depth when it came to situations like this, though. What did people do when their cars broke down? She hurried back into the driver's seat as a lone car whizzed past and climbed inside the relative warmth of the cab. It was going to get cold fast if her car didn't have power. She could freeze to death, all because she didn't know what to do now.

God, how Blake would laugh at her "independence," that asshole.

She drew a calming breath. Anger at Blake always galvanized her. Hadn't he smirked all through their divorce proceedings? Told her she'd be utterly helpless and she'd come crawling back, begging for him to help her. If nothing else in life, she was going to succeed, by golly, just to prove him wrong. Amy pulled out her phone and began to google.

Okay, she could call a tow truck.

Except . . . she didn't have the money for something like that. All she had was the little bit of cash from pawning her jewelry, and she'd been hoping to use it for groceries for herself—and her new friend, Donner—this week.

Oh no. Poor Donner. He was all alone at her house and probably worried. Did dogs get worried? She thought of the dirty, disheveled collie and hoped he was okay. All right, for Donner's sake, she had to get home.

So she went down her list of contacts in her phone instead. Lisa—the high school teacher—didn't have her car at night because she shared with her husband. Jenny—another elementary teacher—had a boyfriend in Ten Sleep who she visited on the weekends. Royce—the principal—didn't answer when she called, and neither did his secretary (and wife) Elizabeth.

She went down her tiny list of friends, panicking. Layla didn't pick up and her phone went to voicemail. Becca—her friend and the local beautician—was out with her new husband tonight. She couldn't call her and interrupt her date, not when she knew that Becca had one of her husband's brothers babysitting for her.

Greg! Her landlord. He was nice enough, wasn't he? And he was always asking her out on a date. She dialed him quickly, her heart pounding. If he came and saved her, she'd absolutely go out with him on a date—

The phone went immediately to voicemail. Not even one ring.

Frowning, she tried again. Same thing.

He was ignoring her calls. So much for him having a

"guy" to come fix things. Now he was just flat-out ignoring her. Amy choked on a horrified laugh. At least she didn't have to date him now.

The only other person on her list was Caleb, and she blanked out for a moment on who he was. Then it dawned on her. Right. Caleb Watson, one of Libby's uncles. The quiet, weird one who had volunteered to be Santa even as he'd crushed his own hat in his hands.

He was a stranger . . . but she was out of options.

Sucking in a deep breath, she dialed his number. Her heart pounded. What would she do if he blew her off? If he couldn't be bothered? If—

"Hello?" He answered on the second ring, his voice slightly surprised.

"Oh my god. Caleb. Hi!" Amy knew she sounded hysterical, but she didn't care. "I'm sorry to bother you but I don't have anyone else to call. I seem to be having some car trouble and I don't have the money for a tow truck and—" She drew in a shuddering breath, trying not to cry.

"Where?" Caleb barked out.

"Highway," she managed. "Coming back from Casper. I'm about halfway—"

"Wait there," he said and hung up.

Wait there? It was on the tip of her tongue to tell him she didn't have anywhere else to go, but she'd be arguing with a dial tone. Did that mean he was on his way? She didn't know. Worried, Amy texted him.

AMY: I'm sorry to be a bother, but does that mean you're on your way?

CALEB: Y

Okay, she was going to take that as a "yes" and relax, just a little. Inhaling deeply, she wrapped her coat around her body tighter and sank low into the bucket seat. She could do this. It was fine. She could be independent and strong and not need anyone tomorrow.

Tonight, she was just grateful a stranger was on his way to rescue her.

CHAPTER FOUR

It seemed to take forever for him to show up. She knew it wasn't that long—she'd been checking her phone in between rounds of sudoku to try to calm her mind—but it felt like an eternity. The car was getting cold, her breath puffing in front of her face in clouds, and her Prada jacket, while lovely and stylish, didn't do much to keep her warm. Her Houston clothes weren't going to cut it in Wyoming. She'd have to get warmer gear at some point.

Like when she got her alimony checks in.

Amy was coat shopping on her phone when a truck pulled up in front of her, then backed up and turned around until the lights shone in through the windshield. Gratitude rushed through her and she unlocked the car door and stepped out, on the verge of weeping. "Hi," she called out in a wobbly voice. "I hope I'm not ruining your evening."

The big cowboy was silhouetted in the headlights, all hat and shoulders, and she'd never been so glad to see anyone. He walked over to the passenger side of his car and pulled a blanket out, then approached her. "You're a bother."

"Oh." Her heart sank.

"No bother," he growled, as if frustrated. "Meant to say *no* bother." And he carefully tucked the blanket around her shoulders, wrapping her in warmth. He handed her a thermos next, then ducked his head as he moved toward her car. "No bother," he muttered again.

"I appreciate it either way," she said softly. "I didn't have anyone else to call."

"Where's your coat?"

She looked down at her lightweight camel jacket. "I'm wearing it."

He shook his head once and pointed at the thermos. "Drunk."

"Drunk?"

"Drink. That." The expression on his face was hard to tell in the darkness, but he looked . . . flustered?

Well, that was two of them. Amy unscrewed the lid while he opened her car door and popped the hood. The moment the thermos was open, the hot scent of coffee wafted through the air and she wanted to cry with how wonderful it smelled. How warm.

Okay, she cried a little. Just a little. She sniffed as she took a sip, and it was sugary and full of cream, just how she liked it, and that made her cry a little more. It was just luck that the coffee was perfect and he was looking at her car and she wasn't alone.

For the first time in months, she didn't feel alone and adrift, and the sensation was overwhelming. More tears came.

"I'm sorry," she said as he moved to the front of the car

to look at the engine. "I tried to see if something was broken but I didn't know what I was looking at. I'm trying to be independent and do things on my own, but I couldn't get it to start when I put the key in again and I tried calling everyone and—"

He looked up at her. "You're great."

She blinked. "Wh-what?"

"Doing great," he managed, voice gruff.

For some reason, she needed to hear that. "Thank you," she told him in a small voice and sipped the coffee again. Her tears dried a little and her panic ebbed. "I know we're strangers but you can't know how much I appreciate you being here. It means everything to me."

He looked up from under the hood of the car, his gaze hidden by the shadows thanks to his hat. For a moment, she wanted to see his face. To see if his eyes were filled with kindness and understanding or scorn. Blake's face would have been filled with irritation, and he'd have made her feel stupid, like it was her fault for the car breaking down.

Just thinking about that made her nervous. "I didn't do anything, you know."

"Huh?"

"To the car. It wasn't me. I was driving it like normal and it just died."

Caleb nodded, his hat bobbing.

"I didn't hit anything in the road," she felt desperate to explain. Like she needed to somehow prove that she wasn't the screwup here. "And it's got plenty of gas. I get oil changes on the regular—"

"It's fine," he said. "Quit apologizing."

Oh. Okay.

She clutched at the blanket and drank a ton of the delicious coffee while he poked and prodded at things. He got in the car and tried turning the key once or twice, pumping the gas pedal, and it was on the tip of her tongue to start making excuses again, but she bit them back. He said it was fine. She had to believe him. He just . . . wasn't the chatty type. That didn't mean he disliked her. It just meant he wasn't much of a talker.

Amy bit her lip as he popped the trunk and got out of the car once more, heading to the back. She followed behind him, a blanket-wrapped, caffeinated lump of helplessness. "I was hitting up an estate sale," she told him breathlessly, remembering some of the contents of the trunk. "That's why I'm out late."

"Didn't ask," he said as he lifted the trunk. He stared at the boxes for a moment, then grabbed a handful of linens and pushed them aside, searching for something.

Not only did it reveal her vulgar Humping Santa and Mrs. Claus, but it activated them, too. Amy watched in horror as Santa made a creaking noise and started bouncing his pelvis against his jolly wife. Caleb watched it for a moment, then cleared his throat and covered it up again. "Cable?"

She wanted to die of embarrassment. Did he think she was a pervert now? That she watched a lot of dirty shows on cable and had to fill her house with . . . humping things? What the heck? "No, I don't watch a lot of cable," she managed politely. "That's not why they're there. I got them to repurpose—"

"Jumper," Caleb choked out. "Jumper cable."

"Oh." She thought for a moment. "Um, what do those look like exactly?"

He made another noise in his throat and then shut the trunk.

Amy cringed, clutching the thermos, and waited for him to blast into her. To tell her what an idiot and a failure she was for taking up his time.

A long moment passed. Then another. Was he waiting for her to say something? She bit her lip, uncertain.

Eventually, he spoke. "Mine are in my brother's truck. Gonna need to drive you in," Caleb said, the words slow and measured, almost as if practiced. "Probably the alternator, not the battery, but I can check it in the morning. You need to get home. It's cold."

She was cold. Freezing, actually. Her little boots were like all her clothes—fashionable but not suited for cold, snowy weather, and only the blanket and coffee were keeping her from turning into an ice-cream cone. "What should I do?"

"Me." He coughed hard, then stammered. "I meant me. I'll drive you home."

Amy blinked at him. He really did say the strangest things. Shyness? A learning disability? Whatever it was, it wasn't her business. All she cared was that he was kind. "Are you sure you don't mind?"

He gestured at her car. "We'll lock it. I can get a few parts in the morning and try things. Take it to a shop if I can't get it started."

The rush of gratitude that surged through her was overwhelming enough that she felt like crying again. "Are you sure?" Amy asked. "You don't mind?"

"Not for you." He coughed and cleared his throat again. "Not at all," he said, louder. "Come on."

They got into his car. It occurred to her that he was practically a stranger and she was getting into his vehicle without knowing more about him than his name, but . . . what else was she supposed to do? A tow-truck driver and an

Uber driver were strangers, too, and Caleb's assistance was free. So she got in, tucked the blanket around herself once more when the seat belt was on, and gave him her warmest smile.

He really was the kindest man.

Hell, he was messing all of this up.

Caleb clutched the steering wheel tightly as he drove back to Painted Barrel, trying not to think of all the stupid things that came out of his mouth whenever she was around, but they kept cropping up as ugly reminders that his tongue played a different game than the rest of him.

You're great.

What should I do?

Me.

God. She'd think he was an idiot. He was trying to say as little as possible so the beautiful Amy Mckinney wouldn't realize what a fool he was, but that was proving impossible. He had to talk to her a little, but every time he opened his trap, dumb shit kept coming out. He was going to have to deal with it; that was all.

He was still more than a little shocked that she sat next to him in his car, quietly sipping coffee and gazing out into the snowy night. Of all the people in Painted Barrel, she'd called him when she needed help, and he wasn't sure what to make of that. He was grateful, all right, but it was puzzling. At least, it had been puzzling until she'd tearfully admitted she didn't have anyone else to call. It made him far too happy until it occurred to him that he was a last resort.

Even so, he'd dropped everything to come and rescue her. A kind, gentle woman like her shouldn't be alone with no one to depend on. That bothered him. Wasn't he the most tongue-tied man alive? He'd grown up in the remote wilds of Alaska with no one but his brothers and a few remote neighbors, and yet he'd have had people to call if stranded. It made no sense.

They pulled into Painted Barrel and he glanced over at her—the only time he'd allowed himself to look over at her tonight. She was far too pretty, and it just distracted him. Her long, dark hair was down around her shoulders, making his fingers itch to touch it, and she wore a pair of blue-framed glasses that just made her bright eyes that much brighter. Her nose was red tipped with cold and her cheeks flushed, and she'd had such a sad expression on her face that it made him want to fling her over his shoulder and carry her away from everything.

Whatever she needed, he'd fix it.

He'd had crushes in the past before, had thought some women were attractive, but it was nothing like the gut-wrenching, tongue-tying yearning he felt when he looked at her. She was special. Pretty. Smart. Kind. His clever little niece loved her.

Caleb had always thought he'd work in Painted Barrel for a year and then go back to Alaska, but the moment he saw Amy, his plans changed. Someone like her wouldn't like living off the grid in the remote wild, and so he decided to stay. His brothers thought he was crazy.

At least, Jack did. Hank understood, now that he'd fallen in love and married the local hair lady, who was also a nice, pretty sort who wouldn't live off the grid. Painted Barrel wasn't such a bad place. It was small and kinda remote, nothing like bustling Casper. And she was here, which made it the only place he wanted to be.

"Address?" he asked when she remained quiet.

"I'm the next street over," she said in a soft voice, pointing. "Just turn right at the bank."

He did, and the truck crept along the quiet street. Painted Barrel was a small town, and an old one. Most of the buildings in "town" proper were a hundred years old, and some had weathered the history better than others. When they pulled up to a dilapidated old one-story at the end of the road, he gave her a curious look.

"That's me," she said, her smile bright. "I never thought I'd be so happy to see the place."

He knew it was rude to ask but figured he would anyhow. After all, he'd said plenty of dumb shit to her all night and she hadn't flinched. "*This* is where you're living?" He looked at the small place again. It wasn't more than a couple of rooms, and the boards outside needed a fresh coat of paint something bad. There was a small yard completely covered in snow, and while the neighbors had their sidewalks and driveways neatly tidied, hers were iced over. The windows looked as if they were sagging right out of their frames, and the blinds were old and crooked. The only thing that seemed to match "his" Amy was the festive little wreath on the door.

"I know," she said with a grimace. "It's a dump, isn't it?"

"Ah . . ." He rubbed his jaw. How to answer that politely? "It's a . . ."

"Dump," she emphasized again.

"House," he managed to say. He'd seen worse, but those had been in the remote Alaskan wilds and . . . actually, no, those places looked better kept up than this.

"I just have a very small budget," she admitted as she opened the car door. "And Greg tells me there's not a lot of rental places around here. I'm on a waiting list to get something better, though."

Caleb jumped out of the car and raced around to her side of the truck, his boots skidding on the icy driveway. Did she not know how to salt the damn thing? Or to scrape it clean? Didn't matter. It wasn't his business. He helped her out of the car, keeping the thick blanket wrapped around her for warmth, and she didn't seem to mind his touch on her shoulder, which made his heart thud as if it were the most intimate of caresses.

"Do you want to come in for a moment?" she asked him, putting her key in the door.

Did he want to go in? Hell, he never wanted to leave her side. He'd take whatever opportunity he had because he wasn't sure he'd get another. Caleb just nodded and stepped inside.

The place was even sadder inside than it was outside. It didn't make sense, because Amy was always beautiful and kept up in her appearance, but this house was . . . well, it wasn't good. The few pieces of furniture she had were old and broken or chipped, the sofa was ugly as shit, and he could hear the wind whistling in through one of the windows. From his vantage point, he could see into the kitchen, and old yellowed linoleum matched the equally yellowed and dingy countertops. The entire place looked terrible and dated and smelled like mildew.

Mildew . . . and poop.

"Oh no," Amy moaned behind him, and rushed into the kitchen. "Poor Donner."

He followed her in, and to his surprise, there was a dog— as mangy as the damned house—sitting in a corner, tucked next to the pea-green stove. In an opposite corner, the dog had clearly relieved himself, but she wasn't focused on that. She knelt in front of the animal and stroked its head, ignoring when it snapped at her.

"Poor baby. You're scared, aren't you? I'm sorry. There's two people here tonight. Here, Caleb, come and let Donner smell your hand so he's not so scared." She turned and waved him over expectantly.

He knelt by the dog, and his estimation of the pretty schoolteacher dropped a notch. This was her dog? It looked like it had been abused and misused for a long damned time. His coat was so knotted and filthy it needed to be shaved, and the cataract-covered eyes were full of fear. This didn't match his mental image of the schoolteacher. Was he all wrong about her?

"Donner?" he asked after a moment. "Like . . . the party?"

Amy turned, her face inches from his as they both squatted by the dog, and there was pure astonishment on her face.

"Sorry," he muttered. He wanted to tell her that he liked history. That he read a lot of books and liked to learn about the Old West and things like that. Now she was going to think he was even more of a weirdo than before.

She just giggled, the sound a little squeaky and rusty, and so adorable that it made him ache. "Like the reindeer."

Ah. Okay, that was a smarter guess.

Amy reached out and gently touched the dog's head, ever so careful and loving as she rubbed one ear. "I found Donner last night out in the snow. He kept growling but he was hungry, so I brought him in. I think he's blind. I was going to put up flyers and post online, but there hasn't been time to do much of anything. And I was supposed to get him some pet food tonight and . . ." She bit her lip, and for a moment, she looked so frustrated that she seemed as if she was ready to start crying again.

"I've got dog food," he managed.

"On you?" She looked surprised. "Really?"

He wanted to slap his forehead. "At home. I can bring some in the morning." It was the longest sentence he'd managed in a while, and he was pretty proud of it. He rubbed the dog's muzzle, then got to his feet. "That okay?"

Amy's eyes softened. "Of course that'll be okay. Can I pay you for it?"

He shook his head and went to the sink to wash his hands. The dog was kind of a mess, and after working in a barn or with livestock all day, you learned to wash your hands often. When he reached for her sink, though, he saw her faucet was dribbling—not just from the tap, but from both knobs, and no amount of twisting made the water turn off. "This is broken."

"I know. My landlord . . ." She trailed off. "It's on the list."

Right. Of course she knew it was broken. He washed his hands quickly, then glanced around at the old kitchen. Just like he suspected, there was a bucket tucked surreptitiously in a corner to catch drips. No wonder the place smelled like mildew. Back home in Alaska, if the cabin he'd shared with his brothers had a leaky roof, they all crawled all over the damn thing to get it patched up. You took care of stuff, didn't let it go to heck. Her landlord hadn't gotten the memo, though, and the entire place needed a good fixing, in his estimation.

Caleb couldn't say that to her, though. It was clear she knew that already. Despite her elegant clothing—*thin*, warm-weather elegant clothing, he noticed—she had an embarrassed expression on her face. She didn't like him seeing this place. Not like this.

He cleared his throat and held his hand out. "Keys."

She pulled them out of her purse and then hesitated. "Why?"

"Gonna fix you."

Amy's jaw dropped and she gave him a look of concern. "Excuse me?"

He flushed. He really needed to learn to stop blurting things out before he thought. He composed himself, thinking through the words before stating them slowly. "I am going to fix your car. I need the keys so I can drive it over to the ranch in the morning to take a look at it. If I can't get it working, I'll tow it to the garage."

"Oh. But . . . if it's the alternator, isn't that expensive?" She held the keys out, hesitating. "I don't know much about cars. And I don't have much money . . ."

Caleb held his hand out, waiting.

Still, she hesitated. "We don't exactly hand our keys over to strangers in the city, you know."

He'd given her a ride home. Even now, she was wearing his blanket around her shoulders. He was in her phone. She'd called him for help . . . but he was a stranger? Amy must have seen something on his face, because she hesitated for only a moment longer before handing her keys over. "Just . . . let me know how much it costs, okay?"

"I'll be back at seven."

"For what?" Her brows furrowed and she gave him a curious look.

"I can give you a ride to work, too."

"Oh. That's very kind of you but it's Friday night. I don't work again until Monday."

"Monday morning, then."

He wasn't being kind. Not really. Caleb managed to nod and then left her house, realizing as he got back into his truck that she'd given him all her keys, even her house keys. Damn, but she was trusting. Someone could take advantage of her if she wasn't careful and if he wasn't around. The thought worried him, but he'd just have to talk to her about that.

Then again, talking was hard. Maybe he'd write her a note. Or would that seem creepy? He didn't know. He watched her house for a bit, and when the lights went out, he drove home, his thoughts on fire with possibilities.

She hadn't known his face before. She knew it now. He'd rescued her. He had her car to tow, and a standing date with her on Monday morning. He'd left his blanket with her. He had her keys.

There were endless opportunities to see her again, not just that Santa crap. He needed to take advantage of these opportunities, too. If he was just chauffeuring her around like a nice guy, he'd get the chance to talk to her, more than just the blurted-out responses he kept flinging at her. He could hold a real conversation with her.

He could bask in her presence.

This was everything he'd wanted from the moment he'd seen her . . . and he needed to not mess this up. Caleb had to tread a thin line—he didn't want to scare her and be too pushy, but he also didn't want her to get away, not when he had the chance to romance her.

So he drove home, his thoughts whirling, and when he got to the Swinging C Ranch, instead of heading to his private cabin back behind the main house, he raced over to Jack's and pounded on the door.

Jack didn't answer—not right away. He slept like the

dead, Caleb knew. Years of dealing with Hank's snoring and Caleb's habit of reading by flashlight, and Jack had learned to sleep through anything. So Caleb continued to pound at the door, waiting patiently for his brother to wake up.

"Okay, okay," Jack finally called out hoarsely. "Jesus. Give me a moment." He came to the door a few seconds later, his hair standing straight up, and gave Caleb a red-eyed look. "Is someone dead?"

"No."

"Well, someone's about to be." He glared at Caleb. "What the hell's so important?"

Caleb pushed inside, ignoring his younger brother's sour attitude. "You have to help me. This is my big chance to win Amy."

"Win Amy . . . what the heck?" Jack scrubbed at his face with a tired hand. "What are you talking about? And where have you been?"

"Amy's car broke down by the side of the highway," Caleb said, sliding into the recliner by Jack's TV. He kicked up his legs and watched his grumpy brother as Jack settled on the side of his bed. "She said she didn't have anyone to call so she called me and I went to go rescue her. She cried the entire time I was there, too."

"I'd cry if your ugly ass showed up to save me, too," Jack teased, and Caleb tossed his hat at his brother. "You think she wants to date you now?"

"I don't think she was thinking about anything except her car being broken down." He thought about the two humping Santa dolls in the trunk of the car and felt his face get hot. That was . . . damned odd. "I'm picking her up Monday morning to take her to work and I told her I'd get her car fixed."

"What? Ya damned sucker." Jack shook his head. "I should have known. She's gonna bat her eyes at you and use you like a sponge."

Caleb shook his head. Jack hadn't seen how distressed Amy was, how utterly alone and adrift she'd looked. "She's not using me. And she needs help. You should see her place. It's a mess. Leaky faucets and a hole in the roof, and she acts like she doesn't know what to do with it. She doesn't know how to take care of anything." He hesitated for a moment. "And she rescued a dog, too. A blind one."

"Oh man, don't tell Uncle Ennis. He's going to practically invite her into the family when he hears that."

Invite Amy into the family? Caleb was okay with that . . . as long as it meant she was marrying him. As long as they weren't, like, siblings or anything. "I need to use this opportunity to talk to her," Caleb said to his brother. "Help me think of what to do."

"And this can't wait until morning?" Jack yawned.

"No, I have to start working on a plan now. I'm giving her a ride to school Monday because her car's busted, remember? Pretty sure it's the alternator."

"If it is, you can fix that," Jack said absently. He rubbed his head, thinking. "Okay. So you want to use this time to romance her, huh?" He squinted at Caleb. "How'd it go tonight? You say anything stupid?"

"Oh yeah," Caleb muttered. "But maybe if I'm around her enough she won't care." Or maybe if he was around her enough, he'd loosen up and stop saying such dumb shit. Either one worked for him. After all, Hank had been married to Becca for about five months now, and Caleb was able to string sentences together around her finally.

Not long ones, but real sentences. It was a start. He was

sure he could do the same with Amy, preferably before he had to dress up as Santa.

"Okay," Jack said, rubbing his hands. "I got it."

Caleb sat up, tensing. "What? What's the plan?" Of the three Watson brothers, Jack was the one who was great with women. If anyone had ideas, it'd be his brother. He always knew what to say.

"You said her car was busted, right?" When Caleb nodded, Jack continued. "And her house was a mess? Broken stuff?"

Caleb nodded again.

"You offer to help her with all this stuff. She's got no money, right? So she could use the help of a nice guy like you to fix her faucet and help her with her car." Jack gave him a smug smile.

That . . . didn't seem like much of a plan. "I was going to do that anyhow, Jack. I can't just leave her with her faucets dripping and her car broken down. That ain't who I am. I can fix all that stuff lickety-split."

"I know you can, dummy." Jack sat up and smacked Caleb lightly across the forehead with the back of his hand. "But for this to work, you need to fix this stuff nice and slow. You take your time. Fixing her faucet? That's gonna take at least a full afternoon."

"It is?" He was pretty sure the wax ring just needed to be replaced on the knobs and—

"It is," Jack emphasized. "And maybe while you're helping her with it, you take your shirt off and flex a little."

That . . . didn't sound much like something Caleb would do. Then again, telling her that he'd "do Mrs. Claus" and then bolting away sounded more like something he'd do, so Jack's idea was better. "Go on."

"You can help her fix her car, but maybe it just takes a long time. And you take a lot of breaks." Jack shrugged one shoulder. "And you chitchat with her. Talk to her about things you like. Things you know about."

"Like the Donner Party," Caleb added immediately.

"Aren't they the ones that ate each other?" Jack furrowed his brows and shook his head at his brother. "You really are terrible at this shit. Don't talk to her about cannibals. Talk to her about things that interest her."

"Like . . . ?"

"Well, the obvious one is that it's the holidays. Ask her about Christmas. Ask her what she's doing for Christmas. Ask her about the kids in her class. There's a million things. Make it seem like you're interested in what she has to say."

That wouldn't be too hard, because he was absolutely interested in what she had to say. Everything that came out of Amy's mouth was endlessly fascinating to him. "And fix things like I planned, but go real slow."

"Super slow," Jack agreed.

"You're a genius."

"I know." His younger brother gave him a smug look. "We'll get you hooked up with this schoolteacher yet. We just need to be crafty."

Jack made it sound like a challenge, and that sat a little wrong with Caleb. Amy wasn't a prize to be won. She was a person—a sweet, gentle woman with a brilliant smile and sad eyes that made him want to give her the world. But Jack was the expert.

Caleb was just a tongue-tied cowboy who was terrible with women. So he'd defer to Jack.

This plan was a good one, though, and Caleb was encouraged. He left Jack's cabin behind and went to his own, but he couldn't fall asleep. He was too busy thinking of all the things he needed to do to help out Amy.

He'd become her new best friend, the one she could lean on for all her troubles . . . and then maybe once they were friends, she'd realize she was in love with him just like he was with her.

A man could dream.

CHAPTER FIVE

*F*ix things slowly, Caleb reminded himself as he drove up to Amy's place at the crack of dawn on Monday morning. He'd dropped off dog food for Donner on Saturday morning but left it on her porch so he wouldn't have to talk to her. He hadn't been ready for that yet. This morning he would help her with a few things around the house, then meet up with Jack after he and Hank finished morning chores at the farm. They'd drive out to Amy's car and tow it, and then Caleb could fix the car at his leisure and romance Amy at the same time.

He was prepared this morning.

Didn't matter that he hadn't slept a lick since Friday—he could sleep some other time. Right now he was fired up with opportunity. He'd been in Painted Barrel for months now and never really had a chance to spend time with the beautiful teacher. Now he was going to take every opportunity and squeeze them for every moment, just like Jack suggested.

So he was bringing over breakfast. Fresh coffee was in

an extra-large thermos, heavily sugared and creamed because she'd sucked his coffee down Friday night and Libby had mentioned once that her teacher liked lots of stuff in her coffee just like her uncle Caleb, and it had stuck in his mind as just another reason why Amy was perfect for him. He'd snagged some of the fresh-baked pumpkin-spice muffins that Becca had sent with Hank, along with a paper bag of Christmas cookies. For her dog—Donner, hell of a name— he'd raided Uncle Ennis's vet clinic and gotten a leash and harness, more dog food, and treats, and he'd tossed the bundle of goods into the back of his truck, along with his toolbox and a shovel.

In his pocket, he had a series of notecards with phrases he could reference when he talked to her. Written on them were good conversation starters that he'd thought up. Things like "So, what's your story?" and "Are you spending the holidays with family?" and "Have you finished your Christmas shopping?" He had one with weather-related phrases, and one with teacher types of things to ask her. He flipped through them as he drove down the snowy roads toward Painted Barrel. He wasn't memorizing them, because he knew himself well enough to know that the moment he saw her, they'd all fly out of his head anyhow. He was practicing saying them aloud, because the more comfortable he was with each phrase, the more likely it wouldn't trip on his tongue.

"So, what's your story?" he asked aloud to the truck as he drove. "What brought you to Painted Barrel? What made you take up teaching?"

Jack would laugh his fool head off if he heard Caleb. Hank would, too. Uncle Ennis and Becca would probably just look at him with pity, though. That might be worse than the laughter.

He got to her house long before dawn was even peeking

through the sky. Caleb didn't ring the doorbell just yet, though. Instead, he parked in the street and got out his shovel and a bag of rock salt. He felt a little bad about leaving it icy all weekend, but she wasn't going anywhere, he reckoned. Caleb cleaned off the sidewalks and the driveway, scraped the ice off the porch and the steps, and because her neighbor's yard was pretty close (and because he was still nervous), he did their drive, too. All the while, he muttered to himself. "What made you take up teaching? What's your story? What made you decide to move to Painted Barrel? What did you do before coming here?"

He was going to nail this shit.

With that confident thought going through his head, Caleb put the shovel away, took a deep breath, and grabbed the bag of food and the extra-large thermos. Hands full, he knocked on the door and waited. It was early. Real early, and he wondered if she was asleep. That might be awkward, especially if she was in her pajamas. He'd had a lot of time to daydream about what Amy looked like when she slept, though, and he didn't think she was a pajama type. More of a silky nightie with a bit of lace and hardly any straps . . .

And now he was sweating.

Caleb sucked in a breath as she peeked through the window in the living room, and then he heard steps coming toward the door. His cock was uncomfortably hard in his pants—all that thinking about her in a nightie—but his coat was long and hopefully she wouldn't notice anything.

She got to the door, and sure enough, she was in a flannel robe, a bright-red-and-green holiday affair that hadn't figured into his fantasies (but would now), and her hair was pulled up into a messy knot atop her head. There were dark circles under Amy's eyes and she blinked at him sleepily. "Oh. You're here early. I'm not ready."

"You're a problem," he blurted, then winced when her eyes widened. "*It's* not a problem."

The dog pushed past him, heading into the yard, and Amy grimaced, heading out onto the porch after him. "No, Donner, wait—"

A runaway dog, he could handle. "I'm on it."

Caleb set the bags down on the porch, dug out the leash and harness, and followed the dog into the snow. Luckily, Donner wasn't going far. He sniffed, looking for the perfect place to do his business, and when he was done, Caleb clicked his tongue and the dog sat as if trained. That answered that— he was probably a ranch dog that had been dumped once he'd lost his eyesight, or wandered away from his home. Either way, he was smart. "Good boy," Caleb murmured, keeping his hands on the dog's matted fur and petting him as he collared him. He kept the leash short and clicked his tongue, then patted his side as he walked so the dog would have a noise to follow. Donner fell into step right at his side, obedient and calm.

Amy beamed at them from the doorway. She was beautiful this early in the morning, so beautiful it made his chest ache just to look at her. "You're a genius," she told Caleb. "He's been running away all weekend and I have to keep luring him back."

"Ranch dog," was all he said, and offered her the leash as he went inside. The interior of her place looked worse now that he'd had the weekend to process things. It didn't match who she was. Amy was always immaculately groomed, and her clothes looked fancy. This place looked as if college kids inhabited it, with its mismatched furniture and bare walls. It was damned odd, especially for someone who was always as elegant as she was.

When Caleb turned, though, he saw that the blanket he'd wrapped around her Friday night was on the small, worn love seat. Had she slept there all weekend? Why? It looked damned uncomfortable. He noticed the musty smell was just as strong this morning as it was Friday night and began to wonder. "Gonna look around."

"Oh, okay." She held the leash and led the dog into the kitchen. "Let's get you some breakfast, Donner."

Caleb did some poking while she fussed over the dog. He opened doors and closets. Saw the neat and tidy bathroom and frowned to himself at the leaking faucets there. The closets were full of clothing, but everything else seemed to be in order. There was a guest room full of boxes, all neatly labeled, but no furniture. Her bedroom was the last spot to check out, and he hesitated for a moment, not wanting to pry into her privacy. Curiosity got the better of him, and he opened the door. He saw the caved-in ceiling and the stripped bed, and the smell of old, standing water was overwhelming. He'd seen enough, and it made him angry.

Why wasn't anyone taking care of this place? She was renting it, right? Whoever was renting it to her was a real dick who clearly didn't care if the place was livable or not. He made a mental note to ask Becca who Amy's landlord was. Becca was good friends with Amy, and she always had all the town gossip. She'd know what was going on.

Until then, it was up to Caleb to help Amy. To take care of her. Jack had told him to take his time and fix things slow. He'd do that with the car, but everything else? There was enough stuff to keep him busy here for weeks on end, no pretending necessary.

So he closed the door to the bedroom and said nothing.

No sense in shaming her. It wasn't her fault the ceiling had collapsed, but it bothered him that she was sleeping on that damned love seat. He paused to text Jack.

CALEB: When you head this way, get the mattress out of my cabin and bring it with you.

JACK: Aww shit. You moving in? You work faster than I thought!

CALEB: No. You'll see when you get here.

JACK: Interesting . . .

He'd let Jack stew on that for a bit. For now, he had work to do. Caleb headed toward the kitchen, where Amy was hugging the bag of dog food to her side and gaping at the cellophane-wrapped plate of muffins that he'd brought, along with the cookies. "Are you sure you meant to bring all this?"

He shrugged, heading toward her sink. "This is a problem."

"I know," she told him, getting a chipped bowl out of the pantry. "My landlord said his guy would be by soon enough to handle it, but I haven't seen him yet. He must be busy."

Caleb grunted. His estimation of her landlord went from rock bottom to even lower. He watched her for a moment, noticing that all her dishes were mismatched. It was just another thing that didn't add up. She fed the dog before herself, and he went out to his truck to get his toolbox. When he came back, she was tackling the muffins and coffee, a look of pure bliss on her face.

"I don't know how to thank you," Amy said to him, a cup of coffee in hand. "This is amazing. You're amazing."

He was going to blush like an idiot if she kept praising him, so he said nothing. Just went to her sink and pulled open the doors underneath to look at the pipe work. There were leaks under there, too, with a bucket underneath to catch water. No surprise. Everything in this dump of a house seemed to be leaking. He got out his wrench, and as he did, he brushed against the notecards in his pocket. Right. He wanted to ask why the hell she was living in this small, crappy place, why she was so broke, why she was alone. Those words would come out wrong, though. He needed to stick to the script he'd made himself, the lines he'd practiced.

What did you do before you came here?

Tell me about yourself.

"What did you do to yourself?" he blurted, then winced. Damn his tongue for being such an idiot.

But she only laughed. "I've been asking myself that for ages."

"Came out wrong," Caleb said, glad he was hiding his face under the sink so she couldn't see his embarrassment. It took him a moment to compose himself, to remind his brain of a proper question. "What brought you to Painted Barrel? That's what I meant."

She gave a slow, sad sigh. "A divorce."

He said nothing. What could he possibly say? He was angry that some jackass had had her in his life before Caleb did and that idiot had tossed her away. He was also ridiculously glad for that divorce, because otherwise he'd have never had the chance to sit in Amy Mckinney's kitchen, his hands on her drippy sink, his heart thumping like an out-of-control freight train.

"Before you ask, no, he didn't cheat on me," Amy offered. "It was my idea."

"Wasn't gonna ask." Though he did like that it was her idea to get divorced. It meant she wasn't hung up on her ex. That made his path easier.

Well . . . not that he had much of a path. When it came to women, Caleb was just completely in the dark.

"It doesn't matter," Amy continued softly. "I'm here now, and I'm on my own. I'm happy. I am." He wasn't sure if she was trying to convince herself or him. "And on that note, I should get ready for school. Are you sure you don't mind driving me? I can ask one of the other teachers—"

"I'll take you."

"I appreciate it. So much." He heard her get to her feet, and then she came over and touched his shoulder lightly before leaving the kitchen. A moment later, he heard the water in the bathroom turn on, and the pipe in his hands gave an alarming gurgle that drew his attention back to it.

He should have told her not to take a shower in a house when a strange man was working on her pipes. Any red-blooded man in his right mind would be tempted to open that door and join her. He knew he was. He scowled at himself and focused on the sink, trying not to think about Amy undressing or soaping her body up.

He was here to help her out, not to be a pervert. She felt safe around him.

Jack would tell him that was a problem. That her being "safe" enough to shower with him in the house meant he wasn't on her radar at all as a man. He was about as important as the filthy dog in the kitchen.

Caleb glanced over at the dog—Donner. "Damned if you do, damned if you don't."

*   *   *

By the time she was ready for work, Caleb had an idea of how to fix the leak under the sink and had already tightened the seals on the knobs to stop the leak above. He had a mental list of parts he needed from the hardware store, and it was getting longer by the minute. Of course, that list flew out of his head the moment she appeared in the kitchen again, her eyes sparkling, wearing a slim, long-sleeved green dress that made her eyes look bluer than the ocean.

It made all the words he'd been saving up fall out of his head entirely.

"Are you sure you want to drive me? I can walk. It's only a few blocks." She smiled at him even as she shrugged on that too-thin coat. He looked at her shoes—beige high heels—and wanted to shake his head at how impractical she was. It was December in Wyoming. Didn't she have warm clothing? Then again, given the state of her place, he supposed she didn't.

He wondered about this divorce. He wouldn't ask, but, oh, he'd wonder.

Caleb just grabbed his keys and headed for the door. Amy followed him, a little hesitant. "Do you think Donner will be okay? I'm afraid to leave him outside without me here. I wanted to give him a bath, but he doesn't trust me yet." She bit her lip, gazing at Caleb. "Does this make me a bad pet parent? I've never had a dog before, so I don't know what I'm doing wrong or right."

"'S'fine."

She watched him a moment longer, biting her lip. "You sure?"

He was going to be there with the dog today, wasn't he?

He added dog bathing to his to-do list. His brothers would just have to pick up the slack with the herd today. They'd understand, and if they didn't, he'd just smack 'em on the back of the head.

Hank would understand at least. He'd been all tore up over Becca all spring.

So he grunted again and gestured at the door, pulling his hat on. She followed him out, shivering when the cold blast of morning wind hit her, and he made a mental note to get her a warmer coat. The thing she had was just ridiculous. Boots and a coat, he mentally added to his list.

They drove one street before she gasped and clutched his arm, nearly making him drive off the road. "Wait! Stop!"

He jerked to a halt, stomping on the brakes as the truck slid, looking for a child or a dog or something that was about to run out into the street.

Amy fumbled with her seat belt. "I need that tree."

"What?" he bit out, not sure he heard her correctly.

She was getting out of the car, though, trotting over on the icy street to the curb, where a dried-up husk of a Christmas tree had been set by the garbage. At first, he didn't think she was serious. But a moment later, she grabbed the tree by one of the branches and he watched as dried pine needles showered to the ground.

Okay, she *was* serious.

Caleb parked his truck nearby and moved to her side. "What the hell are you doing?"

Amy blinked those big eyes at him. She let go of the tree and it gave another rain of crispy, dried needles. "If it's at the curb, they're throwing it out, right?" She looked uncertain for a moment. "I was just . . . I thought I could take it. It's a Christmas tree."

"I know what it is." It was also a dried-out husk that had

been cut too early and not given water. Not only was it dead; it was dry enough to be tinder. It was a fire hazard and her house had enough problems.

"I don't have a tree," she told him patiently, then reached for it again. "Can we put this in your truck and take it to my house? I promise it won't take long."

"No."

"Oh." She looked crestfallen. "Okay. I guess it is a little messy. I've never had a live tree before. Mine always came from the department store." She gave him a timid smile. "I'm sorry. I just got excited. You're right. It was silly of me."

Now he felt as if he'd kicked a puppy. "We can get it."

"No, no, it's fine." Her smile turned even brighter. "I don't need a tree. There's nothing to put under it anyhow. I'm better off saving my pennies for dog food than trying to decorate it. I'm having enough trouble decorating my classroom." She chuckled and headed back toward the truck.

Caleb stared after her for a moment, then shook his head. Hell. Now he was going to have to add a tree to the list of things to get for her. Not a shitty, dried-up tree like that, but a real one. He'd shake the birds out of a tree and cut it down himself if he had to. He'd do everything for her. He just needed a chance for his tongue to loosen up and he could explain himself.

Today wasn't that day, though.

He got back into the truck and they both sat in uncomfortable silence as he drove up to the school. Caleb tried to think of the right thing to say, to tell her that the whole tree thing wasn't a big deal, that he'd take care of things for her, but when he tried to phrase it in his head, his mind went blank. He kept turning over ideas, trying to think of just the right thing, and then they were suddenly at the school. He pulled up to the curb and then got out to walk her to the door.

"Oh, you don't have to do that," Amy said, giving him an apologetic little smile. "You've already done so much."

But it was still dark outside, and the least he could do was walk her to her classroom. It was the polite, gentlemanly thing to do . . . and it gave him another opportunity to talk to her. *Think,* he told himself as he walked at her side into the school. *Think of something to say. Anything. Comment on the weather. Ask if she's enjoying the holidays. Pull out your cards and go over one of the lines you rehearsed.*

He did none of those things. Instead, he was utterly silent as they walked to her door. He opened it for her—at least he remembered that much—and was about to say something, anything, when she gasped.

"What the heck? Is that for me?"

Amy swept forward, and as she did, Caleb got a good look at what was making her so startled. It was a massive bouquet of red and white roses, so large that it nearly took up one-half of her desk. She moved forward in a trance, pulling a glittery card off a stick. "From your Secret Santa." She turned and gave him a startled look. "You . . . ?"

He shook his head.

It wasn't from him. She had another suitor, apparently. Some other guy was giving his woman flowers, and she was beaming ear to ear, utterly surprised and delighted at the sight of them.

This put a kink in his plans. He'd been planning on taking his time with her, getting comfortable enough to have real conversations, maybe eventually ask her out on a date in a couple of months, when he felt like he could relax around her and just be himself.

Clearly that wasn't going to work. If she had another guy interested in her, Caleb had to beat him at his own game.

He just had to figure out how.

CHAPTER SIX

The enormous bouquet of flowers puzzled Amy all day long. Every time she sat at her desk, the perfume of them practically choked her. They were gorgeous, granted, but now that she was a broke teacher, she knew how much this sort of thing cost, and the price tag of it made her uncomfortable.

From Your Secret Santa.

She'd read the card a half dozen times in the last hour, hoping for a clue as to who that Secret Santa could be. The card was from the local florist, the scribbly handwriting probably from whoever took the message. And there were two dozen red roses with another dozen white roses sprinkled in the mix. The vase—and spread—was enormous.

All the other teachers in the school were envious. She got visits from all of them as they took breaks, each woman asking Amy about the flowers and gently prying as to who sent them.

Amy had no clue. She barely knew anyone in town. Who would send her flowers?

At first, she worried that they were from her ex, Blake. That this was him paving the way for a reconciliation. The thought upset her so much that she moved the roses into the coat closet after lunch so she wouldn't have to look at them. After a little more time passed, though, that didn't seem like it could be the case.

Blake was still angry at her. The last time they spoke, he'd sneered and told her that she'd come crawling back to him. He wasn't the type to bribe or play coy. No, Blake was good at destroying her self-confidence and making her "easier to manage" that way. Flowers weren't his thing.

Someone else, then.

A name popped into her head—Greg, her Realtor-slash-landlord. Immediately, she hoped that wasn't the case. Greg was nice . . . at least, nice enough. But he reminded her far too much of Blake and she wasn't interested in that kind of guy right now. She was more interested in getting her darn faucet repaired.

Over and over, these thoughts whirled in her head as the day crawled past. They did math songs in the morning, and after recess—an indoor recess—they'd started quiet time. Right now, they were reading books, which was a welcome distraction from the flowers.

"Miss Mckinney?" one of the children asked as they sat on the floor and she read them a book.

"Yes, Ella?"

The little girl put her hand down and wiggled on her mat, happy to be called on. "Are we going to have a Christmas tree in our classroom? Miss Lindon's class has one."

Her heart sank a little. Miss Lindon loved spoiling her kids, and unfortunately, the other teachers struggled to keep up. Miss Lindon's tree was currently covered with gourmet candy canes and chocolate foil stars, and kids that answered questions correctly got to eat those candies. A pile of presents was under the tree, and Jenny—Miss Lindon—had been shopping for months for her kids.

Amy hadn't bought a thing for her kids yet, unless they wanted some of the ramen out of her pantry.

But she couldn't tell them that. It wasn't their fault their teacher had gone through a contentious divorce and her crappy ex-husband wasn't paying the alimony payments that would help her start her new life. They deserved to have the same classroom experience that other students did.

So she lied. "Your tree was in my car, but it broke down. I'll bring it in when my car is fixed, and then we'll all spend a day decorating it. How does that sound?"

The students cheered, and Amy mentally went through her wardrobe and shoes. Could she pawn Louboutins to get money for the tree? Did pawnshops even take shoes? It was worth asking, she supposed. She went back to reading, determined not to think about the tree issue until later.

By the time the day was ending, Amy had a headache from the cloying rose smell, she'd made a list of potential items to pawn, and she'd texted Layla twice about the alimony payments. Still nothing, but that wasn't a big surprise. There'd been nothing since she'd moved out of state, and Amy knew he was doing it to punish her.

Okay, she'd need a plan B. Maybe she could babysit to make some money? She'd talk to Becca—Becca would know people around town that might want a babysitter. And wouldn't a schoolteacher be the perfect one?

Then it was time to do the end-of-day cleanup song, and the schoolroom was tidied, and gloves and coats were put on and checkmarked on Amy's list. She marched everyone out front, dropped off the bus riders, then checked off heads that already had parents waiting out front. Becca gave her a quick wave as she picked up her stepdaughter, Libby, and even Amy's normal straggler, Billy, was out the door on time. Huh. Amy went back to her classroom, cleaned up, and prepared for the next day. She "graded" papers and put stickers on them, cut out construction paper strips for Christmas garlands, and prepared supply buckets for the next day's activities. As she put the final pair of safety scissors into Tammy's bucket, she looked up.

Caleb was in the doorway.

She jumped, startled, and her hand went to her chest. "Oh dear god, you scared me."

His hard face was impossible to read. He said nothing to her reaction. Didn't greet her. Didn't laugh. Didn't apologize. Said nothing at all. He just leaned against the doorway and waited.

Caleb unnerved her.

He'd been nothing but nice, of course, but the man was silent to the point of distressing.

Even so, he was doing her a favor. He was picking her up from work so she wouldn't have to walk in the cold, just like he'd picked her up on Friday. He'd been her knight in shining armor when he'd arrived to rescue her, and he'd wrapped her in a blanket and gave her a warm drink and he just . . . fixed things.

She'd been so completely and utterly relieved that someone had arrived to take care of the situation that she'd cried tears of joy. So now, today, she didn't even mind his cranky expression.

Well, she minded it a little.

He'd just . . . he'd be such a handsome man if he smiled every now and then. He had the most amazingly beautiful eyes with long, unfair lashes. He had a rugged face and a thick beard, and the cowboy hat he wore made him look damn good . . . or at least it would if his mouth wasn't flat in a somber expression. She'd met his brother Hank a few times, and while the man was an intimidating mountain of a human, he smiled when his playful, talkative little daughter was around, or when he looked at his new wife. Becca spoke glowingly of Hank, so Amy just figured he was quiet around strangers.

But Caleb? Even his sister-in-law said he was a very silent type and he rarely spoke to her.

Amy beamed at him, because it didn't matter that he was gruff and surly. His actions were everything. "Are you sure you don't mind? I can walk. It's probably good for me."

He glanced down at her shoes, then gave his head a small shake and stepped out into the hall, a silent signal that he'd wait for her. She tidied things one last time and then pulled on her jacket, readying to go out into the bitter winter wind. He really was the nicest man. "I hope I'm not taking up too much of your day."

He didn't respond to that. Not even a grunt.

Gosh, he'd talked to her Friday night and this morning, hadn't he? She hadn't imagined that? He was so silent right now it was starting to unnerve her, though. Amy tucked the vase of flowers against her side and walked out into the hall with him.

That got his silent attention. He frowned at the flowers as if they offended him.

"Oh, I'm sorry. Are you allergic? I didn't want to leave them here because the smell was a little overwhelming in the classroom. I can put them back . . . ?"

He shook his head. "'S'fine."

Well . . . that was a word. Maybe even two, if she used

her imagination. It was a start. "I appreciate you taking all this time to help me out, Mr. Watson. I don't know how I can thank you." He said nothing, but that didn't surprise her, so she continued on. "I hope I'm not pulling you away from something urgent. If I am, I totally understand and I can always just . . ." He kept walking, utterly quiet.

If she didn't know better, she'd say he didn't like her. But he'd been so kind Friday night. Kind this morning, too. Even now, he wasn't being rude. Just . . . quiet. So she tried not to take it personally. Tried not to think about Blake, who was never silent, who liked to tell her in great detail all the things she did wrong on a daily basis.

But she was done with Blake. He wasn't worth spending a single moment thinking about.

It was an awkward ride back to her house, but she audibly gasped when they pulled up and her car was in the driveway. "You fixed it already?"

Caleb shook his head.

"It's not fixed?"

"Needs alternator part."

Oh. She wanted to ask if that would take long to get, but a more worrying thought hit her. "Is . . . the alternator expensive?" She'd add it to her list of things she'd have to pay for by pawning things. A Christmas tree for the classroom, presents, an alternator, a new ceiling for the bedroom, a new mattress . . . it made her stomach hurt just thinking about all of that.

Caleb shrugged, as if that answered everything. She wanted to scream in frustration at him, but she took a deep breath, clutched the cloying roses, and got out of the truck.

When she got inside her house, though, something seemed . . . different. She set the roses on the counter by the sink and it took her a moment to notice that her faucet wasn't dripping. Surprised—and pleased—she turned the water on and off to test it. It worked perfectly, and not a single drop spouted from the handle. When she turned the water off, nothing dripped. "You fixed this."

Caleb grunted.

She looked around the kitchen, but the dog wasn't in his corner. His food bowl was empty, too. "Have you seen Donner?"

He nodded and walked into the living room. She followed, and to her surprise, he opened the bedroom door and waited, watching her. Amy stepped inside and bit back another gasp of surprise.

The ceiling, once a gaping wound that led to the attic, had been covered. A blue waterproof tarp stretched from one end of the ceiling to the other, taped at the edges of the wall. He'd done this for her. And there was a freshly bathed Donner on a big, plaid cushioned dog bed at the foot of her bed. Her bed wasn't a water-bloated mildew-scented mess, either. The bed had been made, a new set of sheets and blankets that she didn't recognize neatly tucked in. She touched the bed, wondering how he'd gotten the mattress so clean after she'd spent days trying to get the smell out . . . and realized it wasn't her mattress at all. This one was softer and didn't have a broken coil at the foot.

It was a different bed.

He'd done all this for her.

More tears misted her gaze, and she stared at her room with a sense of wonder and a growing sense of panic. Amy turned to Caleb, swallowing the knot in her throat. "You did all this?"

He watched her with those long-lashed eyes, and after a moment, he nodded.

Amy was overwhelmed. He'd fixed things in a day that

she'd been asking to be fixed for months now. He'd gotten her a new bed so she wouldn't have to sleep on the uncomfortable love seat again. He'd retrieved her car and ordered a part for it.

He'd even washed her dog.

She was really going to cry now, because it was wonderful, and yet she couldn't appreciate it, not truly. "I can't afford to pay you," she whispered. It was humiliating. When she was with Blake, they'd had lots of money. Her parents had had money, too. Now that she was alone and on her own, she was utterly penniless, and it was a hard contrast to get used to.

Caleb just blinked. He walked away from the bedroom door, and she followed him, uncertain and guilty. She waited for him to chastise her, to tell her to come up with the money.

Instead, with his back to her, he pointed at her living room window. "Gonna caulk that tomorrow. Take a look at the roof, too."

"Did you hear what I said? I can't pay you. This is nice, Mr. Watson. It's overwhelmingly nice and I can't get over it. But I don't have the money. I don't have the money for anything." She really was going to cry. Even now she was fighting the tears that threatened to burst free. "Please, just tell me how much an alternator part costs and don't fix anything else. I can't afford to pay you and while I appreciate it more than you know, I can't—"

"Pay. I know." He closed his eyes, as if bracing himself for some odd reason, and then slowly spoke. "The part for your car won't be in for a few days."

"Oh." Maybe she'd have time to get some money together between now and then. "I see—"

He turned toward the door and pulled out a piece of paper from his pocket and glanced at it. "My uncle is a vet," he said after a moment. "We'll take the dog to him tomorrow. See if he's chipped."

"Tomorrow?" she asked. "You want to do this again tomorrow?"

He nodded and then left, and she just stared at the door. Interacting with Caleb Watson was baffling. He acted as if he didn't like her. Like he didn't want to look at her. Like she was a pain in the ass he was simply tolerating. He sure wasn't talking to her much.

And yet . . . he was doing all these kind things for her. And he'd return tomorrow to do the same things.

She moved into her bedroom, where Donner was still curled up in his bed. He lifted his head as she sank down next to him and offered her hand for him to sniff. When he licked her hand, she petted his soft head. He was clean and dry, and to her surprise, he wasn't gray all over but a mix of black and white and gray. He looked handsome and smelled so much better. It was just another thing Caleb had taken care of for her.

"He must feel really sorry for me," Amy whispered to Donner.

The dog licked her hand as if in agreement.

CHAPTER SEVEN

For the next few days, Caleb continued to silently show up to Amy's house and get to work. One day, he crawled all over her roof, patching and shingling until it got dark. The next day, he stayed late and put up a new ceiling in her bedroom. It wasn't plastered, but with drywall up, it made her feel so much better. Her house was coming together, and it was all thanks to a silent, handsome cowboy that she wasn't entirely sure didn't hate her guts.

He never asked for money, either. He just drove her to school and got to work on her place. He was affectionate to the dog—who wasn't chipped, it turned out, so now Donner was more or less hers—and always made sure to carry a couple of treats. Donner loved him. Amy was having a hard time finding fault with him herself. Caleb was punctual. He was nice. Useful. Polite. He was also utterly silent and never smiled at her, which only made Amy more self-conscious in his presence. Even charity stopped being so generous after a while, right?

To make matters even more stressful, her Secret Santa had gone gifting crazy. A fake tree had shown up on her porch the next day, boxed. All it said was *From Secret Santa*, and she'd been so delighted that she took it to school and her students had a full day of helping her put it up and making paper ornaments to decorate it. They'd loved making it special. Amy had, too.

She was positive one of the other teachers—or a parent—had heard that she didn't have a tree and had stepped in, but when she asked around, no one confessed to the deed.

Another present had shown up at her desk at work, much to her chagrin. This time it wasn't flowers, but a huge box of chocolates, so she shared them with her students and saved them for rewards.

The next day, another fake tree was on her porch. This one, she dragged into the house. Caleb said nothing, just frowned at her as he worked on recaulking all her windows.

At work, this time there were new flowers—carnations—and a lovely rose-gold bracelet. She'd asked Caleb to drive her into Casper so she could pawn it, but he'd just narrowed his eyes at her and gone back to plastering the ceiling in her bedroom, so clearly the pawning would have to wait until she got her car back. It seemed like every time she turned around, Caleb was fixing something new at her house. It was the ceiling. It was the faucets. It was the cracks in the windows that were so bad that her heating bill was through the roof. It was fixing the creaky step on the front porch. It was rewiring the lights because when she plugged in her artificial tree (complete with prewired lights), everything in the living room went dark.

He said nothing at all, just went to work as if it was his place he was fixing up.

It was baffling to her. Caleb said even less than he ever

did. When she'd first met him, at least he'd blurt out jumbled sentences, but now he'd fallen into utter silence, and it unnerved her. She'd rather have him talking, even if he said the wrong thing. She hoped he wasn't angry at her, or offended at her helplessness. She tried to help him out as he worked, but he'd just take the tools from her hands and narrow his eyes at her, and she got the hint.

More presents rolled in at work, too. A thick jacket in the perfect size. Lined, heavy boots. More flowers. Christmas tree ornaments of crystalline birds that clipped to the branches and made her tree at home look festive and glittery. A box of holiday cupcakes. There was a randomness to the gifts that made them puzzling. Some were practical and appreciated—like the thick scarf and cap that went with the heavy coat—and some were just flighty and ridiculous. On Friday, she got a locket, a stuffed bear, and a fancy coffee maker.

Her coworkers were fascinated. The other teachers stopped by at recess or after classes were over to see what Amy had received that day. They oohed and aahed over the jewelry and flowers and gave her puzzled giggles at the more practical presents. Ironically, she was most excited about the coffee maker, because it would make heating water for her ramen that much easier.

"You're *sure* you don't know who it is?" Mrs. Lawrence asked her for the third time that Friday.

Amy shook her head. "Everything's signed Secret Santa."

"Sure they are." She gave an exaggerated wink. "You can't keep a boyfriend secret in this town. Wait and see."

"I don't have a boyfriend." That part was getting frustrating, too. With the constant barrage of gifts and flowers, everyone assumed she had someone. You didn't receive jewelry out of nowhere, after all. Even Amy knew that, and each time a new piece showed up, it made her uncomfortable.

"Well," Mrs. Lawrence said with a know-it-all expression on her face. "You should go out with whoever's sending these to you. It's clear he's in love."

Amy laughed awkwardly. "Maybe I should." It was flattering, even if it was a little mystifying. She couldn't figure out who the gift giver was. Every time she thought she had it figured out, a new gift would show up and mystify her. The gifts really did seem like Blake, trying to woo her back . . . except for the trees and the coat and the coffee maker, all things designed to make her life here more comfortable. She thought maybe it was a parent or a friend, or even the principal, who'd been known to cheat on his wife in the past. Awkward. But then she'd received a massive bouquet of mixed red and white flowers. There was a large poinsettia or two, red-edged white roses, and sprays of white flowers. It was beautiful . . . only the small white flowers looked like lily of the valley, a poisonous plant. Amy wasn't sure . . . but she was also going to be darn careful, and she'd immediately taken them to the school office to lock them away. Her class was made up of the youngest kids in the school. Who was so thoughtless to send flowers to a kindergarten teacher without checking to see what was in the bouquet?

It made no sense. None of it.

Every now and then, she wondered if it was Caleb . . . but he seemed just as surprised as she was every time she showed up with flowers.

Besides, she was pretty sure he didn't like her at this point. His silence told her he was doing things out of the goodness of his heart, not because he wanted to date her. He acted more like she was a nuisance than anything.

It wasn't Caleb.

So . . . who was it? And why? Someone who gave jewelry to a stranger wanted something from them. But . . . what?

It was constantly on her mind, to the point that she constantly texted Becca throughout the day. Like when the locket came in on Friday—she immediately texted Becca. She'd grown close to the beautician over the summer when she kept showing up at the salon, just desperate for female conversation that wasn't about classrooms or school starting. Becca was about the same age as Amy, single at the time, and they'd bonded right away. It was so nice to have a girlfriend in town, one who wouldn't immediately assume Amy was secretly seeing a rich man because of all the gifts. Someone who'd be just as mystified as she was.

> AMY: So in addition to the flowers and the coffeepot, I just got a locket.
>
> BECCA: WTF
>
> BECCA: Is there a picture inside the locket? Anything?
>
> AMY: No, the only thing inside says that it's 10-carat gold and the stone in it is a real ruby.
>
> BECCA: This is insane.
>
> BECCA: Do you think it could be a stalker?

AMY: Well, crap, now I do!

AMY: Do you think I'm in danger?

BECCA: Right now, no. But if it keeps escalating, it might be a problem.

BECCA: I would just keep a log of everything and don't wear the gifts.

AMY: I was going to pawn the jewelry, but I guess I'll hold on to it for now. Shoot.

AMY: Becca, I'm at my wit's end. Who could it be? I swear I haven't been giving anyone in town the wrong ideas.

BECCA: You're sure it's not Caleb?

AMY: God no, he hates me. You should see the dirty looks he gives me every time he picks me up.

BECCA: Caleb's harmless, I promise you.

AMY: He's the nicest, and he's fixed so much for me, but he's not doing a good job of hiding his dislike.

BECCA: Should I say something to Hank? Get him to straighten him out?

AMY: No! I feel guilty for saying anything at all. Just that it's not him.

AMY: I did think it was my ex, but some of the gifts don't make sense. Like they wouldn't be from him.

BECCA: Greg?

AMY: Ugh, I hope not.

BECCA: If it makes you feel any better, I don't think it's him, either. Flowers sound like him, jewelry and a coat do not.

BECCA: Maybe it's one of those cowboys at Sage's ranch? The vets? Have you met any of them?

AMY: I don't think I have?

BECCA: I'll ask around. Maybe one of them has a kid going to school. Let me see what I can find out.

AMY: Thank you, Becca. I appreciate it.

BECCA: Until then, stay safe! And don't take rides from strangers! ;)

AMY: I have to take a ride with Caleb, remember? He's still waiting on that part.

BECCA: Okay, if you have to get a ride with a stranger, Caleb's the one to trust. Later!

AMY: Later.

The conversation did nothing to settle her nerves. By the time Caleb showed up on Friday afternoon to drive her home, Amy was rattled. Did she have a stalker? She clutched the coffeepot to her chest, the new jewelry in her purse, and tried not to think about it as she got into his vehicle. She'd moved to Painted Barrel to start her life over, to get away from Blake and his controlling attitude and her parents' disapproval of their divorce. She just wanted a fresh, simple, easy life.

And now she had a freaking *stalker*?

Amy took a deep, shuddering breath. She could handle this. She could.

"You okay?"

She jumped at the sound of Caleb's gravelly voice, her heart pounding. She tried to smile over at him. "Fine. Great. Thank you for asking."

He gave her a curious look, those long lashes blinking, and then turned the truck on.

They drove in silence as they always did, and Amy clutched the coffeepot. To think she'd been overjoyed to get it, and now it was as tainted as the rest of the presents. She'd put them all in a box in the kitchen and decide what to do with them after the holidays. Hopefully her Santa would reveal himself between now and then. If not, it was all going into a donation box somewhere. She wouldn't even pawn it for money; she would just get it as far away from her as possible.

They got to her house and Amy immediately went into the kitchen as Caleb followed her in. "Any news on the part for my car?" she asked, even though she suspected the answer.

"Monday," he said.

Of course. A few more days without a vehicle, which meant she couldn't go grocery shopping or to a pawnshop or anything. She had no cash, no word on her alimony, nothing. Amy pursed her lips and set the coffee maker down, pushing it to the back of the counter. She went back to the living room, and Donner was on her love seat, curled up on one cushion and getting dog hair everywhere. She couldn't be mad, though, because his tail started thumping happily as she approached, and when she sat down, he immediately crawled over to her and started licking her face as she rubbed his ears.

For a blind dog, he knew just how to cheer her up. She hugged him close, burying her face in his soft, thick fur.

Okay. She could do this. Donner needed her.

And she still had a few things up her sleeve, a few options to explore. So she straightened her shoulders and looked at Caleb as he went to the window and ran his hand along the edges, testing for air. "I need to run some errands. Would you help me? If you're busy, I understand, but I need to get these done before the Christmas Carnival at the school tomorrow night."

He nodded, once.

"I can pay you for gas and for your trouble. I just need to go by my accountant's office first."

His eyes narrowed but he said nothing.

"Give me just a minute to get ready," she promised him brightly. She snuggled Donner a little longer and wanted to take him with her. A dog at her side would make her feel safer if she had a stalker. But she remembered how scared he was alone in her backyard, and when she'd taken him to the vet, so it was best that he stayed inside where it was safe and warm and familiar. She put extra food in his dish and waited, petting him a bit more as he sniffed the floor until he found his bowl. Then she washed her hands in the bathroom, pulled out a very specific purse from her closet, and reached for her new, warm coat.

And stopped.

The coat and her nice new boots, her scarf and her hat? Those were all tainted until she found out who was gifting them. Frustrated, she put on her lightweight camel jacket instead. She'd just shiver, damn it.

When Amy came out of her room with her bag, she beamed a brilliant smile at Caleb, who was frowning at her. He looked vaguely displeased, and so she said, "I hope it won't be a problem to take me out? If it is, I can call an Uber."

"I got it," he mumbled, ducking his head as he went to the front door and held it open for her.

All right, then. She gave him her most brilliant smile, determined to be cheery despite everything going wrong. If he was going to help her out, the least she could do was be good company. So she kept smiling all the way out to the car, and she smiled on through the brief drive to Main Street, where her accountant's office was. She arrived just as Layla was putting the key in the door.

Her friend's eyes widened at the sight of Amy. "Oh! Hey there. Did we have an appointment? I was going to run out early and do some shopping—"

Amy put a hand on Layla's arm and leaned in. "Can we talk in private? Five minutes, tops."

Layla glanced at Caleb's truck and then nodded, opening the door to the office again. "Of course."

"Any sign of my alimony?" Amy asked as they paused in the entryway.

"Girl, you know that answer as well as I do." Layla pushed up her heavy glasses. Unlike Amy, who only wore her glasses to read, Layla wore hers constantly. Her long, silky straight hair was caught up in a bun with three pencils shoved through it, and she was wearing a blazer over a *Star Wars* tee. "It's not coming anytime soon."

"I know, but I need money." Amy held out her bag. "You remember this?"

Layla froze. Her fingers fluttered as her hand went to her own purse. "Your Birkin?"

"Yeah. It's too expensive for me to use day to day, so it's just sitting in my closet." She'd gone into her first meeting with Layla with the purse, back when she'd first moved to Painted Barrel. Layla had absolutely swooned over it. "I'll sell it to you for a hundred fifty."

Layla shoved her glasses up her nose again. "Um, aren't they worth like ten grand or something?"

"Maybe. I don't know. My ex bought it for me. I could really use the money, Layla." Amy held it out to her accountant and friend. "Please."

The other woman touched the bag with trembling fingers. Through a few casual texted conversations, Amy knew Layla loved funky accessories and expensive shoes. Apparently she also loved expensive bags. "I shouldn't."

"Please. It's either you, or I take it to a pawnshop and hope they give me money—"

Layla squeaked in distress and clutched the bag to her chest. "You will not pawn my precious!" She mockingly pretended to claw at the air. "But you have to ask for more money, Amy, that's just not right."

"Two hundred?" Amy joked.

"I won't give you a penny less than three hundred," Layla said, hugging the purse to her. "Will you take a check?"

"Only if the bank will let me cash it tonight."

Layla grimaced. "Friday night after five? Cash it is. Give me a sec." She trotted back to her office, leaving Amy nervously waiting in the small lobby. To her relief, Layla reappeared a minute later with a stack of twenties. "Here you go, and Merry Christmas to me. You're sure you want to do this?"

"I'm sure." She was so relieved to see that money that she couldn't stop smiling. "You're the best. Thank you so much, Layla."

"Girl, no, thank *you*." She stroked her hand over the purse again. "If you change your mind, I'll give it back to you, I promise."

Amy wouldn't change her mind. She hugged Layla, thanked her again, and then tucked the money into her smaller Prada purse and headed back out to Caleb's truck. As they pulled away from the curb, she watched Layla leave the office, petting the massive new purse on her shoulder.

"Wasn't that yours?" Caleb asked, sounding as surly as ever.

"Yeah. I sold it to her for some quick cash." Amy sighed with relief. She already felt ten pounds lighter, some of her worries gone for the day. She could buy groceries. She could get presents for her kids to give to them at the carnival tomorrow night. She could pay Caleb back for some of the things he'd done. "Can I give you two hundred now and more later when I get back on my feet on payday?"

"No." He glared at the windshield. "Where to?"

"I need to give you some money at least," Amy protested. "Let me—"

"Where to?" he repeated again.

She lost her temper. Maybe it was all the weirdness of the week or the worry about her car and her finances, but she was tired of his short, shitty mood. "You are the most stubborn son of a bitch ever, I swear."

He looked over at her in surprise . . . and then laughed.

That surprised her just as much. Not the cussing—it was a habit she was trying to break—but his smile. It changed his somber, bearded face into something breathtaking. Oh. He had beautiful teeth, too, white and straight, and he was just . . . charming as hell when he smiled.

For a brief moment, she wished he was her Secret Santa after all. That someone as kind and thoughtful as Caleb was her secret admirer. Maybe that would get him to open up and really talk to her. In this moment, that was what she wanted more than anything, her loneliness a constant ache in her soul.

"Where to?" he asked again, a little more gently this time.

Amy sighed, the moment gone. "To town hall. I have to pick up my costume for tomorrow night. Have you gotten yours?"

He glanced over at her as he turned the truck. "Costume?"

"For Santa? You know, to play Santa Claus? I'm going to be Mrs. Claus?"

Caleb nodded slowly, though she could tell from his expression that he'd forgotten all about it. "The children will appreciate it," she said. "But they'll probably appreciate it more if Santa actually talks to them."

He grunted a response.

"For the record, Santa doesn't grunt, either."

He gave her a sharp look out of the corner of his eye.

She didn't care. It wasn't like she'd forced him to sign up. He'd volunteered. He had to know what was involved with playing Santa. If he wasn't going to do the job, he should have never thrown his hat in the ring. "I know you probably don't want to hear this, but some of those children have been looking forward to seeing Santa for weeks now. There's no mall around here for them to go and see him, so this might be their only chance to have this experience. However you feel about things, please keep that in mind and try to make this as wonderful for them as you can."

There was a long pause. "I'll try."

Amy let out a slow breath. "Thank you."

"It's . . . hard for me."

No shit, she wanted to say, but she didn't. He was nice, for all that she couldn't understand what he was thinking. He had a kind heart, she knew he did, so she needed to just smile and encourage him past it. "Just remember that they're children. Small children. All they want to hear is that they've been good enough to get a present from Santa. That's all."

He nodded again as he pulled the truck up to the municipal office. Painted Barrel was small as far as towns went, so the post office, water department, library, and pretty much everything else were all in the same building. Amy thought it was adorable and part of the town's charm. You literally knew everyone who lived here and what they did. It felt like a big family . . . even if she felt like the weird cousin who'd just arrived to spend the summer with relatives she barely knew.

As they parked, Caleb frowned at the building in front of them. "It's closed."

"It's not," Amy reassured him. "Sage said her new baby was fussing and her husband has a cold so she closed up early. She texted me to tell me she left a key under the mat so I can get in and take care of things. Come on." She slid out of the truck and headed for the building.

The key was just where Sage said it would be, and Amy flicked on a few lights, feeling a little uneasy as Caleb followed her in. She'd been glib about going in to retrieve the costumes, but now that she was inside, she felt like an intruder. Sage had told her that the costumes were in her office, so Amy headed in that direction and pushed the door open gently and turned on the light. Hanging from a hook on the wall were dry cleaner bags with *AMY* and *CALEB* paper signs taped to them. The rest of the office was covered in Christmas decor, interspersed with family photos of Sage and her husband cuddling their children. Amy picked up a recent photo, absolutely in love with Sage's brilliantly happy smile and the dimples on the fat baby she was holding.

"Ugly sweater," Caleb told her, leaning over her shoulder to look at the photo.

She chuckled. "It is not," Amy said, feeling the need to defend Sage and her child even though they really were quite hideous sweaters. "They're just festive. I like that they're so happy." That was the thing with Sage—she really was the happiest person Amy had ever met. It was impossible not to adore her. Amy set the photo down and moved toward the hanging costumes. "We'll have to try them on—"

"What?" Caleb blurted, looking at her with surprise.

"We'll have to try them on," she stated again, pulling the hangers labeled *AMY* off of the hook. "Sage said there were a few different sizes of costumes, and if none of them fit, we're going to have to do some emergency letting out. Santa can't wear skintight clothes, you know."

He just stared at her, his eyes wide.

She lowered her hanger, frowning at him. "You do know

what Santa looks like, right? Kinda fat and jolly?" She wiggled a finger in his direction. "While I appreciate the fitness you've got going on, the kids are going to want to see a jolly old elf, so you're going to need to stuff with a pillow."

He pulled off his hat and rubbed his head, and she noticed his face was bright red. Aw. He was embarrassed. Poor Caleb.

"It'll be fine," she reassured him. "I'll be at your side the whole time. The kids will love it. Here." Amy tucked her designated costumes against her body and gestured at the bathroom down the hall. "I'll go try mine on in the other room and you can shut the office door and try yours. If they don't fit right, we can go to my place and fix things. That way we're all set for tomorrow. Okay?"

He said nothing, as usual. Just slowly took down the garment bags with a pained look on his face.

"I'm going to take that as a yes," she told him merrily. "Be right back."

Amy headed down the hall and closed herself into the tiny municipal office bathroom. The building was an old one, which meant the floors creaked and weren't all that even, and all the fixtures were old. Even so, it was clean and neat, and she pulled out the first costume and tried it on.

To her dismay, it was far too tiny. Sage was a tall, sturdy woman and so Amy had been hoping that the costume would be roomy, but it was clearly for someone several sizes smaller than her. She put it aside and pulled out two others, giving them both a shot. One was like a tent and draped so low in the front that Amy's boobs were practically hanging out, so that one wouldn't work, either. The third dress would have to do. It was a nice costume, red with faux fur trimming around the collar and matching hat and curly, white-haired wig. The skirt was a little shorter than she'd have liked, puffy with a crinoline, and went barely to her knees because it was supposed to show off matching knee-high black boots with white fur cuffs. There were a few problems with the costume, one being that it was extremely tight across the chest and made her nipples and bra show through the fabric. Okay, she'd have to use some tape instead of a bra tomorrow. She'd done that for special occasions in the past and she could do so again. The boots were the other problem—they were tight on her feet and made her toes cramp painfully after a few minutes. She'd take them home anyhow and hope to find something that would look okay with the costume. If not, well, she'd put up with a bit of toe cramping. Amy eyed her figure in the mirror critically. She knew Mrs. Claus was supposed to be frumpy, but the costume was an odd mixture of cheesecake and holiday. Maybe it was her hourglass figure, which had seen far too many nights with Ben & Jerry's on the couch to be lean. Her butt was bigger than it should have been, and her boobs were, too, and maybe that was what was making the costume look so odd. Or maybe she was just paranoid. With a white wig on, wire-frame fake glasses, and some red circles on her cheeks, she'd look like a regular Mrs. Claus.

There was a knock at the bathroom door.

Oh. Was he waiting on her to come out? She *was* hogging the only bathroom in the municipal office, after all. Amy opened the door and grimaced an apology . . . which died in her throat.

Caleb was shirtless in front of her.

Words failed Amy as she stared at him. She knew he was fit. He had to be the way he crawled all over her roof, and he worked as a cowboy. That meant he was in shape. She just hadn't realized how in shape until she saw him now. His hand was on the Santa pants, holding them up around his slim waist, and he wore no shirt, which meant she had an impressive look at his lean, muscled chest. Dark hair lightly sprinkled firm pectorals and led down to a six-pack and obliques that rivaled any swimmer's. She'd never seen a chest like that outside of Hollywood.

"Oh," Amy breathed. Her face went red as she realized she was staring at his chest like a horny teenager. "Oh. Sorry." She forced herself to make eye contact with him.

He was bright red in the face, as well, the flush showing above the dark beard. "Need you."

"Sorry, what?" Her heart thudded.

Caleb cleared his throat and, if it was possible, turned even redder. "Can't figure it out. The costume." The words were choked in his throat, and he thrust an arm out to her, holding the Santa coat out.

Oh. She took the jacket from him, trying to figure it out. It was surprisingly heavy and seemed like far too much material, so she turned it in her hands, examining it. At least, she pretended to. She couldn't focus, because she kept thinking about Caleb's chest.

She really was going to be a creepy Mrs. Claus, wasn't she?

Forcing herself to focus, Amy held the jacket back out to him. "I think it has a loop that wraps around the arm from the inside, like a hospital robe . . ."

He jerked his gaze away from her and snatched the coat. "I'm sure it's fine."

Amy looked down and her breasts were squeezed like sausages against the front of her costume, her nipples clearly outlined. Well, good lord, it was worse than she'd thought, and seeing him shirtless had just made things worse. Covering her boobs with an arm, she shut the door again.

"Mine's fine, too," she called out. "Let's get dressed so we can finish running errands."

CHAPTER EIGHT

Caleb was sweating.

Of all the things he'd expected to see when she opened the bathroom door, her breasts practically presented to him was not one of them. Thanks to the ill-fitting top of her costume, he'd been able to see everything outlined. Her nipples stood out against the shiny material, and he'd been unable to stop staring.

He'd wanted to touch her so badly. Instead, he couldn't think straight with those plumped-up breasts practically staring him in the face. It had made him react in all kinds of ways. His mind blanked out. His face turned red.

His dick turned hard.

Having an erection in a Santa suit seemed . . . wrong. So he'd hastily retreated, glad for the pants that fit in a weirdly baggy fashion.

Now if he could just get through the rest of the evening without making a fool of himself again, it'd be great. He got dressed, making sure his winter coat covered his erection, and shoved the costume back into the bag. She met him in the hall, all smiles, as if he hadn't seen her glorious tits practically naked in that costume, and he started sweating all over again.

He was sweating when he drove her to the closest big-box store, several towns over. She talked and chattered as if determined not to notice his silence. Inside the store, she picked through everything as he walked a few steps behind her, pausing at the clearance aisle and looking at the prices of everything before putting something into her cart. She was making gifts for her class to give out tomorrow night, she told him, and put a roll of wrapping paper into her cart. Amy fingered some of the pretty, festive bows before buying the cheapest bag possible, and then at the last minute put those back, too.

She was breaking his damned heart.

He noticed she bought dog food and a squeaky toy for Donner, and the largest pack of ramen noodles he'd ever seen. When they got to the register, she carefully counted each dollar out and dug around in the bottom of her purse for two pennies. He didn't understand her—money was clearly an issue, but she wore expensive, impractical clothing. Did she have a shopping addiction or was it something else? He suspected it had something to do with the ex-husband, but he didn't ask.

Couldn't ask. He'd just mess it up.

But he lingered in the store and bought the biggest bag of damned Christmas bows himself and shoved it into her bag when she wasn't looking.

"Thank you," Amy said to him softly as they drove back to Painted Barrel. "I know I'm taking up a lot of your time, but it really is appreciated."

As if he had anything better to do. As if he wasn't basking in every single moment spent in her presence. He was soaking up every smile, every note of her musical voice, every time she touched her hair. This was what he'd dreamed of for months now—just being with her—and he was going to take every opportunity he could.

"Once my car's fixed, you won't have to be my chauffeur anymore." Her voice was light and almost playful. "And after the holidays I can work on paying you back."

Caleb frowned. Why was she so damn obsessed with paying him back? He considered a variety of answers, some longer than others, and eventually settled on a simple, "Nope."

"Don't tell me that." She chuckled. "I'm not trying to be a charity case and you've done so much for me. I'm just waiting on a few payments to come in and then I'll have a lot more breathing room with my finances. When that happens, I'm going to look up the costs of repairs for all the things you've done for me and pay you for your time. I promise."

He didn't want to be paid for his time. He wanted to spend more time with her. He scowled at the windshield. She still thought this was charity, then. Even after all the gifts he'd showered her with this week. Maybe his message wasn't getting through.

Story of his life—Caleb's messages never got through.

When they got to her house, she greeted Donner with a happy hug, and he noticed the old dog was curled up on her love seat in an old blanket. He was glad to see she was spoiling the old man, and went over to rub the dog's ears. Amy spent a moment squeaking Donner's new toy and talking in baby-speak to the dog, so Caleb took her things into the kitchen.

The coffee maker he'd bought for her and wrapped up carefully was still sitting in the box. He thought for sure she'd want to use it, since she microwaved everything, even her morning instant coffee. He glanced over his shoulder at her again, frowning to himself. She hadn't worn her new jacket tonight, or the scarf and hat, or the boots he'd given her. He'd done flowers one day—carnations—but had opted for more practical gifts after she'd come home and promptly dumped the flowers.

That had confused him, too. Hadn't she been excited over the other flowers she'd gotten? Or had she figured out that he was now giving her gifts, too, and didn't like that? Did she know it was him?

"Sorry," Amy breathed as she came up to his side and helped him unload one of the bags. "I just wanted Donner to know he wasn't abandoned. I should take him out for a quick walk after this, too."

He nodded, and because he couldn't resist, gestured at the coffeepot.

"Oh, that? It's a gift someone got me." Her tone turned flat. She dug in her purse and then pulled out a couple of small, blue velvet cases and tossed them atop the coffee maker. "It's been a real heck of a week."

She sounded . . . disgusted? That was odd. He knew someone else had sent her flowers, more than once, but what were these cases? Donner trotted up to Amy's side and whined, so she got out the leash and took the dog into the backyard. The moment she did, Caleb couldn't resist his curiosity. He opened one of the cases . . . and saw a bracelet. There was a necklace in another, and a pin of some kind in another. All of them looked glittery and very expensive.

What the hell? No wonder she didn't like his coffeepot.

How could he compete with gold? He'd sent her fucking boots like an idiot. A coffeepot. Should he have been sending her jewelry all this time?

Caleb clearly had to step up his game. He needed to talk to Jack.

Love notes," Jack declared with a firm nod. "Girls love that sort of thing."

"Love notes?" Caleb echoed, just a hint disgusted. "Are you serious? When I gave her a coffee maker?"

Jack just nodded and leaned in, his arms crossed as he sat at the table with his brother. "I'm telling you. Women love a romantic note. You need to up the ante. This guy's sending her jewelry. Unless you wanna clean out your savings account, you gotta go super-romantic. Big gestures. Love notes." Jack pushed a pen and a piece of paper toward Caleb. "Now, start writing."

Love notes.

Big gestures.

That part did ring true. He remembered that when he'd first seen Amy, Hank had been asking her for advice about how to woo her friend Becca. Amy had suggested a big gesture of some kind, something to let her know she was appreciated.

Hell . . . Jack was probably right. Making a noise of protest in his throat, Caleb pushed aside his cup of coffee and took the pen. "I can't even talk right in her presence and I'm supposed to somehow come up with a love note?"

"Not just one," Jack said, grinning ear to ear. He was clearly eating this shit up. "I think you need to send her a bunch of them."

"Exactly how many?"

Jack shrugged. "A big gesture would be to send her one an hour every hour while she's at work."

"What, and I just show up and deliver them by hand? You know that won't work. I can barely speak around her. She'll think I'm an idiot." Caleb stared down at the paper in front of him as if it was offensive. "What if she wants me to read it aloud?"

Jack considered this, scratching his chin. After a moment, he snapped his fingers. "You send flowers. One rose with each love note, every hour."

Flowers? Caleb scowled. "I'm pretty sure she's flowered out at this point."

"Women are never flowered out," Jack said confidently. "And she'll love the notes. Who's the expert here, you or me?"

"Expert on what?" Hank's voice boomed into the Swinging C kitchen a moment before the door slammed shut behind him.

Caleb just put his hand on his forehead, fighting back a groan. Great. The last thing he needed was his older brother showing up to offer advice and make fun of him. Like this wasn't hard enough as it was.

"The expert on romance," Jack said with a grin and gestured at Caleb. "The teacher's playing hard to get."

"I can't compete with jewelry," Caleb muttered.

"You can . . . It just usually involves more jewelry." Hank flipped a chair around and straddled it, sitting with his brothers. "Someone's giving her jewelry?"

"Her other secret admirer," Caleb admitted, and then gave his brother a curious look. "What are you doing here this late at night? Becca okay?" Now that Hank had married, he and his daughter lived with Becca in town, and Hank was normally gone from the ranch after dark to spend the rest of the day with his family. Uncle Ennis went to bed early, so it was just Jack and Caleb . . . or so Caleb had hoped.

Hank just grunted, shrugging his shoulders. "Libby's been checking all the closets constantly to see where 'Santa' is hiding her presents, so I hid them up here in my old room. I came by tonight to wrap 'em, but I see we have other entertainment planned." He nudged Caleb.

Caleb just scowled.

"I thought you were there all week helping her out," Hank said. "Isn't that why Jack and I have been covering your chores all the damn time? So you could romance her?"

"Ain't working," Jack declared. "He's still tongue-tied around her."

"Have you tried getting drunk?" Hank asked.

Caleb glared at his older brother. "I'm not getting drunk just to be around her."

"Turns out our girl has another admirer," Jack went on, ignoring the look Caleb shot him. "She's been getting roses and jewelry all week while our boy gave her a coffee maker."

"And boots," Caleb muttered. "She needed warm boots."

"Oh boy," said Hank. He rubbed his mouth. "And so now you're gonna write her love notes?"

"Every hour on the hour on Monday," Jack declared. "With more flowers."

Hank shook his head. "You're gonna scare her. Does she know she has two admirers?" When Caleb shrugged, Hank rolled his eyes. "She's gonna think it's all just one really crazy, obsessed guy. Sending her love notes is just gonna scare the shit out of her."

Caleb threw the pen down. He was glad to nix the idea

of the love notes—what the hell could he possibly say?—but then that meant he had no ideas. "What do I do, then? If you're the expert?"

"How about you do what you were supposed to do a few days ago?" Hank retorted. "Suck it up and ask her out. Before this other guy gets the balls and beats you to it."

He had a point, Caleb had to concede. He did need to ask her out. Even now, after all the things he'd done to help her and the time he'd spent with her, he wasn't sure that she saw him as more than a buddy. He thought of her smile and the way she doted on the blind dog. He thought of the determined way she shopped, pinching every penny. He thought of her chuckle when she was amused by something.

He thought of her tits in that damned Mrs. Claus outfit.

He thought of the way she'd paused and stared at his chest in surprise, as if she was suddenly realizing that Caleb was a red-blooded man standing in front of her.

It was that look of surprise that made up his mind. For better or for worse, he had to ask her out, because she'd never realize he was doing all these things because he was in love with her.

And he had to do it before someone else swooped in and took credit for some of the gifts he'd given her.

Tomorrow, then, at the Christmas Carnival. He'd ask Mrs. Claus out on a date.

Somehow.

Amy's Mrs. Claus boots hurt her feet five minutes after she put them on. It was like the world was reminding her not to get too comfortable tonight. Which was a real shame, because otherwise, the Christmas Carnival looked as if it was going to be a success.

It was early yet, of course. Amy and all the teachers had shown up early to help decorate the school. She'd texted Caleb and told him she didn't need a ride today, that one of the teachers was swinging by to pick her up, but that he would need to be at the school at six sharp. It was still a few minutes before six, but Amy loved how things were shaping up.

The interior of the school glittered with clouds of fake snow, puffs of cotton sprinkled with fake crystals. Paper "sidewalks" made of cutout gumdrop shapes lined the halls, leading up to the different carnival booths. Directly across from "the North Pole" was a dunking booth that the principal would sit in, dressed as the Grinch. Somewhere in the school there was a Cake Walk, and piles of presents were being watched over by volunteers. Amy's gifts were all ready and waiting for her students, but some of the wrapped boxes were raffle prizes. The gym smelled like hot cocoa and peppermint, and Amy loved it.

She wasn't the only one. Parents were arriving early with excited children, and so were other townspeople. She'd run into Hannah, who owned a small hotel downtown, and her husband. She'd met a few other ranchers with small children, and the mayor, Sage, had come through with her babies and husband, all of them in matching ugly sweaters.

This was nothing like home, Amy thought with happiness. Back when she lived in the big city, no one cared about community events. Here, everyone turned out to support everyone else, and it was lovely.

Everyone, that is, except for Santa Claus.

Amy checked her watch. He still had five minutes, but they had a line forming, waiting to get their chance with Santa. She chewed on her lip, nervous.

"Where is he?" A hand touched her shoulder.

Amy whirled around, sighing with relief when she saw her friend Becca. The hairdresser was adorable in a fur-lined coat of red and white, her dark hair pulled into a braided coronet. At her side was her stepdaughter, Libby, dressed in a matching outfit.

"He's coming, right? He told Hank he was coming," Becca said, squeezing Libby's hand. "I'm going to send Hank to kick him in the pants if he doesn't get here soon."

"I'm sure he's coming," Amy reassured her. "He hasn't said otherwise."

"He probably hasn't said anything," Becca grumbled. She bent down and smoothed a lock of hair off Libby's brow. "Why don't you go see if your daddy will win you a stuffed snowman, baby girl? We can come back for Santa. I know he'll want to see you."

"Okay! Bye, Miss Mckinney!" Libby waved and dashed off, disappearing into the crowd.

Amy smiled nervously at the people waiting and then leaned in toward Becca. "Do I look okay?"

"You look great," Becca reassured her. "Nice and flat up top."

Whew. She'd texted Becca a picture after she'd taped down the girls, making sure that nothing could be seen, but it was nice to get reassurance. "Good."

"The hair's a nice touch." Becca reached up and fingered one of the fake white curls on Amy's head. "Glasses, too. It's all really cute and you look adorable. Are you having fun?"

"I will soon," she reassured Becca. Just as soon as Caleb got here.

Becca leaned in. "Any word on your gift giver?" When Amy shook her head, Becca gave her a knowing look. "I found out who it is."

That had Amy's attention. "You did?"

"Yeah, and he's going to be here tonight. Are you . . . sure you want to know?"

Uh-oh. Amy swallowed hard, willing down the knot in her stomach. "I guess I do now. Is it bad?"

"All I can say is that I'm sworn to secrecy about the fact that Greg sent you those roses." Becca fluttered her lashes innocently. "So I can't tell you that."

Amy groaned, wanting to stomp her feet like a child, but the pinching boots hurt too much for that. "Greg? Really?"

"That's what I heard from the florist." Becca shrugged. "I mean, it's really generous of him. When we were together I had to really drag any sort of gift out of him, so the jewelry is a nice touch. The good news is that it's not a stalker. The bad news is that it's Greg."

Amy bit back a sigh. It wasn't that she disliked Greg. It was just . . . she was hoping for someone more exciting. But that was unfair of her, wasn't it? She'd said in the past that if her Santa wasn't a stalker, she'd go out with him if he asked. After all, wasn't she lonely and wanting to get to know people in town? And yet . . . she hadn't felt all that lonely this week with Caleb's company every day. It had been easy to forget that she'd vowed to try to date more.

Strangely enough, she thought about shirtless Caleb and felt her cheeks grow hot. "Greg's perfectly nice," Amy admitted. "If he asked me out, I probably wouldn't say no." She'd have a nice dinner, see if there were any sparks . . . and maybe find out what the deal was with the maintenance guy that never showed up.

"Well, I can tell you that I dated him for ten years and he is absolutely not worth the effort, but maybe he's turned over a new leaf." Becca shrugged. "You deserve to be happy, and he's not a stalker, so I'm just happy for you."

Amy laughed. "You think he'll ask me out, then?" She tried to be excited about it and not think about Caleb's shirtless chest again.

"If he doesn't, then he's crazy. Who wouldn't want to date Mrs. Claus?" She winked at Amy. "And speaking of, I think your Prince Charming has arrived."

Amy turned as Becca moved away, but instead of Greg approaching, it was Caleb—or rather, it was Santa Claus. He swept into the school with authority, all swagger despite the bright red-and-white costume. He'd figured out how to wear it, apparently, the belly stuffed to roundness, and his face concealed by a big, fluffy beard. He wore the Santa hat with the same authority he wore his cowboy hat, and when he approached, he gave a big, hearty laugh.

"Ho, ho, ho, look at all these little ones waiting for me!" He put his hands on his big fake belly and gave the best Santa laugh she'd ever heard.

Oh my lord.

She'd been hoping—at best—for Caleb to just get through the night. That he wouldn't be the best Santa the kids had ever seen, but he'd do the job and she'd be grateful for it.

The man in that costume was hamming it up. He hugged the little ones as they reached for him and headed for the chair set up in their "North Pole" for him to greet children. Jenny, who was running the camera, gave Amy a look of surprise.

"Ho, ho, ho," Caleb said again, and made it up to his seat. "Is it time for me to greet the good boys and girls?"

"I-I think so," Amy stammered, flustered. "Shall we get started?" She turned to the front of the line and beamed at them, remembering that this wasn't about her; it was about the kids. And Caleb was going to be magnificent, so it made her job easier. Her smile was huge as she turned to the first shining face. "All right. Who's ready to see Santa?"

CHAPTER NINE

Caleb watched Amy all night.

It was a little difficult to do so, given that children with sticky hands and runny noses were plopped into his lap over and over again, and he had to play the role of Santa. Because she was Mrs. Claus, she was in eyesight at almost all times, talking to parents, collecting tickets and distributing photos, and moving the line along. He'd thought Painted Barrel had a small school system, but there was an endless line of kids here to see him, so he kept ho, ho, ho-ing and stroking his big fake beard and hamming it up.

Strangely enough, this Santa shit was easy.

He'd been petrified at first, certain that his tongue-tied habits were going to get in the way, but the moment he put the beard on, he realized no one could see his face. Those kids didn't know it was him under there. And really, kids were easy to talk to. They didn't have expectations like adults did.

So it was easy to be Santa. Easy to haul each kid into his lap and listen to them talk about what they wanted for

Christmas. One little guy immediately started crying and confessing that he'd been bad, and Caleb had to talk him off a ledge before the poor kid had a breakdown. Most just wanted to sit in his lap, wide-eyed, and ask for Legos or books or dolls. It was easy. It was kind of fun, too.

And Amy was delighted with him. She was beaming in his direction, her smile so wide that he felt as if he'd hung the moon. Shit, if he'd known this would get that much of a reaction out of her, he wouldn't have been dreading it so much. His gaze moved over her as the latest kid got out of his lap and Amy ushered him away. Her hips swished in the skirt, and even though she was supposed to be his elderly, pink-cheeked wife, all Caleb could think about was the way her tits had practically jumped out of that costume yesterday, her nipples at attention.

She was a lot less chesty tonight, and he wasn't sure if he was disappointed or relieved. Relieved, he eventually decided. It would be a nightmare if Santa popped a boner.

Even so, he couldn't resist reaching for her. She was his wife in this little game, right? As she walked past, he noticed she hobbled a little, her feet hurting. So he reached out and boldly snagged his arm around her waist, drawing her into his lap.

A few of the parents chuckled.

Amy went stiff in his arms, her eyes wide with surprise behind Mrs. Claus's wire-rimmed glasses. Their gazes met, and this was his moment. He wanted to ask her out. He wanted to confess that he'd been the one that gave her some of the gifts this week, and while they weren't jewelry or endless vases of flowers, he hoped that she'd go out with him. Just once. Just a coffee.

But as he stared into her eyes, no words came to mind. He just held on to her and gazed into her eyes.

"You okay?" she whispered. "Do you need a break?"

He nodded once, mentally cursing himself. It was all right. There was still plenty of evening. He could ask her out later, maybe, when all this was done. They could go for coffee afterward. There was a little coffeehouse about a half hour away and—

She patted his shoulder and turned to the others, climbing off his lap. "Santa needs a fifteen-minute break, guys. We'll be back." When the child at the front of the line groaned, Amy picked up her clipboard and wrote with a candy-cane pen. "Don't worry. We'll keep your place so you won't lose your spot in line, I promise."

Someone handed Caleb a bottle of water, and, damn, he was thirsty. He sucked it down, but it tasted like fake beard and dribbled everywhere. He watched Amy as he took his "break," noticing that she didn't take much of a break herself. She paused and talked to the woman running the camera and then got stopped by a parent who she recognized and started a conversation with. As she talked to the parent, he watched her and drank his water. *Okay,* he told himself. *When she comes back, you ask her out. You tell her you can give her a ride home and did she want to get coffee afterward. It's easy enough. It's the perfect opportunity, and you're not going to have many more.*

He could do this.

He could.

"Amy?"

A man called her name out and pulled her aside. Caleb frowned as she disappeared down a hall, and long minutes passed as he waited for her to return.

When she did, she was alone and had a single red rose in her hands. She looked flustered, too.

He offered her his water bottle.

She took it, shooting him a grateful look and then taking a sip. "I hope it's okay that we're sharing spit," she whispered to him. "We're supposed to be married, right?"

"Married spit," he agreed, and then mentally cussed himself up one side and down the other. *Now's your chance, idiot. Say it.* "Want to get coffee after this?" The words blurted out of him before he could think twice, before he could mess them up.

Before he could take them back.

Amy gave him a look of surprise. Her gaze flicked to his chest and then she gave him an apologetic little grimace. "Coffee sounds great, but . . . it seems I have a date." She waved the rose in front of him. "Secret Santa asked me out."

Caleb gritted his teeth.

Some asshole had beat him to the punch.

A my had been having a wonderful time until Greg showed up. She'd been delighted with how Caleb was interacting with the children. For all that he was quiet and practically unpleasant to her at times, he was fantastic with the kids. He'd gone above and beyond as Santa, and every child and parent left smiling. Amy enjoyed herself, too, and she didn't even mind the pinch of her boots because she was having too much fun. Then he'd pulled her into his lap.

And she'd thought about his shirtless, gorgeous chest again. She'd gotten all flustered and breathless and climbed off him right away, mumbling something about the students. She wasn't thinking of them at all, though. She was thinking of those long lashes and that hard chest, and, good lord, when had surly, silent Caleb Watson become so irresistible?

When Caleb said he needed a break, Amy had thought that would be the perfect time to grab some hot cocoa for herself—the smell had been tempting her all night. It was also the perfect time to get her head on straight and stop thinking about the man playing Santa right now.

And then she'd seen Greg, a rose in his hands. He was wearing a suit, and he called her name.

She put a smile on her face and went to him, even though it felt—oddly—like her evening was about to be ruined.

But that wasn't fair to him. All he'd said was hello. So she tried to smile brighter. "Happy holidays, Greg."

"Nice outfit."

She did a mock curtsy that was hell on her cramping toes. "I'm helping out with the carnival."

"Obviously. Can you get away?" He held the rose out to her. "I think we should go on a date."

Amy suddenly wanted to snarl at him. She'd learned after years of being married to Blake that it was the little ways that words were said that told her what he was really thinking. Greg wasn't asking her if she'd go out with him. He was more or less demanding it, and tossing in a charming smile to take the sting out of his bold words. He wasn't asking what time she would be done, either. He was asking her to abandon the carnival so she could spend time with him.

Blake would have done the same. Years ago, when she was young and wide-eyed and wanting to get away from her parents' strict control, his utter confidence had been exactly what she was looking for. Now she knew better, and it just irked her.

He must have noticed her hesitation. "We don't have to, you know. I just thought I'd ask." He gave her a sheepish smile. "It gets lonely being single during the holidays."

Some of her unease vanished and she gave him a more genuine smile. She wasn't being fair. He wasn't Blake, and she wasn't the Amy she'd been a few years ago. It was just a date between two lonely people and he was right—the holidays were rough when you didn't have anyone to spend them with.

Weirdly enough, she thought of Caleb. She hadn't felt so lonely with him around. Donner, either. But she knew what it was like to be alone, and Greg had said the right thing to make her heart squeeze with sympathy. She took the rose from him and tilted her head. "Were you my Secret Santa?"

"Busted." He winked. "A little birdie told me that you wanted to go out with whoever had sent the gifts, so I thought I'd come and ask in person."

She'd *what*?

Amy was about to protest that she'd said no such thing when her conversation with Mrs. Lawrence yesterday came back to her. *You should go out with whoever sent these gifts. He's clearly in love.*

Oh. Amy had agreed awkwardly . . . and now she was being called on it. She licked her lips, thinking. Would it be the worst thing to go out with Greg? Greg, who was a little too overbearing and sales-y to suit her, but who'd also sent thoughtful gifts and was here even now with a flower and giving her puppy eyes? Could she let him down when he clearly had spent so much time and effort to get her to notice him?

Had anyone ever put so much effort into getting Amy's attention? She hesitated and then threw caution to the wind. "I guess I did say something like that."

"Great." He beamed, thumbing an impatient gesture at the door. "My car's just outside. Does that mean we can leave this place?"

Immediately, Amy felt like she'd made a mistake. Her stomach sank, but she took a deep, steeling breath. Nothing to do but go through with it. Maybe he had a reason for being such a bad landlord and all she needed was the chance to get to know him. Maybe. "I can't go until we're done," Amy told him. "All the teachers have to stay. But maybe we can do something afterward?"

"That sounds great. I'll be waiting. You want to text me and I'll swing back and pick you up?"

"Sure, that'd be wonderful." She bit back the sly comment that sprung to mind about how he tended to ignore her texts when it was about her house and leaky faucets, but that was unfair. She wasn't going to be unfair to him, darn it. She was going to give him a chance. He'd been so generous this week and he was just trying to be nice. Maybe he didn't realize he'd gone overboard with the gifts.

He leaned in to kiss her and she automatically tilted her face so he could kiss her cheek instead. "Children are watching," she pointed out, though she didn't think anyone was going to notice. They all knew she wasn't Mrs. Claus. She was Miss Mckinney. But kissing Greg here in the hall didn't feel right.

None of this felt right, and she couldn't put her finger on why.

It was just a date.

It was a date with someone who'd thought about her enough to get her multiple Secret Santa gifts this week. And while some of them were thoughtless, like the bouquet with lily of the valley, some of them, like the coffee maker, were downright genius. She could go out with him one night and see where it led.

Distracted, she headed back toward the chair Caleb sat in as Santa. He offered her his water bottle. He asked her out for coffee, just being polite as he always was.

And for a stupid, wistful moment, she wished it was Caleb who had showered her with gifts this week. If Caleb had been her Secret Santa, she'd have thought very differently about her upcoming date. Well, no, she wouldn't even be going out with Greg if Caleb was her Secret Santa. She'd have taken him up on that coffee and tried to peel back a few layers of his silence to see what was underneath.

But this was real life, not fantasy, and she had to be practical. She handed Caleb back his water bottle, took up her clipboard of children waiting to see Santa, and beamed at the first one back in line. "Are we ready to get started again?"

CHAPTER TEN

By the time the last child finished his visit with Santa, Amy's feet were throbbing nightmares. The thought of another hour in the boots made her murderous, so when one of the teachers saw her hobbling, she gave Amy a sympathetic look. "Why don't you call it a night?"

This time, she didn't argue. "Thank you, I will."

Amy looked over at Caleb, who got to his feet. He still wore the beard and suit and hadn't issued a word of complaint. He'd been a perfect jolly Saint Nick and she felt overwhelmed with appreciation for him. He hadn't fussed or griped as kids sneezed in his face or dripped their hot cocoa down his front. He'd listened calmly and stayed in character all the while, and every child left happy. He didn't have to do this, either. He wasn't a parent, just a volunteer with a good heart, and it made her appreciate him so, so much. "I can't thank you enough for what you did tonight," Amy told him. "You were an absolute rock star."

He said nothing again, just shrugged, and she wondered

if it was she that he was utterly silent around, as if he had absolutely nothing at all to say to her. For some reason, that was vaguely hurtful to think about, and so she gave him a tight smile and gestured at her phone. "I don't need a ride home, just FYI. Greg's picking me up."

Caleb responded with a derisive little snort.

That irked her. It was her decision to go on a date with Greg, and it was a good one, damn it. She deserved to give such a devoted, generous guy a chance, didn't she? So she ignored Caleb's response and hobbled away with her phone, texting Greg.

AMY: I'm done here. We still on?

GREG: Be there in 5.

Amy shrugged on her light jacket over her Mrs. Claus outfit and went outside to wait for her date. There was a large plaque in front of the school, dedicating it to the first principal in the area, and she sat on the edge of it to take the weight off her feet. They throbbed and ached, and she wanted to rip the boots off and get a good look at the variety of blisters that were surely forming. Also, the tape wrapped around her boobs itched like mad and she wanted to take it off, too. Maybe she should have suggested that they go out another night. Tonight, she felt pretty done.

She looked at the array of streets in front of her. She was only a few blocks away from her house, and while it was cold and slushy, she could be home shortly. Maybe she should cancel on Greg.

Her feet said otherwise. They told her she wasn't walking five feet, much less five blocks.

Okay, date it was. She held her purse and jacket in front

of her and waited. Greg had said five minutes, hadn't he? She checked her phone as the minutes ticked past. Ten. Fifteen. Twenty.

At twenty-three minutes, a sports car pulled up to the school, blaring rock music and nearly drowning out the endless Christmas carols still playing in the auditorium. He parked and then grinned at her, sticking his head out the window. "You ready?"

Amy supposed she was. She got to her feet—tried to hide the wince of pain with a smile—and walked slowly forward. He didn't get out and get the door for her. That was fine, really. Not every guy had to do that, she told herself. It was just that Caleb had been doing it all week and so she was used to it. She got into his car, breathed a sigh of relief when she got off her feet, and looked over at him. "Hi there. Where are we headed?"

Greg just gave her a slow grin. "You'll see."

Well, wherever he took her—and they were limited in options after nine at night—would be fine. She didn't care as long as it was a seated sort of date.

He pulled away from the curb . . . and then drove around to the back of the school and parked.

Amy's brows furrowed. "We're staying here?"

He turned the radio off, and the only thing she could hear was the distant sound of "Carol of the Bells" leaking out from the school. They must have left the music on as they cleaned up the mess, and for a moment, she wanted to be in there helping them, blistered feet or not.

Greg put his arm over the back of her seat. "Thought we could get to know each other a little better. Besides, you're not exactly dressed to go out much of anywhere."

"Oh." What could she say to that? *No, I don't want to get to know you better*? It seemed rude, and if he tried anything, she was fine with rude, but maybe she was just overreacting. Maybe he just didn't want to be seen with Mrs. Claus. "Thank you for the gifts. I didn't know who they were from."

"It was the least I could do, since you've had so much trouble with the rental." He beamed at her, then toyed with a curl of her white wig. "Does this come off?"

"It's just a wig," she said, and tugged it off her head and into her lap. Her hair was smooshed into a flat bun and slicked down, and she was pretty sure it wasn't a hot look for her, but at the moment, she didn't care. The wig itched. "As for the rental, your guy never showed up. He hasn't fixed a thing. Not one."

"Mmm. I'll have to give him a call and see what's going on." He slid a bit closer to her.

This was cartoonishly bad. It seriously reminded her of one of those horrible dates in the 1980s films where the overbearing boyfriend forces himself on his girlfriend. She didn't think real people acted like this, but Amy supposed there was a first time for everything. She slid a little further away. "I didn't know who was sending the gifts," she said again. "I can't wait to use the coffee maker. It—"

"Coffee maker?" His brows drew together and he chuckled. "What are you talking about?"

"The coffee maker you sent yesterday? The single-cup percolator? With the hot-water fixture?" She tilted her head, studying him. "Did you not send that?"

"I sent roses a few times," Greg said. "Flowers for a beautiful flower."

Oh, barf. "You really should be careful what flowers you send to a kindergarten teacher," she began. "Some of the flowers you sent were poisonous, and some little ones still like to put things in their mouths and—" She broke off in a shrill little cry as he lurched in and planted his mouth on hers.

Greg smelled like breath mints, and his lips were hard on hers. A second later, he shotgunned his tongue into her mouth, working it like a piston as his hands went all over her torso. Dear lord. This was not her idea of getting to know each other. She should have known better the moment he parked behind the school. Amy pushed at his chest, leaning back against her car door, but Greg was impossible to push away. His hands were everywhere, his mouth surging against hers, and—

The car door opened and Amy tumbled backward.

She let out a yelp of surprise, expecting to hit the icy pavement. Instead, strong hands caught her and hauled her out of the car, setting her on her feet. Dazed, she stared at the man in the overstuffed Santa suit. He'd taken off the beard and hat and had switched to his wide-brimmed Stetson. There was a look of pure fury on Caleb's handsome face as he set her gently onto her feet. He checked her over, then turned toward Greg.

"What the hell, man?" Greg stared up at him in disbelief.

"That's my wife."

Both Amy and Greg stopped in surprise. "She's what?" Greg asked.

"She's Mrs. Claus." Caleb stabbed a finger at her. "I'm Mister. That means you don't get to touch her unless she wants it." He turned and looked back at Amy, a question in his eyes. "Looked to me like she didn't want it."

Amy shook her head. "I just want to get out of here."

Caleb nodded once. Before she could say anything else, he moved to her side and put an arm behind her knees. Within the space of a breath, he hefted her into his arms and stormed away, back toward the school.

"Now, wait just a minute," Greg said, marching after them. "You can't just do that! We were on a date!"

Amy bit her lip. She wanted to stay with Caleb, but she also didn't want them to fight.

As if he could read her mind, Caleb gently set her on her feet again. "Gimme a moment."

Amy nodded, wide-eyed.

Greg made it to Caleb's side a breath later and grabbed the large cowboy by the shoulder. She put her hands to her mouth, worried, waiting for someone to throw the first punch. Instead, Caleb just grabbed the keys out of Greg's hand before he could speak and pitched them as far as he could into the night. They sailed through the air and landed in the snow . . . somewhere.

"You son of a bitch," Greg exclaimed. He stared at Amy, wide-eyed, and then stormed off into the snow to hunt down his keys.

"Let's just go," Amy whispered.

Caleb nodded and lifted her into his arms again. She held on to him, arms around his neck, and wondered if this was her getting swept off her feet. It made her want to laugh hysterically . . . okay, and maybe cry a little, too. Her weird night had taken a rotten turn, and she could still taste Greg's awful kiss. If Caleb hadn't been watching them . . .

She shook her head. No, he would have gotten the picture eventually. She'd have kneed him in the balls if he hadn't taken no for an answer. This way, Caleb had solved the problem. Even now, when she looked over his shoulder, she saw Greg hunting for his keys in the snow, no doubt cussing up a blue streak.

In this moment, Caleb was her knight in shining armor. Or rather, a Santa in a padded suit. She looked at him, worried that she was too heavy—she'd never been carried before and she was at least two sizes larger than she was when she got married for the first time. "You can put me down. It's okay."

He shook his head. "Your feet hurt."

He'd noticed? She hadn't said anything. And they did hurt. Badly. Right now she wanted nothing more than to pitch the hated boots into a fire, but she had to return them. "Can you take me home?"

Caleb nodded and then hesitated, his gaze out on the parking lot. He swore under his breath. "I'm boxed in. Someone's parked behind me."

Which meant they were stuck here, unless he wanted to heft Amy through the entire town. She inwardly winced as Greg let out a triumphant hoot somewhere far behind them. He'd found his keys. Suddenly, the urge to run away hit her like a load of bricks. She patted Caleb's chest as they got to the front of the school, indicating he should set her down. "Come on. Let's go inside. I don't want to make a scene and I'm afraid that's exactly what Greg wants."

Caleb hesitated, as if he wanted to stay outside and fight for her honor—in a Santa suit, no less—but she grabbed his hand and hobbled inside as fast as she could.

Adrenaline made her feet hurt less, oddly enough. Amy was able to race down one hall and toward her classroom. She pulled the door open and shut it behind them, then looked around for a hiding place. Greg would find her classroom. He would know that was where they went.

She turned, and Caleb was staring at her. "What—"

The coat closet! Amy grabbed his hand and hauled him after her, racing toward the small closet in the back of the classroom. Once they were both inside, she shut the door and turned off the light.

Now there was no sound but that of their breathing.

Caleb cleared his throat. "Any particular reason why we're hiding in a closet? In the dark?"

"You're awfully chatty tonight," she sniped back.

He grunted.

"That was mean of me. I'm sorry. It's just been a hell of a night." Amy buried her face in her hands and then bit back a groan because she'd probably just smeared her Mrs. Claus makeup all over her face . . . if it wasn't already smeared from Greg's punching-tongue kisses. Ugh. "I'm sorry. This just . . . all went to shit in an instant."

Silence.

"You cuss a lot for a kindergarten teacher," he whispered.

"It's a habit I'm trying to break," she whispered back. "And we're hiding in a closet because Greg is going to know this is my classroom and he's going to come looking for us."

"And we're hiding from that shit stain why?"

That made a horrified giggle rise in her throat, and Amy clamped a hand over her mouth. Oh god, Greg *was* a shit stain. It didn't matter that he was her Secret Santa. It didn't matter if she was trying to be open-minded or not. She didn't want to date him, especially not after that fiasco.

Parking the car behind the school and immediately molesting her was just . . . ugh. Who did that?

Greg, apparently.

"We're hiding because I don't want anyone to get into a fight," Amy said in a soft voice as she sat down on the shoe bench and noticed he sat down next to her. "If you can promise me that you aren't going to get into a fight with him, we can get out of this closet."

It was all quiet for a minute. Their breathing evened out. Strains of "Silver Bells" carried through the school's PA system.

"Guess we can stay for a bit," he finally said. "Because I can't promise I won't punch his smug face."

She let out a small laugh. "It is rather smug, isn't it?"

"And punchable."

Amy was pretty sure that Caleb had said more words to her in the last thirty seconds than he had in the entire last week, and, oh . . . she liked it. She liked it far too much for her own good.

"How long are we going to stay in here?" Caleb asked, and she jumped, startled at how close he was. Maybe it was the darkness in the closet or maybe it was just his sheer size, but he seemed to be everywhere. His shoulder was brushing her shoulder, his leg against her leg.

All this closeness? All this darkness? After he'd carried her away from the worst (and shortest) date ever?

She'd never been so turned on in her life.

Amy licked her lips nervously and shifted on her feet. "I don't know how long we should stay in here. How long do you think it'll take for him to give up?"

"Dunno. How are your feet?"

She was touched that he'd noticed. "They hurt like the dickens."

"The boots?"

"Yeah, they're awful."

"Well, if we're going to be in here for a bit, take 'em off."

"Oh no, I'm sure it's fine," she began, only to let out a yelp of surprise when big hands clasped her calf and started working the zipper down her leg. Okay, she'd gone from turned on to practically coming out of her skin, all from that small touch. Why was his taking off her shoe so damn sexy? Lord have mercy, if her date had gone like this, she'd have never gotten out of the car. She clutched one of the low coat hooks jabbing into her shoulders as he moved across from her in the darkness and tugged one boot off. "You don't have to . . ."

Her words died in a moan. The moment that boot came off her foot? It felt like paradise.

"Other foot," he told her in a gruff voice.

She immediately obeyed. It didn't matter that she was sitting in a poofy crinoline with smeared makeup on her face and duct-taped boobs as long as she could get those hated boots off. He pulled the other one off her foot with gentle, enormous hands . . . and then began to rub her foot through her sock.

His hands felt so good she nearly came. Instead, she bit her lip and fought back another moan. "You . . . you don't have to do that," she managed, breathless.

"Does it feel good?" His voice was low and gravelly again, and, oh god, he sounded amazing.

Sexy. Arousing. He could read her the phone book in that voice and her panties would get wet.

"It does feel good."

"Then I'm happy to do it." And those magical fingers rubbed the arch of her foot. This time, she couldn't bite back the whimper of pleasure that erupted from her. God, he was going to think she was perverted with all the noises she was making. Greg was going to hear them simply from all the moaning she was doing. The other teachers would think . . . well, they'd think she was getting worked up by a cowboy in a coat closet, and they wouldn't be wrong.

She'd never known her feet were such erogenous zones. Yet he kept rubbing them with those strong, amazing hands, and she never wanted him to stop.

Heck, if this kept up, she'd never want to leave the closet. Ever. She could just have her students bring her meals in here or something and she'd set up shop permanently with Caleb at her side.

"So . . . that was your date," Caleb said after a long moment.

"Ugh. Yeah."

"You can do better."

He sounded so disgusted, his voice so flat, that she giggled. "It's been a strange week. He was my Secret Santa, and I've been telling myself I need to get out more, you know? Get back on the wagon and start dating again. I told myself that whoever was my Santa, I'd go out with him and give him a chance. Unfortunately, it was Greg." She sighed. "I wasn't thrilled, but I thought I'd give him a chance, since he was my Santa and all."

Caleb made a sound of disgust in his throat.

"I know, I know." Amy felt a little disgusted herself. "It was just . . . some of the gifts were so thoughtful, and I guess I felt like I should get on the wagon again, you know? So it seemed like a good idea. Sort of. It meant ignoring a lot of other things about his personality, but . . . yeah." Sometimes she was really stupid when it came to men.

"Which gifts?"

"Huh?"

"Which gifts were the ones you liked?" he asked again, his fingers moving over her foot. "The jewelry?"

She chuckled, grimacing in the dark as she thought about the locket and the bracelet and how uncomfortable they'd made her. "The coffee maker, really. It wasn't something I expected, but it was kind of perfect for my needs."

"You should have been excited about the coat," he muttered.

She pulled her foot out of his lap, curious. "How did you know I got a coat?"

It was silent for a long, long moment. Then he reached for her foot again and began to rub it once more. She should have protested, but she didn't. It felt too good. "He wasn't the only one giving you presents. That's all I'm saying."

"You?" she breathed, utterly surprised. Other than tonight, he'd always acted like he barely tolerated her. Like she was an idiot he was just being nice and helping. He'd given her presents?

"Not all me," Caleb confessed. "I sent you the carnations, but it just seemed silly to send you more flowers when you needed practical things. So I sent you the trees, the ornaments, the boots, the coat and scarf, and the coffee maker."

Here Caleb had been the one sending her the most thoughtful gifts. The ones that made her pause. The ones that made her want to go out with her Santa in the first place. "You . . ." she repeated again. "You never said anything."

There was a long, heavy sigh in the darkness. "Don't know if you noticed, but I'm not real good with words."

"You seem to be fine right now."

"I'm in the dark. I can't see your face or the look in your eyes. That makes it easier." He rubbed her foot hard, working her arch. "That, and your feet. For some reason, that helps. The rest of the time? It's just . . . hard for me. My tongue gets tied up in knots."

She was speechless. All this time and he'd been her Santa? Well, one of her Santas? He'd said nothing as she brought home present after present? No wonder a second tree had appeared on her doorstep after she took the first one to school. How that must have made him crazy. "Why did you give me all those things?"

"Why do you think?" His big fingers—calloused but

strong—moved over the front of her foot in the best massage ever.

"You *like* me?"

Those magical fingers paused. "You didn't know?"

"No. Of course I didn't know!" She was still in a state of shock. He'd thought she'd known that he liked her? She couldn't have been more surprised if he'd told her that Santa Claus really did exist. "You . . . you're always so short with me. Like I'm doing something wrong, or like I'm an idiot that you're forced to put up with."

"What, just because I ain't chatty, that means I can't like you?" He sounded defensive.

"You're not chatty. You're, like . . . silent. And it seems to be just around me. You were amazing with the kids."

"Well . . . they're just kids."

"And I'm just me."

"You talk like you're not something special."

"I'm not!"

He grunted, the sound one of disbelief. Carefully, Caleb set down Amy's foot, and she could have cried at how gently he did it . . . or the fact that the foot rub was coming to an end. She stayed in place, even as she heard the bench creak as he got to his feet. Heard his footstep as he crossed the small closet over to her.

His voice was gentle as he finally spoke. "I'm not good around women. Never have been. Grew up just me and my brothers. Every time I saw a pretty girl, my tongue just . . . knotted up. It's hard for me to talk. Everything comes out wrong."

"You seem to be doing okay right now," she breathed, aware of his nearness. For some reason, she was picturing him shirtless again, like a pervert. She really needed to stop focusing on his chest. It was just . . . it was such a nice chest. She'd never been one to get bowled over by the physical form, or so she'd thought. But Caleb's chest? Caleb's chest had changed her mind on that. "It's a social anxiety thing, then?"

"I guess."

Amy wasn't good at making speeches in front of crowds, so she understood that. There was no reasoning behind a phobia of that kind, just that it happened. "You could do what I do when I have to give a presentation—picture everyone naked."

"If I picture you naked, that's not gonna help me talk," he said with a low chuckle that warmed her down to her toes.

She'd opened her mouth to speak, when she heard the creak of the door opening in the other room. Amy sucked in a breath and grabbed for Caleb's hands to quiet him. He was standing near her, she realized, and she felt him lean against the wall right next to her, as if there wasn't an entire coat closet full of space.

She remained still, waiting for Greg to show up, for him to fling the closet door open and see them hiding like a pair of kids. And why *was* she hiding, really? Other than she just didn't want a confrontation with him?

As if their minds were on the same wavelength, Caleb leaned in and whispered in her ear, "I know I already asked, but are you *sure* we have to hide from him?"

"I don't want to talk to him, and I don't want you to fight him," she whispered back, breathless. Then she added, "Don't change the subject. I can't believe you really like me."

"I washed your dog," he pointed out in a low voice.

She smothered a laugh behind her fingers. He *had* washed

her dog, and poor Donner had been *filthy* filthy. "I thought you were being nice."

"You're sleeping in my bed."

Amy gasped. "That's your bed?"

"Shhh," he whispered, his fingers brushing over her mouth.

They both froze at that small touch. She didn't know if he'd meant to touch her like that, or if it was an accident, but it had sent a reaction through her body that made her senses tingle like mad. "That's your bed?" she whispered again, even softer. "You brought me your bed?"

"Yours was ruined," he murmured, and Amy felt his breath tickle her ear. "Didn't like the thought of you sleeping on that love seat."

"That's . . . very nice of you."

"And I'm fixing your car. You think I'm that much of a Good Samaritan?"

She loved the amusement in his voice. It made her all warm inside, and it made her toes curl. Caleb with a touch of amusement in his tone did all kinds of things to her body. "So I should fling myself into your arms out of gratitude for the mattress?"

"That wasn't why I did it."

Her breath caught in her throat. He was definitely leaning in, and she could feel his breath hot against her ear. Her skin prickled with awareness, her body pulsing. "Then why did you do it?"

"Same reason I volunteered to be Santa, I suppose."

"I still haven't figured out why you did that, either."

A long pause. Then she got her answer. "Because . . . it made you smile."

Oh god. Why was that the sexiest thing she'd ever heard? Had anyone ever been so generous? She was stunned by just how much he'd done over the last week, and how clueless she'd been. Amy was kicking herself for even spending five minutes focusing on Greg when this knight in shining armor of a cowboy was right under her nose.

Silently under her nose, of course, but still there.

Harnessing just a hint of daring, Amy turned and faced him—at least, she thought she was. She turned in the direction of his breath and hoped she was facing him. The skirts of her costume were pushing against him, and she suspected if she leaned forward, she'd press herself against his chest. It was all very intimate . . . and she was eating it up. "I have to say," she whispered, "I much prefer the Caleb that talks to me. I like it when you speak."

"It's easy in the dark." His nose bumped hers, and she realized just how close together they were, how far he was bending over to be face to face.

She wanted to kiss him. Just close that distance between them and kiss him before he got all shy on her again. Would it be a bad idea? He barely even said two words to her, half the time, and yet here she was, getting all turned on by the feel of his breath against her skin. By the way his laughter slowly rumbled through his chest, like a train car taking the long way around. By—

A hand touched her hair, her cheek. It disrupted any thoughts she had in her head, and Amy froze.

In the next moment, Caleb's mouth was on hers.

It seemed they had the same idea.

She'd been expecting a tentative kiss from him, something that a shy man might start with in order to open up to something more. Not Caleb. The lips that descended on hers were utterly ravenous. He kissed her so hard that their mouths smashed together and their teeth clicked. She tried to laugh, to make a startled comment, but then that devouring mouth continued its conquest of hers and she forgot all about an apology.

He absolutely did not kiss like a shy man.

There was no finesse in Caleb's kiss. It was raw hunger, full of longing and heat and so much need that it took her breath away. His lips were fierce on hers, his fingers grazing her jaw as if he wanted to hold her, to cup her face and just kiss the hell out of her until her toes curled.

They were curling right now, so mission successful.

But then he changed the kiss, and it became something less frantic and intense and shocking, and his tongue grazed against the seam of her mouth in a silent question. She moaned and opened up for him, and then they were making out like teenagers, his tongue slowly stroking against hers in the deepest, wettest kiss she'd ever had. She clung to him, wanting to whimper with each drag of his tongue against hers. To just dive into this kiss and never come out again. Her hands curled in the front of his Santa suit and she pushed him backward, just a little, even as the kiss intensified.

Something fell on her shoulder. A hat, probably. It startled her enough that she broke the kiss, though, and stumbled backward in the dark.

One strong hand was at her waist immediately, propping her up. "You okay?"

"I'm fine," she said, breathless. "Do you think he's gone?"

"Not sure I care," Caleb drawled, tugging her a little closer.

Oh god, she wasn't sure if she cared, either. Amy slid her hand to his nape and brushed against the short hair there. "We can kiss other places than the closet."

He chuckled, the sound so raspy and delicious that it made her all tingly inside. "I'm sure we can. It's just . . ." He hesitated, then continued. "I had a big plan, you know. How to win you over."

"You did?" She was stunned.

"Yeah. Been working on it for a few days now. Had to compete with the jewelry, you know?" His fingers brushed over her jaw in the darkness and she wanted to lean into that touch like a kitten. "Tell you all about how amazing you are. How you take my breath away every time I see you. How special you are. Was gonna start first thing Monday morning."

She was melting. Positively melting.

"But I guess that was a waste of time."

Okay, she'd stopped melting. Amy frowned in the darkness. "Why was it a waste?"

His thumb skated over her lower lip, sending quivers through her belly. "Doesn't make sense to send you a bunch of anonymous notes when I've revealed my hand right here."

He had a point. And more than that, he hadn't realized how much the whole Secret Santa situation had stressed her out. "Anonymous notes would have scared me," she admitted. "So I'm glad it didn't happen."

He stiffened. "Scared you? Why?"

"No reason," Amy said quickly. She didn't want to get into the details about her ex-husband. Not right now. It'd ruin this wonderful mood she was in. "I don't suppose you'll kiss me again?"

"Only if you want me to."

"I really, really do," Amy whispered. She could have sworn she heard a low groan from him as his mouth brushed over hers, and then they were kissing again and she forgot everything but the touch and taste of his lips. She'd never been kissed so completely, so thoroughly, and with so much intent. It was like she could feel every bit of his hunger for her, and it took her breath away.

When they finally separated, she let out a sigh of contentment.

"What now?" Caleb murmured.

"I'm a little sad I don't get my notes now. I'd like to hear about how beautiful and special I am."

He laughed, just a little. "I had one a day for twelve days. Twelve days of Christmas. And I was going to do something special each day."

"Well, now I'm really disappointed," Amy teased. "We should have held out on the making out for a few days more so I could clean up for Christmas."

"I can still give you the notes. But this time you'll know who they're from . . . and I'm probably going to want kisses for each one."

"As long as you talk to me, I'm fine with that." Amy smiled into the darkness. "Just . . . don't be silent, all right? I don't mind shy, but when you're quiet, I feel like you don't like me."

He grunted. "Just be patient with me. I'm trying."

Oh, she would totally be patient. She would be so damn patient they would sing songs about it. "I can do that."

"Maybe I'll just grab you and kiss you every time my tongue stops up," Caleb said.

Okay, she liked that idea. "That sounds good to me." For a moment, she hesitated, then glanced in the direction of the door. It was all quiet in the classroom, but maybe it was the darkness fooling her. She noticed the Christmas music had turned off, too. "Do you . . . do you think he's gone? We should probably head out soon. I don't want to get locked in."

"If he's not gone, I'll deck him. How's that?"

Oddly enough, that worked for her. "Sounds good to me. Um . . . can I ask you for a ride home?" She grimaced, feeling sheepish. "I know I've been a total freeloader, but I swear it'll end soon."

His hand brushed against hers. "You know that's partially my fault, too?"

"What is?"

"Your car. I might have dragged my feet on it so I could be around you."

She gasped. "You didn't."

"I did. I ain't sorry about it, either."

Come to think of it, she wasn't sorry, either. She'd just had no idea all this was going on under her nose. Gosh, she was clueless sometimes. "I'm still going to pay you back."

He grunted a response that might have been a no, but that didn't surprise her. He took her hand in his and opened the door to the closet, just a crack. Light played on his handsome face, and it took Amy's breath away at just how handsome he was.

"Coast is clear," he said, and then opened the door wider. He looked over at her and then went silent. His face flamed bright red.

Uh-oh. "What? What is it?" She looked down at her chest, but no nipples had escaped the duct-taped band of doom.

"Your face." He gestured at her jaw.

Amy touched it, then realized it was sensitive when her fingers brushed over it. Oh, she knew what that was. Beard burn. She'd felt it brushing against her skin as they'd kissed, but she just hadn't cared. "Is it bad?"

"It's not good," he admitted, voice strangled.

"Then we'd better get home quickly," she told him, and hobbled forward on sock-covered feet. Now that he'd stopped the foot massage, the pain was coming back, and she tried to hide her grimace.

"Stop," he barked at her.

She froze.

He did, too. Then he leaned forward and kissed her, hard. He sucked in a deep breath and closed his eyes. "Easier to talk to you when you're in the dark."

Amy giggled, because it was . . . absurd. Cute but absurd. "You want to put a paper bag over my face, then?"

"No." He gave her a scowl and kissed her again. "Wait here. Boots." He cleared his throat as he walked away. "I'm getting them."

Already he was so tongue-tied around her? Her heart squeezed. Poor Caleb. Was she really that scary? She bit her lip and then ran her fingers over her sensitive jaw. No regrets about the kissing in the closet; that was for sure.

Maybe they could just make out in the dark a lot. She was down for that.

CHAPTER ELEVEN

By the time they got out to his truck, the parking lot was nearly empty. Greg's sports car was nowhere to be seen. Caleb opened the door for her as she tiptoed out on aching, cold feet—which was still preferable to the boots—and made sure she was comfortable before he got into the truck himself. He paused and looked over at her, his gaze on her mouth, but didn't lean over to kiss her again.

Amy was a little disappointed at that. It looked as if the moment the lights came on, Caleb's shyness returned. It was like the man in the closet with her had disappeared and his surly, silent replacement returned. For a few moments, she wondered if she'd simply had a mental break and imagined all of it. There'd been no kisses, no heated conversation, no nothing. Just her mind snapping or something.

But then they'd pulled up to her house and he'd circled around the truck to get her door again. The moment he pulled her free, he picked her up.

"I can walk," she protested, even as he carried her to the

threshold like she was a dainty, virginal bride instead of Mrs. Claus with blistered feet. When he set her on the porch, he gazed down at her and then kissed her again.

And that made her smile.

"I'll be by in the morning."

"Oh, but tomorrow's Sunday. I don't have anywhere in particular to go . . ." The words died in her throat as he gave her another intense look. "Okay."

"First note," was all he said.

Right. She'd told him she wanted her Christmas notes after all. That was a little selfish of her, but she was going to take it. After all, when was the last time she'd felt so very wanted by a man? His thoughtful gifts (and his kisses) made her feel as if she could float on air. "Tomorrow, then," she murmured. "See you then."

He didn't kiss her good night, though from the look on his face, he probably wanted to. Instead, he just nodded and headed off the porch and back to his truck. She watched him leave, then went inside.

Donner immediately got up off the love seat, his tail wagging madly as she came in. He circled around her, all wiggly dog, sniffing the air until he found her, and Amy hugged him as he licked her face. "What an evening, Donner. It has been a wild ride."

The dog just whined and licked her jaw some more.

"You want me to tell you all about it? While we go for walkies?"

The dog went from wiggling to beside himself with excitement. Oh yeah, Donner knew what a walk was. Some jerk had missed out when they abandoned this sweet, wonderful old dog. She hobbled into the bedroom and got her most comfortable pair of shoes, then leashed Donner and took him outside, all the while telling him about her eventful night as if he was a close confidant.

Maybe he was. She was starting to see why people loved dogs so much. He was always excited to see her, always happy to eat whatever she gave him, and never complained. Yep, she was definitely becoming a dog person. Living in Wyoming was changing her, but she liked to think it was for the better, all around. She was becoming a person with friends of her own, a person with a career. A person with a rent payment, and a dog, and . . . a boyfriend. Potentially.

Actually she wasn't sure what she and Caleb were right now. Maybe she should ask him in the morning. He'd probably blush, but she bet she could get it out of him . . . between a few kisses at least.

Amy smiled into the darkness as she held Donner's leash.

Caleb avoided talking to his brother Jack when he got home from the carnival. He headed straight to his cabin and kept the lights off as he pulled his costume off and lay in bed. He knew Jack would want to know all the details, but . . . he couldn't share them just yet. He wanted to keep tonight bottled up in his head for a bit, to mull over the details without hearing Jack crow about one thing or another.

He'd kissed Amy Mckinney. Made out with her in a closet.

And he hadn't fucked it up.

That might have been the most unbelievable part in all of this—that he'd somehow pulled himself together to hit on her. He'd been a changed man ever since he saw her get into Greg's car. Saw that jackass pull around to the back of the school instead of taking her to a legit date, and Caleb had known—he'd *known*—what that jerk was up to. It didn't matter that Amy was an adult and she wasn't his girlfriend. He stormed his way over to the parked car because he had to make sure that this was something she wanted. She hadn't seemed excited about the date all night, the sparkle in her eyes gone. If anything, she looked as if she'd been dreading going out with Greg. That didn't sound like a girl that wanted to park and presumably make out.

He'd been right, too. It had been dark, but not so dark that he couldn't see Greg practically fucking pounce on Amy. She'd flailed, and so he'd started marching forward. When he got just outside the car, he saw her pushing against Greg's chest to no avail, and something in him had snapped.

This asshole had the nerve to kiss Caleb's woman.

He'd seen red. He'd flung the car open and pulled Amy out, and for a moment, he'd been torn between whuppin' Greg's ass and just hauling Amy away from him. His girl came first, though, so he'd focused on her. Then she'd hid in the closet with him and started talking, and . . . he'd just talked.

And talked.

For him, it was a revelation. He knew it was hard to talk to her when he was looking right at her face. Knew he needed to say more to her, and yet the words never seemed to come to mind. But in the darkness? He couldn't seem to shut up. She'd sounded so soft and sweet and sexy that he'd been unable to resist approaching her.

Kissing her.

She'd been his first kiss. He was old for that sort of thing, but Caleb figured once you found the right person, that sort of thing would just kick in. It certainly had for him. He'd loved kissing her. He'd wanted to kiss her soft mouth for hours and hours on end. She'd been clueless that he liked her, which was startling to him. He'd thought he was pretty obvious about his crush, but she'd been genuinely surprised. Clearly, Caleb was going to have to constantly show Amy just how much he liked her. How much she meant to him.

Even if he had to turn the lights off just to have a conversation with her.

Because he'd known the very first time he saw Amy Mckinney that he was going to marry her. Now he just had to convince her . . . and he was one step closer to that.

His phone pinged with a text.

HANK: Howdgo

HANK: U

HANK: U nd th tcher

HANK: jst call me

Hank hated texting—said his fingers were too big for the tiny keyboard—and so the curiosity must have been eating him alive for him to text Caleb this time of night. He ignored his brother, though, turning off his phone's screen as he put his hands behind his head and thought about Amy.

Amy and her mouth.

Amy and the little sounds she'd made as he kissed her.

The way Amy had felt when he'd carried her in his arms, and the soft expression in her eyes when she looked at him on the porch, as if she wanted him to kiss her all over again.

He'd almost done it again, too, but he knew that if he kissed her again, he'd never want to leave.

And he had a Christmas romance plan to enact. By the end of it, he figured he'd propose. No sense in beating around the bush for months and months like his brother Hank had with Becca.

Caleb knew what he wanted: Amy. He just had to romance her good enough that she wanted him, too.

The next morning, Caleb took pains to avoid Jack. His younger brother would be waiting for Caleb to arrive so he could grill him on how the evening went, and Caleb wasn't ready to share it just yet. So he woke up and showered early, jerking one out quickly so he'd stay in control—hopefully. He trimmed his beard and took care to splash a bit of cologne on as he did, just in case Amy liked a boyfriend that smelled like a piney forest or some shit. He didn't have much experience in that sort of thing, so he was just winging it. But he thought about how red her face had been after he'd kissed her, how scratched up from his beard, and he rubbed his jaw thoughtfully. Time to cut the beard off? Perhaps. He intended to kiss Amy every day from now on, so it might have to go.

He gathered up the notecards of his plan, his carefully crafted Day 1 letter, dumped all the supplies in a box, and got out to his truck in the dark. It was very early, earlier than Jack even woke up, so he was safe in that regard. When he got to Amy's, he knocked quietly, mindful that it was still dark outside and her neighbors were probably asleep. He'd been practicing all night what to say to her. How to greet her. Easy conversation topics. Surely it'd be easier for him to talk to her now after what had happened last night. They'd gotten past the awkwardness . . . surely.

But the moment she opened the door, his mind blanked out.

Amy was beautiful. It didn't matter that it was predawn and she was in a night robe, her hair a tousled mess and her eyes heavy with sleep. She wore no makeup, the flaws in her skin visible, but to him, she was utterly gorgeous. She'd look like this when he woke her up, he realized, and it filled him with yearning. He wanted to be the one in bed with her, to give her a cup of coffee every morning. To lean over and kiss her before she got out of bed, because she was his and he wanted her to start every day knowing that.

The words glued themselves to his tongue. He was empty.

Caleb stared mutely at her as she yawned, touching her hair even as Donner pushed against her leg, his tail wagging. "Is it morning already?" Amy asked, sleepy.

He should answer her. *Close enough. Yes. Yes, it's morning.* "Morning enough."

She smiled. "So it is. Good morning, Caleb."

Damn, but she was pretty. His brain melted down when she turned that smile on him. He nearly dropped the box in his hands, distracted, and juggled it in his arms as he headed inside. *Greet her,* he told himself. *Talk to her. Small talk. Kiss her. Something. Don't just stand there like a mute when she talks to you.*

"What's all that in the box?" she asked in a drowsy voice, padding behind him as he went into the kitchen.

He wanted to tell her. He wanted to say a million things to her, but they were all frozen inside his paralyzed brain. It was like his damn jaw wouldn't unclench to say a proper greeting. How was he ever going to date her—or romance her—if he couldn't even talk to her? He set the box down on the counter and noticed that the coffee maker he'd gotten her was now out of its box and plugged in. Good. That meant she wasn't rejecting him or his gifts like he'd worried. He could talk to her. He could.

Caleb turned around and focused on her. She gazed up at him with those heartbreakingly blue eyes, her hair messy as if she'd just risen from bed. Her feet were bare and her robe gaped in the front, just a little, showing inviting smooth skin that begged to be touched and . . . and he still couldn't think of a thing to say. He tried focusing on her face, the expectant look in her eyes as she waited for him to say hello to her just making things worse.

Then he saw the light switch on the wall behind her. Without thinking, he reached over and flicked it off. The kitchen immediately became dark again, the only light behind them from the small window over the sink. Amy's face hid in shadows, and a tiny chuckle rose from her throat.

Caleb crossed the two steps between them and kissed her. She made a sound of surprise; then her hands slid to his waist as his tongue slicked into her mouth and he kept kissing her. Amy moaned against his mouth, her tongue flicking to greet his. It didn't matter that she tasted like morning breath—hell, he probably tasted like the two cups of coffee he'd already downed—she was the best thing he'd ever tasted and he wanted to keep kissing her forever. Eventually, though, he pulled away, giving her mouth one last gentle peck.

"Good morning," he managed.

"Hi," she said, dazed. Her hands still clung to his waist. "We . . . we better now?"

"I think so." It was true. Something about crossing the distance between them and claiming that first kiss of the day had helped. It helped that she melted against him, encouraging his kiss. It meant he was doing something right and that she wouldn't laugh at him if he was tongue-tied. That she liked him anyhow. Reluctantly, he moved over and flipped the light switch on again.

Amy's mouth was pink and swollen from his kisses, her skin reddened from his beard. He wanted to caress her face, to take away whatever discomfort he'd caused her. But she smiled at him, that gorgeous, brain-numbing smile, and he forgot near everything.

"Did you bring coffee?" she asked. "Or do you want me to make some?"

Her prompt helped. It reminded him that he'd arrived with a box of useful things. Unable to resist, Caleb leaned in and pressed his mouth to hers one last time and then turned to the box of goods he'd brought. "I brought some to brew," he told her. "Wasn't sure what flavor you liked."

"I like hazelnut," she admitted, moving to his side. "But I just buy whatever is cheapest at the store."

He made a mental note. Hazelnut. And she liked her coffee sugary sweet with tons of cream. He knew that much, and he'd brought both just in case. He started to unload the box, setting things on the counter. "I brought things for you."

She peered around him, her chin practically resting on his sleeve, and he wanted her to move closer. "I see flour and sugar, and . . . garlands?" Amy giggled. "What exactly are we making here?"

"We're decorating your tree for Christmas," he told her. "And we're making cookies."

"Oh, I love that idea," Amy gushed, all enthusiasm. "Do you know I've never made Christmas cookies?"

He hadn't, either, but he knew she loved sweet things, and so it seemed like a smart idea. "I noticed the tree I got you was naked," he pointed out, his face heating at the word "naked."

"I've been so busy that I haven't had time to work on re-purposing the decorations I bought." She nudged him with her hip as he opened the bag of coffee. "Remember the box that was in the trunk of my car? I bought some stuff at an estate sale but it's all pretty old. I was hoping to be able to use some of it."

He remembered a humping Santa. "Those weren't yours?"

"They are now." She chuckled, pulling out one of the tinsel-covered garlands and red and green wooden beads. There was a box of pretty glass ornaments, too, and she sighed happily at the sight of them. "I think I like this stuff better, though."

"I'm sure we can mix both," he told her. "Your stuff and mine."

"That sounds wonderful." Her face held a dreamy smile. "I love Christmas. A real Christmas, you know? Where the presents mean something and aren't just status symbols."

He was pretty sure he'd never been given a "status symbol" present in his life, but not everyone grew up in the remote wilds of Alaska. So he grunted a response, then added, "I wrote you a note, too."

Her lips quirked into a small smile. "So you, Mr. Shy, were going to show up to my house with a secret note and bake cookies? This was the plan?"

"No," he admitted. "The plan was to order some stuff from the bakery and send it to you with an anonymous note. But this way I get to spend time with you."

Amy chuckled and bumped his hip again. "No complaints here, but I have to admit I'm not much of a cook."

"Here I thought you were a gourmet chef, what with all that ramen."

She laughed even harder. "Don't you know? Ramen is dirt cheap, my friend." She peeked through the box, then gasped and pulled out a bag of chocolate chips. "Now we're talking." She tucked his note into her hand and began to open it.

"Wait," he said, the shyness attacking him out of nowhere. He put a hand over hers. "Don't read that while I'm here, okay? Just . . . wait for me to go."

Her expression turned to one of sympathy, but she beamed at him and held it to her chest. "I'll go put it in the bedroom so I can read it later."

She practically danced out of the room with the letter, much to his amusement. Hell, he guessed he was going to have to put more effort into the next one.

She returned, dressed in yoga pants and an oversize sweatshirt that hung off one delicious shoulder, and pulled her hair into a clip. The coffee brewed, and Caleb pulled out everything in the box. The decorations were on the table and Amy moved back and forth from the kitchen to the living room, putting decorations on the tree and eating chocolate chips from the bag as she did.

She was adorable. He couldn't stop staring at her, even when he was supposed to be (secretly) looking up cookie recipes on his phone. Because he'd arrived with a bunch of ingredients and realized he'd left Uncle Ennis's old cookbook back at the ranch.

"What are you doing?" she asked as she came to get a refill of her coffee and caught him peering at his phone.

He quickly hid it. "Nothing."

She arched a brow and waved her fingers at him, indicating he should show her.

"I might be looking at a recipe," he confessed after a moment. "I'm not experienced with this kind of thing. I can dress a deer, but make a cookie? Not so much."

"Dress a deer?" she asked, wrinkling her nose. "Like . . . in a sweater?"

Caleb stared. "Like . . . kill it and skin it and cut the meat up?"

"Oh." Her face turned bright red. "Well, that makes a lot more sense."

His nostrils flared. He was not going to bark with laughter in her face. He was *not*. "You thought . . ."

"That you were dressing them in little sweaters like people do their dogs, yeah." She gave him a sheepish look. "I did mention I'm from the city, right?"

"I think that's pretty obvious."

She laughed again, the sound silly and light, and it made him smile. "Speaking of animals in sweaters, do you think Donner needs one?"

"Why?"

She shrugged, pulling a jar of peanut butter from his supplies and digging a spoon into it. She immediately sat down on the floor and offered it to the dog, pulling the old collie into her lap as it licked the spoon. "I don't know. People are always dressing their pets in sweaters online. I don't want Donner to feel left out."

"I don't think you have to worry about that. Just feed him and give him attention and let him stay inside at night, and I imagine he'll be in love with you in no time." If he wasn't already. Amy was easy to love.

"You're the expert," she said cheerily.

"I am . . . at dogs, at least. Maybe not with cookies." He tapped on his phone's screen again. "You have any lard?"

Her eyes widened. "I don't even know what that is."

He thought for a moment. "Maybe we should just make pancakes instead. I know how to make those."

"I like pancakes," she said hopefully, smiling at him.

After that, it got a little easier to hang out. They ate stacks of pancakes and did the dishes by hand, talking about nothing in particular. After that was done, they went to the living room and he watched as she finished decorating the tree, then put Humping Claus and his wife underneath it. "Seems a shame to separate them," Amy told him with a mischievous look.

"Looks like he's giving her the gift that keeps on giving."

Amy broke into peals of laughter with that, collapsing next to him on the love seat. "Now I'm imagining Santa's stamina, and that's something I never wanted to think about, ever," she wheezed.

"Is this not the time to make a joke about North Poles?" He managed to say it with a straight face, to his credit.

She laughed so hard that she wiped tears from her eyes. Still chuckling, Amy looked over at him and sighed, and then the moment changed from silliness to . . . something a lot more charged. "What are we, Caleb?"

That old, familiar nervousness shot through his throat, locking his vocal cords. "What." He cleared his throat and tried again. "What do you want us to be?"

She bit her lip and leaned in closer. "I'd like to try dating, I think." Her gaze fell to his mouth. "I really liked kissing you."

Hell, he'd liked kissing her, too. "We can do that." He pulled her close and she automatically tilted her head back, welcoming his kiss. Caleb's lips were barely on hers when her phone buzzed with an incoming text. She grinned at him and broke off the kiss. "Someone's timing is terrible." Amy reached for the phone in her pocket and put it on the end table . . . then paused.

She just stared at that damn phone screen. At the text she'd gotten.

She was utterly silent for so long that he began to feel uneasy. "Everything okay?"

"Hm?" Amy turned back to him, her eyes a little too bright, her face a little too pale. "Oh. Yeah. I'm okay. It's just personal business." She smiled again but this time it didn't seem to reach her eyes. The happy sparkle in them was gone.

He hated that. He wanted her happy, always. "Do I need to beat someone up for you?"

"Not yet," she told him, and her expression seemed somber. It had been a joke, but she didn't seem to think of it as one, and that made him curious. "I'm sorry," she said after a moment. "I need to make a few calls and then walk Donner . . ."

"It's okay," Caleb said, getting to his feet. The moment was gone. He was new to dating, but he knew when he'd overstayed his welcome. Clearly whatever was in that text message had upset her, and she needed to handle it. He wanted to fix it for her, but it was also clear that she didn't want him to be the one to fix it. So he had to leave it alone, even though it was killing him to wonder about it. "I should get going anyhow. I've been slacking on my chores at the ranch, so I need to go and put in some extra time before Jack loses his mind."

She got to her feet, too, clutching her phone to her chest. "I'm sorry. I'm not trying to run you off, Caleb. I just—"

"Hey, it's okay." He wanted to kiss her again—a hundred times over—but now didn't seem like the time. "Just text me if anything changes between us."

Her brows furrowed and she frowned. "What do you mean, changes between us?"

He gestured at the phone.

"Oh." She shook her head, almost violently. "That's something else entirely. You and I . . . we're still a thing, right?" Her expression was full of hope.

She still didn't get it. Didn't grasp that he'd do absolutely anything for her. Caleb nodded slowly. "You and I are still a thing, absolutely. I'll be back in the morning to drive you to work."

"And with another note?" She wiggled her eyebrows at him. "There's still eleven more days until Christmas."

It was amazing that even when he didn't feel like laughing, she still managed to make it rumble out of him. He chuckled, nodding. "Yeah, with another note."

"I'll see you then." She clutched her phone to her chest and gazed up at him. "Thank you for coming by and making me breakfast."

"It was supposed to be cookies."

"It's the thought that counts," she replied, managing a smile. "And you're very, very thoughtful, Caleb."

Now he wanted to kiss her again. But she was distracted, so he'd be a gentleman. He nodded and pulled his Stetson onto his head, then headed out the door and into the snow.

Tomorrow would come by soon enough, and he hadn't lied—he did need to pitch in more at the ranch. There was plenty to do to distract himself and to stay busy. He knew one thing was going to be on his mind all day, however. He needed to know what had caused Amy's smile to die, and how he could fix it.

CHAPTER TWELVE

Amy clutched at her phone, her heart pounding. She wanted to tell Caleb not to drive away. Heck, she wanted to get into his truck and tell him to just drive and never stop. Just keep going forever, live like vagabonds, moving from town to town, and hide from all their problems.

The real world didn't work like that, though, and Amy sucked in a deep breath and then read the message on her phone again.

BLAKE: I'm sending you a courtesy message just to let you know that I'm filing for bankruptcy.

BLAKE: The latest start-up has been bleeding money and there's nothing to send you. Everything's overextended and mortgaged to the hilt, so you won't be seeing a cent of the alimony.

BLAKE: But I know you're hard up for money.
I'm willing to send you a little from my personal
account to tide you over . . . if you apologize for
humiliating me.

BLAKE: If you don't, you won't see a cent.

BLAKE: That jewelry I sent was just a taste of what
you used to have. Remember? You can have that
again.

BLAKE: But you have to be sorry that you put me
through this . . . and you have to make me believe it.

Amy wanted to vomit.

He was basically going to hold her money hostage. She
would never see a dime of it. There'd be no way to get on
her feet now, not with the alimony money gone. Her car
payment was behind, and the small credit card limit she
had was maxed. She was running out of things to pawn or
sell. She was . . . well, she was screwed.

And Blake would send her some money if she groveled.
If she called him and cried and stroked his ego. If she admitted she was "wrong" and he was "right."

She knew how that went. She'd spent years in their marriage constantly apologizing if she so much as put a glass
in the wrong spot in the dishwasher. If she'd worn a dress
that clashed with his tie. If she hadn't seemed "appropri-
ately" supportive at an entrepreneurial conference or a
business dinner. For years he'd controlled her life, doing his
best to make her feel stupid and helpless and like she was
the problem. Her parents had just contributed to that, too.

They'd told her to go along with her husband, because he was the man in the relationship and clearly the one in the right.

She'd hated all of it. She'd never known how much she'd hated it until she went to a therapist because she was so . . . angry at the world.

Well, she wasn't angry anymore. Now she was just frustrated at how awful Blake was and how he wouldn't leave her alone. She scanned his texts again. The nervous pit in her stomach had returned, as it always did when she dealt with Blake.

The comment about the jewelry made her pause. *He'd* sent that? She laughed, the sound sour in her throat. What a fucking week.

The good news was that she could pawn that jewelry and not feel a thing other than bitter joy.

She'd never beg him for money. Never, ever again. She was going to be independent, even if it meant eating ramen for the rest of her damn life. She'd never give him the satisfaction of her asking for money ever again.

Even so . . . the loss of all that income stung. She chewed on her lip, thinking, and then dialed Layla's office, intending to leave a voicemail.

To her surprise, Layla picked up. "Layla Schmidt Accounting."

"Oh . . . you're there? It's Amy."

"Hey! And, yeah, I'm at the office but I'm not officially working. I'd just left my crochet up here and came to retrieve it." Layla's bubbly voice was so fun and bright, completely at odds with the dry job of accountant. "I'm making winter cozies for the fire hydrants in town just because I thought it'd be funny to dress them up."

Er, okay. Layla did love a weird project. Her office was filled with all kinds of cross-stitched slogans like "A Woman's Place Is in the Resistance" and "Fight the Patriarchy" and "Do No Harm, But Take No Shit." This winter, she'd been wearing crazy colored scarves that were absurdly long and also absurdly huge. Layla didn't seem to care that she didn't fit in with the conservative, traditional town—she marched to the beat of her own quirky drummer.

It made her fun. It made her easy to talk to.

"I have a problem," she confessed to Layla. "My ex sent me a text and said I won't get any alimony from him because he's filing for bankruptcy."

Layla clicked her tongue. "Boy, he's really pulling out all the stops, isn't he? Is he broke?"

"I don't think so." Amy thought for a minute. "It's not the first time he's filed for bankruptcy, either, I don't think. He's done it before with other businesses. He makes one, lets it run into the ground, then folds it and starts a new one. I don't know for sure because he never let me touch the finances, though."

"Mmm, a tax dodger. I've seen that before."

"You have?" She was surprised.

"Yeah. It's a shitty way to do business, but you see people do it more often than you'd like."

"So what can I do?"

"Well . . ." Layla sighed. "Not much? Wait until his bankruptcy is filed and go before the judge to make them shake the pennies out of him? Lawyer up? Actually, lawyering up is the best idea."

"I don't have the money for a lawyer! He knows that."

"Which is probably why he's doing it, Amy," Layla said sympathetically. "He knows you won't fight him. Or if you do, it'll cost you so much money that you won't come out ahead anyhow. This is a dick move, a big one, and he knows it."

She wanted to cry, but Blake wasn't worth her tears. "So what do I do?"

"Document everything. Batten down the hatches. Keep shopping the clearance aisles." Layla paused. "And . . . I'm sorry. We'll keep track of things paper-wise and appeal, but for now, it's business as usual."

As in, no money.

Well, at least she had some jewelry to pawn. It was the one silver lining in all of Blake's garbage.

Caleb tossed hay with the pitchfork, mucking out the stalls. It was dirty, filthy, sweaty work . . . but it was also the kind of work that allowed your mind to wander while still getting a lot done, and so it was perfect for him today. He tossed the old hay into a wheelbarrow, filling it, and as he did, he thought about Amy.

Kissing her in the light was even better than kissing her in the dark. In the light, he got to see the expressions change on her face, the way her eyes got all soft with pleasure, the way her hands fluttered before she touched him, the way she sighed with bliss when he pulled away from her. It made him want to keep kissing her, over and over again. He was utterly besotted. Just thinking about kissing her made him want to toss the pitchfork away and drive over to her place and just stand on her doorstep until she let him in again.

But something was bothering her. She'd gotten a text that had killed her smile, and he wanted to know what it was. He wanted to know who he had to beat up. It wasn't that he was a violent man. But when it came to Amy . . . he'd do anything to protect her smile. Frowning to himself, he stabbed at another forkful and tossed it in the direction of the wheelbarrow.

"Do you mind?"

Jack's voice cut into Caleb's thoughts. He straightened and turned, seeing his brother standing just behind the wheelbarrow, manure-filled hay dusting the front of his plaid shirt and his dark jeans. He scowled under his cowboy hat, and a few steps behind him, at the entrance to the stall, was Hank, the oldest brother. He wore practically the same thing Jack did, but his beard was big and scruffy and he wasn't wearing the manure . . . which explained why he was smirking and Jack wasn't.

"Didn't see you there," Caleb said by way of apology. "I was thinking."

Jack shook off his shirt. "Obviously."

"Got something on your mind?" Hank asked.

Caleb felt himself flush.

"That answers that," Jack teased. "So, how'd it go?"

Caleb turned and shoved the pitchfork into the dirty hay again. "How'd what go?"

Hank just snorted.

"Oh, come on," Jack said. "We've lived with you all your life. We know how you work. You've been avoiding both of us ever since the whole Santa thing on Saturday night."

"Avoided my texts," Hank added, grumbling. "You know I hate texting."

"That's right," Jack continued. "Fess up. Tell us what happened on Saturday. Did you get your girl? Did you ask her out?"

Caleb felt his face turn even redder. He stabbed at the hay again, as if he could somehow squeeze more onto his pitchfork. "Maybe."

"You jackass. Just spit it out." Jack stepped forward and grabbed the handle of the pitchfork, trying to get Caleb's attention.

He let Jack take the tool away from him, and a smile of pride curved his mouth as he looked at his expectant brothers. "I kissed her."

Hank smacked his fist against the wooden stall door in pride. "Damn right you did. I knew you'd get the guts for it."

"You did?" Jack looked stunned. "And she liked it?"

"She didn't complain," Caleb drawled. "Not the first time or the fifth time."

"Fifth?" Jack's eyes widened and he hooted with laughter. "You scoundrel. Tell us all about it."

So Caleb leaned against the empty stall and told his brothers about his Saturday night. About how she'd almost gone out with Greg and he'd rescued her. How they'd ended up kissing, and how he'd gone over there again this morning and made pancakes with her. It was a brief summary, probably briefer than it should have been, but it didn't feel right to tell his brothers all the details. Some stuff you kept private. They could know the gist of things but not everything.

Some stuff was just for Caleb's memories.

"Proud of you," Hank said. "Does this mean I can tell Becca what's going on? She's been up my ass trying to figure out who Amy's Secret Santa is. It's been killing me not to tell her."

Caleb frowned. He liked Becca, but she ran a beauty salon, and Hank sometimes grumbled that people just showed up there to gossip. "Keep it quiet for a bit longer. I'm not sure if Amy wants anyone to know she's with me."

"Why wouldn't she?" Jack clapped him on the shoulder. "You're the third-handsomest Watson in town."

He just snorted.

It made sense to let Becca know. Heck, he wanted to tell everyone in town that he was with her. Everyone in the world, even. His brothers—and Uncle Ennis—already knew that he had a massive thing for the schoolteacher. What would be so wrong in letting the world realize that she was interested back?

But he kept thinking about that text she received. The one that she wouldn't show him. The one that made the sparkle in her eyes die. Maybe it was because of something to do with him. Maybe she didn't want people knowing they'd kissed.

So for now, he needed to be silent about being with Amy. He needed to just keep wooing her until she wanted them out in the open. Until she was the one that suggested they tell the world.

He wasn't going to mess up what they had for anything.

CHAPTER THIRTEEN

Amy forgot all about Caleb's note until the end of the night, when she was getting ready for bed. She found it tossed onto her pillow, and the realization that she still had to open it and read it somehow improved her mood.

It had really been in the dumps all afternoon. She'd moped about Blake. It wasn't the money as much as the fact that he was deliberately maneuvering to keep things away from her. He was making things complicated because he wanted to force her hand, and by doing nothing, she felt like she was subtly letting him win. He wanted her to either fold or fight him and spend her money. If she did neither . . . the one that lost was her. But she was losing all around, wasn't she? More than that, she just hated that Blake was trying to weasel back into her life.

Bad enough that he'd texted her and would pop up in her "recents" every time she looked at her phone.

Even worse that he'd sent jewelry as a gift to mock her. He probably wanted her to get all excited about the pricey gifts and then pull the rug out from under her. That sounded like the kind of head games he loved.

But Blake's efforts had shattered her hard-won peace and sense of pride. How long was this going to go on after her divorce? It had been a year since the divorce had been finalized, longer since they were "together." She'd been in Wyoming for more than six months. How long could she expect him to keep cropping up? Five years? Ten? Would she ever be free of his controlling ways?

The thought was depressing.

She'd spent most of the afternoon walking the dog. Just up and down the street with a short leash, because he was blind and didn't know they weren't going very far. He still loved the walk, his tail hesitantly wagging the entire time, and she let him stop to sniff every bush, every tree, every parked car. Donner's happiness at such a simple thing made her happy. She loved this silly dog. His gray muzzle, his cloudy eyes, his wiggidy-waggedy tail—all of him made her so stinking happy.

Really, it had been a wonderful day when he'd landed on her doorstep.

Thinking about her dog made her smile, and she patted the bed as she sat on the edge. "Come up here for snuggles, good boy." She patted the blankets and Donner hopped up, trusting her, and wiggled happily over to her side. She tucked him against her, petting him, and pulled Caleb's note out. The envelope was green, and when she pulled it out, the paper was white and red, edged with candy canes and reindeer. He'd gotten Christmas stationery just to write her notes? Her heart melted a little at the thought of the big, burly, silent cowboy going to the store and picking through the stationery aisle. It made her appreciate his efforts all the more.

She opened the letter and began to read.

Amy,

Not sure what to say. My original plan was to have a special holiday poem written about how beautiful and wonderful you are. How I've been unable to get you out of my mind since the moment I first saw you. Maybe throw in some Christmas trivia just to fill space. I don't know. If you're reading this, you know I'm not good with words. I'd rather recite a few facts about how the first Christmas trees in history were pagan symbols, but that kills the mood.

I'd much rather talk about you. You're the kindest woman I've ever met. The prettiest, too, but I think it's better to be kind. You've always been patient with me even when I stumbled over my words and acted like a fool around you, and I'm grateful. You're an easy woman to have a thing for. A popular one, too, it seems. I never thought I'd have to fight another Secret Santa for your attention, but here we are. I'd do it again, though.

(Confession: Throwing Greg's keys away was a lot more fun than it should have been.)

This isn't the most romantic letter. I wish it was. Now that you know I'm your Secret Santa, it's hard for me to confess everything I wanted to say, knowing that you know it's me writing this. All I'll say is that I'll do my best to make your Christmas merry and bright.

Yours,
Caleb Watson

PS—If you want the Christmas facts, let me know. I can probably go on far too long about that sort of thing.

She clutched the note to her chest, utterly touched. Then she read it a second time, just absorbing the words. He thought she was wonderful. He thought she was kind. And pretty. And she laughed every time she read the line about Greg's keys.

For a man that claimed to not be good with words, he certainly did charm her with his.

Amy read the letter a third time, then picked up her phone.

AMY: Hi, it's Amy. You there?

He might not answer, she told herself. He might be watching a movie, or doing things with his brothers. He might be handling whatever it was that cowboys handled on a ranch. It was silly of her to just—

Her phone dinged with a response almost immediately.

CALEB: I'm here.

She felt a thrill in the pit of her belly and texted him back, one arm wrapped around her sleeping dog.

AMY: What are you up to?

CALEB: Reading.

AMY: What are you reading?

CALEB: Salt: A World History

AMY: That's . . . interesting?

CALEB: It was at the library. I just like history books. Learning how other people lived.

AMY: Some teacher out there taught you right. :)

CALEB: Actually I was homeschooled by my father.

AMY: He was a teacher, then.

CALEB: Guess he was.

AMY: Soooo . . . I read your note.

There was a long pause.

CALEB: Did I embarrass myself?

CALEB: I don't want you to feel uncomfortable around me.

CALEB: If you do, I can have Hank come and pick you up in the morning and I'll fix your car when you're not there.

CALEB: I don't want you to feel pressured to talk to me.

AMY: Stop panicking. It was a wonderful note.

CALEB: I think my heart stopped for a full minute, just so you know.

She laughed aloud.

AMY: Why would you think I wouldn't love this note? It's very thoughtful.

CALEB: I can't remember a thing I wrote in it.

AMY: You did mention pagan Christmas trees.

CALEB: Ah, shit. I'm sorry. I probably rambled.

AMY: It was cute rambling. I liked it.

AMY: Does this mean I can look forward to twelve days of rambling instead of the poems you had set up?

CALEB: I should confess most of my poems were along the lines of "roses are red" and less Shakespearean.

AMY: I'm not much of a Shakespeare girl anyway. And I still want you to come by in the morning.

AMY: Not your brother. I still like you. :)

CALEB: I like you, too.

CALEB: I probably wrote that in the letter.

AMY: Once or twice. :)

AMY: Should I let you get back to your book?

CALEB: I'm in no rush. How was your day?

AMY: Shitty, if I'm being honest.

CALEB: My fault?

AMY: Nope. Just other stuff. I hope tomorrow will be better.

CALEB: I'll do my best.

That made her smile. Sure, there were crappy things going on in the world, and she had an awful ex-husband . . . but she had a happy, warm dog in her arms and a handsome cowboy texting her and writing her letters.

All in all, it was still pretty good.

CHAPTER FOURTEEN

Amy was humming the next morning and awake before dawn. She knew Caleb was an early-riser type, so this time she wanted to put on her makeup and fix her hair before he showed up. The playful side of her was tempted to stay in her robe, though, just to watch his face get red and his body react to that. She loved the way he stiffened and watched her like a hawk. For all that he was a gruff, silent sort, he absolutely could not hide his emotions lately when it came to her.

It was refreshing, after years of being married to a man who liked nothing more than to manipulate her. She knew where she stood with Caleb.

The day was a good day. He'd taken her to work that morning, utterly silent, but she hadn't minded his quiet. She had her students make holiday cards for family members, and when class was over, she didn't linger to decorate her classroom or work on lesson plans. School was out on Friday for the Christmas holidays, so she just needed to get through the week. Easy peasy.

Caleb was there waiting for her when she got out of school, and to her delight, he was in her car. It was freshly cleaned and vacuumed, and the engine purred like a kitten. For Day 2 of their dates, they grabbed a couple of fancy coffees from the bakery in town and a dog biscuit for Donner, and then spent the next few hours driving and looking for Christmas lights. It was a magical evening, really. They listened to Christmas music and laughed, and Caleb seemed to be more talkative, though she suspected the darkness probably helped. They didn't make out—it was hard to make out with a collie sitting between you on the front seat—but it was a nice date anyhow and she was sad when they turned into Painted Barrel and began to head to her house.

Her happy bubble disappeared the moment they pulled up to her place. A sports car was parked in her driveway. A familiar sports car, one that she'd been hauled out of just a few days ago when her "date" was mauling her.

Greg.

Caleb made a disgruntled sound in his throat. "What the hell's he doing here?"

"I don't know," she whispered. Her gut was knotting in that uncomfortable way. She hated confrontation. Hated it. This was churning up all kinds of bad memories, and she wanted to cry. How was it that she attracted the ones that never seemed to go away? First Blake and now Greg. She just wanted to be left alone by everyone.

Everyone except Caleb.

Worst of all, she couldn't get away from Greg because she was his renter. Even now, she could see the light on in her house, the lights on her Christmas tree twinkling. "He's sitting in my living room," she whispered, and it felt like a violation. He had a key. She knew he did; he was her land-lord. Didn't matter. It felt . . . uncomfortable. He might as well have been going through her damned panty drawer.

Caleb let out a hard breath. "I'm going to take care of this for you. Stay here."

For some reason, those words reminded her of past arguments. Of Blake "handling" everything so she wouldn't have to do a thing. So she could be the little housewife and not look at a bill or have a thought in her head except how to please her husband.

"It's my house," Amy blurted. "I'll talk to him."

"Not alone, you won't," Caleb growled.

Well, that was okay. If he wanted to come in with her, she wouldn't stop him. She took Donner's leash and petted his head so he wouldn't panic, then led him out of the car. Caleb moved to her side, staying right next to her as she marched to her front door. As she got to the doorway, she felt the absurd urge to knock . . . except it was her own damn house. She opened the door with a frown.

Greg sat there in her living room. He'd made himself comfortable on her love seat and was drinking one of her knock-off clearance-aisle sodas from her fridge and flip-ping through an old, battered magazine that Becca had given her. He looked up in surprise when he saw Amy and Caleb . . . and his gaze swung to the dog.

"There's no pets on the lease," Greg said by way of greeting.

She opened her mouth to protest, but Caleb stepped in front of her. He was furious. She could tell just by the set of his broad shoulders. "What exactly is on that lease?" he asked, and his voice was deadly calm.

Greg got to his feet. "I'm not trying to be a jerk. I'm just pointing out the facts. Her contract was very clear that this is a pet-free property."

Amy sank down, her arms going around Donner. He was her dog. He needed her. He was blind and abandoned. He licked her face happily, tail wagging, as if he had no clue the conversation was about him. "He doesn't have anywhere else to go."

"Send him home with this guy." Greg gestured at Caleb. "I need to talk to you privately anyhow, Amy."

"I don't want to talk to you," she told Greg. Not when she felt like crying at the thought of giving Donner up. It had only been a few days but she'd grown to love the old dog. He made her feel not so alone at night. He snored, sure, and he got lost in the hallway, but his tail wagged when he heard her and he danced like a puppy in the snow.

He was hers, damn it.

"I find it real ironic that you're here to talk about Amy's lease," Caleb continued in that too-calm voice. "Seeing as how when I got here, her ceiling had caved in and destroyed her bed."

"I went into her bedroom to take a look. Seemed fine to me," Greg said.

"You went into my bedroom?" she said, her voice sharp with surprise.

"To take a look at the ceiling, yeah. It looks fine—"

"That's because Caleb fixed it!"

"I also fixed the sink," Caleb continued in that same quiet, firm voice that told her he was barely holding on to his shit. "I fixed the faulty wiring, too. I fixed the windows. I fixed every leaking faucet. I fixed the hole in the roof, and the steps on the back porch because they were dangerous. You know why?"

Greg was silent.

"Because I don't like the thought of anyone living in a place like this. I don't like the thought of anyone having to worry that their house isn't safe, or warm. I know Amy's brought these problems to your attention multiple times and you haven't done shit. In fact, I think the reason you're here tonight"—Caleb's voice took on a note of menace—"is because you're interested in going out with her, not in the problems with her house."

Greg's gaze flicked to her, but he remained quiet.

"So are you really going to dither about the damn dog, or are you going to let her have it and maybe I won't bring up to law enforcement that you're having a schoolteacher live in a house that should be condemned? And you're charging her for it? Because if word got around with all the problems poor Amy's had—"

"Fine." Greg put his hands up and took a step backward, and Amy realized Caleb had taken a few steps forward, getting in Greg's face. Her eyes were wide as she looked between the two men. "You can have the dog. I can see you're busy. We'll talk more later."

"If she wants to," Caleb added as Greg scuttled past him. "And you don't let yourself into her fucking house when she's not here without her permission."

"It's my property—" Greg began, but went silent at the glare Caleb gave him. "Fine. Amy, I'll talk to you later."

"Why?" she blurted, a little disgusted at him. "You just came into my house when I wasn't here. I don't want anything to do with you."

He frowned in her direction, glanced at Caleb, and then said quickly, "Rent is due on the first, remember that." He cast one last look at her and then headed out.

Caleb immediately went to the front door. She thought

he'd lock it, but instead, he went to the doorway and stood in front of the screen door, arms crossed, until Greg's car pulled away.

Amy was in shock. Could one person be such an unrelenting creep? How had she let a man have such power over her again? She'd panicked when Greg had said that she couldn't have Donner. It was probably on the lease paperwork, sure, but she hadn't given it much thought. When he said she couldn't have him . . . she'd just frozen in place. She wanted to cry with relief that Caleb had been here. That he'd stepped in and neatly reminded Greg of everything he'd done. So she hugged Donner again. "Thank you, Caleb."

He ran a hand down his face, then sighed. "That guy's a real piece of work."

She laughed—it was either that or start crying. "He's something, all right." She hugged Donner again, burying her fingers in the soft fur. To think Greg could have so casually taken her dog away from her. "I didn't think . . . it didn't occur to me that he wouldn't like the dog here . . ."

"He's an asshole," Caleb said flatly. "I like how he was fine with all the problems you have in this shithole but isn't okay with a dog."

A shithole? She was almost offended . . . except, well, this place was a shithole, wasn't it? But it was her shithole. At least, it had felt like it until she'd seen Greg sitting on her couch. Now she just felt unsafe in her own home. Amy hugged Donner one last time and then got to her feet. Caleb still had a look of fury on his face, as if he wanted to destroy the world on her behalf. That was . . . gratifying. She approached him, a dozen worries racing through her mind. "Do you think he'll be back? While I'm here?"

Caleb's jaw clenched. "When I come by in the morning, I'm going to change the locks for you."

"Oh, but my car—you fixed it—there's no need—"

"When I come by in the morning," he continued, repeating himself as he stared into her eyes, "I'm going to change the locks for you."

She nodded, a knot in her throat. "Do you think I need to find Donner a new home?" The words choked her. Amy didn't want to find him a new home. He was safe here. More than that, he made her feel safe. He was hers. In these few short days, she'd become so attached to him that she couldn't bear the thought of giving him up.

Caleb put his hands on her shoulders, and just that small touch was comforting. "If Greg gives you any kind of trouble, *any kind at all*, you just say the word and I'll take care of him."

God, she loved that. She loved how fierce he was in his protectiveness of her. How he never questioned how she felt, or if she was the problem. He just took her side . . . and that was incredibly sexy. Amy took another step forward, because she wanted to kiss that frown off his face. She wanted to kiss him all over.

Their eyes locked.

She realized he was breathing hard, his shoulders heaving, and she didn't know if it was anger from Greg's intrusion or if it was her nearness. All she knew was that she wanted to kiss the hardness from his mouth. To make all that intensity about her.

So Amy shrugged off his hands, put her arms around his neck, and pulled him in for a kiss.

She was going to be tender, she really was. But the moment he realized what she was up to, he met her halfway, and then they were kissing, and it wasn't tender at all. It was fiery and wild and left her panting and breathless, and she wanted more than just a kiss.

She wanted to hold him.

She wanted to be held.

She wanted to strip off his shirt and run her mouth all over those insanely gorgeous muscles.

Amy broke the kiss and grabbed him by the front of his shirt. "Come with me."

He didn't say anything, just gave one of those grunts that told her he was listening, and she dragged him into her bedroom and shut the door, leaving Donner on the other side. Then she pulled him toward her again, their mouths locking as she maneuvered them toward the bed.

"This isn't sex," she told him between kisses.

"Okay."

"It's just . . . a little touching." She didn't want him to get his hopes up. She kissed him again, her tongue flicking against his, and it sent a spiral of pleasure right through to her core. "A little kissing . . . on the bed. And some other stuff."

He groaned, his big hands tangling in her hair, and then she wasn't sitting on the edge of the bed anymore. She was underneath him, his mouth devouring hers even as his weight pressed her into the mattress. Oh sweet lord, he felt good. He was making her wild with need. How was it that this shy, silent cowboy managed to kiss her just the right way? How was it that his tongue and his lips seemed to light all kinds of fires deep in her belly, when kissing Blake had felt like a punishment for those last few years? Kissing Caleb felt like . . . bliss.

Bliss she wanted more and more of.

She moaned as he nipped at her lower lip, taking it between his teeth and gently tugging. "How is it you taste so good?" he murmured between nips. "How is it you make me so damned crazy?"

Good, then she wasn't the only one that lost her mind

every time they touched. That was a relief to hear. She kissed him again, her tongue gliding against his as the kiss grew deeper, more urgent, and her hands slid down his chest, rubbing against him. She explored him through the material of his shirt. Every inch of him was hard and muscled, and it just made her want him even more. As he kissed her, she dragged her hands lower, feeling bold and sexy. She paused at his belt, and then cupped his length.

It wasn't entirely for his benefit, of course. She wanted to see if he was as turned on as she was. She wanted to feel all of him . . . and she wanted to show him how much she liked him.

Her hand encountered . . . a lot.

Caleb Watson was packing some serious heat downstairs, and Amy gasped, moving her hand over his length as if needing to double-check that all of that was really him.

He groaned into her mouth, kissing her harder, and his hips pushed against her grip.

Okay, yeah, that was all him. Wow. That was . . . impressive. "Caleb," she panted, stroking him through his jeans. "Can I touch you?"

He kissed her again and then pressed his forehead to hers. "You mean you aren't right now?" His voice was strained with effort, as if he was holding back.

She smiled and put a hand on his chest, easing him backward until they had rolled and he was the one on his back. Amy rested on her side and put a hand to his belt, undoing the buckle. "I meant underneath all this."

He exhaled a deep breath, his eyes practically smoky with need. "You can do whatever you want with me, Amy." Caleb reached up and gently touched her cheek, rubbing his knuckles along her jaw in a tender caress. "But know that I plan on doing the same to you."

What, was that supposed to be intimidating? It sounded like a good deal to her. She leaned in and kissed him again, working on his belt buckle as she did. It wasn't easy to manage one-handed, but she eventually got it and worked on his zipper next, easing it down. She changed her kisses to softer, gentle ones, toying with his mouth even as she eased his boxers down over his length.

Then he was hot and hard in her hand, and Amy gasped at the feel of him. She couldn't resist a peek, so she ended her playful kiss and then sat up to look at him.

Lord have mercy, but he was gorgeous. Caleb's cock was impressive. She'd only ever slept with Blake before this, but her memories of him were pale in comparison to what she held in her hand. He was hard and thick, and a vein traced along the shaft of Caleb's cock, inviting her touch. The crown of him was flushed deep with color, thick and prominent and beaded with pre-cum. With a little breath of excitement, she grasped him again, tightening her fingers around his shaft, and realized her fingers couldn't quite touch.

Size wasn't supposed to matter, was it? Looking at all this in front of her, though, Amy couldn't help but wonder if those people were wrong. Because she was really, really liking his size.

"Is this okay?" she asked him, breathless. "I'll stop if you want me to—"

He groaned and pulled her down against him in a hard, fierce kiss, even as his hips surged up against her grip.

Amy moaned into his mouth, squeezing his cock and sliding her hand up and down on him. Okay, he was definitely good with things. She worked him gently, her movements slow because her hands were dry, and the last thing she wanted was to give him a dry hand job. A mental image came to mind—of greasing up her hand with her body lotion and working him until he came—and the idea was so breathtaking and naughty that she felt wicked for even thinking about it.

. . . which meant that she totally, completely wanted to do it.

"Can I make you come?" she whispered against his lips between kisses.

He groaned and bit down on her lower lip again, then licked the nip away. "You know I'm yours. Whatever you want with me, take it." And he pumped into her hand again, rocking against her grip.

"Okay." She let go of him, oh so reluctantly, and reached over the bed to pull the bottle of lotion from her nightstand drawer. The movement put her breasts in his face and he immediately palmed them, seeking out her nipples, and she cried out. Oh god, that felt amazing. She froze, not wanting to move from this spot even as he lifted his head and nuzzled at her breasts, working them with his hands and burying his face in them.

"Gonna make you come, too," he rasped. "God, I want to touch you."

Heat ached between her thighs, deep inside her, and Amy wanted that, too. She was so damn impatient, because she wanted everything all at once, but the enticement of making Caleb come was first and foremost on her mind. Even as he plucked at her now-hard nipples through her cashmere sweater, she managed to lean over and set the bottle on the nightstand. She pumped a large amount into her hand and clasped it tight, getting it all over her fingers and warming the slippery stuff.

She was panting as she slid her hand over his length, because he was still teasing her breasts with those big hands, as if as determined to toy with her as she was with him. And dear lord, it felt so good. When was the last time she'd been kissed and teased so much? When was the last time she was filled with so much aching need that she felt hollow?

His breath hissed out between his teeth as her slick hand glided over his length. He pulled and teased at her nipples as she clasped him in her fist and began to slowly pump his shaft, working him up and down. Caleb's body was stiff as she leaned over him, his breath panting out with every stroke of her hand over his length. He pinched her nipples, hard, and she cried out, even as she felt him shudder and hot, wet heat spilled over her hand. She leaned down and kissed him furiously, still working him with her sticky hand, determined to give him every bit of pleasure she could.

When at last he groaned and pulled her hand off of him, she felt a curious sense of accomplishment. He hadn't lasted long under her touch—she'd made him come hard and fast. That was a heady feeling, and she liked the dazed expression on his handsome face as he pressed his forehead to hers and worked to catch his breath.

That had been so very worth it. It didn't matter that she was aching deep inside. He didn't have to keep his promise— the pleasure had been hers just giving him that release.

He kissed her, all the frantic need drained out of him, and the kiss was slow and sweet and oh so languid. "Towels?"

"Bathroom," she whispered. "I can get it—"

"I'll do it. Wait here."

She watched him like the greedy woman she was, devouring the quick glimpse of dimples at his lower back as he got to his feet and hefted his pants back up. When he returned, they were done up except for his belt, and he had a warm, wet washcloth that he ran over her hand to clean her off. Such a kind, thoughtful man . . . and yet such a protective warrior streak, too. It was a combination that was like catnip to her.

He dumped the washcloth into her hamper, and she started to get up out of the bed.

Caleb immediately grabbed the front of her sweater in a handful and pulled her against him. "Don't I get my turn?"

His husky voice made her body flood with heat. "Oh, you don't have to . . ."

"You think I don't want to?" He gently pushed her back onto the bed. She sat down on the edge, fascinated by the hungry, possessive look in his eyes. "You think I haven't been dreaming about this ever since I saw you?"

She sucked in a breath. "Have you?"

"You have no idea," he murmured, and then gave her shoulder a little push—the same one she'd given him—to drop her back on the bed. Amy lay backward, her legs dangling over the side, and she noted absently that she was still wearing her heels from work that day. Actually, she was still wearing all of her work clothes—her pale cashmere sweater, her green flared skirt, and those nude heels. It seemed a strange, too-prim outfit to be making out on a bed with a big, sexy cowboy, but it didn't matter. He wanted her, and she wanted him to kiss her and make her feel good.

She watched, feeling like a silly virgin, as he lay on his side next to her, close enough that she could practically burrow against his broad chest. Caleb gazed down at her, watching her face, but he didn't kiss her. It was making her crazy, all this wanting. Was he just going to stare at her for a while, then? What was he going to do?

Then his hand went to her knee and slid up her skirt.

Amy sucked in a breath, her eyes widening. It felt so damned intimate to lie next to him, not kissing, and just staring up at his face as his hand crept up her thigh.

"You tell me if anything I do bothers you. Or if you want me to stop," he murmured. "And I will stop." His hand moved high up along the inside of her thigh, practically brushing against her panties.

Her nipples were hard and aching, desperate for him to touch her again. "What do you want me to do?" she whispered, feeling vulnerable and exposed despite the fact that she was fully clothed.

"Just look at me when I touch you," Caleb murmured. "I want to watch your face."

Oh.

She gasped, one hand flying up to clutch at his shirt, as he carefully slid his fingers past the leg band of her panties and pushed into them. His hand was on her pussy, and she was embarrassed at just how incredibly wet she was. She'd soaked her panties with her need, making a mess, and she wanted to squirm with girlish horror.

"Look at how damn wet you are," he murmured, his fingers gliding up and down the seam of her folds. "Never thought you'd get so fucking wet just from touching me."

She whimpered, her lips parted, her breath panting. It was so hard to keep eye contact. She wanted to close her eyes and lean into the sensations. She wanted to hide away from him while he touched her—but with their eyes locked like that, there was no hiding. She felt utterly exposed with her arousal, and it was an alarming sensation. "Caleb," she whispered, clutching harder at his shirt. "Please."

His fingers parted her folds, and then one big, thick digit stroked up and down, moving through her slippery pussy in an erotic glide, and she gasped again.

He found her clit, and his stroking changed to teasing little circles, toying with her there like he had with her nipples. It made her entire body quiver, and she spread her legs wider even as she panted like a shameless thing, clinging to his shirt as he rubbed her toward an orgasm, staring down at her with those intense eyes. She tried to remain still, she really did, but he'd graze his fingertips over just the right spot and then her legs would jerk like a marionette's and a little cry would escape her.

"You're beautiful," he whispered, watching her.

It made her feel beautiful, even when she felt awkward. The orgasm built and rose in her body, making her buck shamelessly against his hand as he teased her clit. She panted his name, wild, and ground against his hand, chasing that release. When it finally came, she cried out, her entire body arching with the force of her release, and her pussy flooding against his hand.

Just like she'd done to him, he kept touching her, wringing those last bits of pleasure out of her body, making her orgasm seemingly last forever until she drew up her legs, trapping his hand, and panted out a protest.

Instead of taking himself to the bathroom to wash his hands, though, Caleb just gazed down at her and licked his fingers clean of her taste, and that made her gasp all over again.

He leaned in and kissed the tip of her nose as she snuggled up against him, basking in the aftermath of her orgasm. "Do you want me to stay tonight? Just to keep you safe? I can sleep on the couch."

Did she want him to stay? Part of her wanted it desperately, but she also didn't want to seem too needy, too clingy. She didn't want to be that pathetic, useless woman like she'd been when married to Blake. So she shook her head. "I'm okay. I have Donner here. I'll just push the couch in front of the door and if he tries anything, I'll call you."

"If you're sure. I don't mind staying. It's a completely platonic offer." He kissed the tip of her nose again, his expression tender.

It made her melt, but it also made her that much more determined to handle it on her own. Hadn't she already leaned on him far too much? "It's okay, really."

"All right, then." Caleb looked as if he didn't quite agree with her choice, but he wasn't going to fight her on it. "Want to see me out?"

She nodded, and it was hard to stand up with her legs as wobbly as a colt's after that orgasm. How was it he could recover and seem so normal, while she felt as if she'd been pieced back together with string and bubble gum? Good lord. She felt wrecked—a good kind of wrecked, but still wrecked. Amy trailed at his side as he put his hat on again and gave Donner a quick goodbye rub—and she remembered how he'd licked his fingers after teasing her to a climax—and then he kissed her again. Hard. Possessive. Achingly wonderful.

"Almost forgot to give you your note today," he murmured, and handed her the envelope.

She clutched it like it was a precious gift and watched from the doorway as he headed down the porch and toward his truck. Once he left, she shut and locked the door, slid the love seat in front of the doorframe, and then collapsed on the cushions to read her note.

Amy,
I had a great time tonight. I know I'm writing this hours before I even get to see you, but it doesn't matter. I know I'm going to have a great time tonight. Just being with you is the best thing to happen to me, so there's no "bad time" when you're around. I get to look at your pretty smile and hear your voice. I get to talk to you. I get to be around you. Nothing about any of that could be a "bad time." Anyone who says otherwise needs a punch to the face.
    That includes Greg.

I've run out of things to say and I still have too much paper to write on. I guess I'll tell you a bit more history trivia. Did you know that the Christmas tradition of mistletoe originated because mistletoe was considered a fertility drug? It's another pagan ritual. Just between you and me, those pagans sounded like party animals.

I like the idea of a kissing ritual, though. Mostly I just like the idea of kissing you more.

Yours,
Caleb

She clutched the note to her chest and sighed. How was it that he could make each note funny and yet utterly romantic at the same time? She was going to be seduced by these notes by the end of the week . . . or less, given what had happened tonight. One more mention of fertility festivals and she'd be flinging her panties at him. He'd spend the night . . . and it wouldn't be on the love seat; that was for darn sure.

Were they moving fast? Absolutely. But she was an adult, a grown, divorced woman. She could do what she wanted, and tonight, she'd wanted to touch Caleb and give him pleasure.

She had no regrets.

CHAPTER FIFTEEN

The rest of the week passed in a holiday blur. On Tuesday, he took her out sledding. They didn't have actual sleds, but Caleb had assured her that a large cardboard box would be just as effective. She hadn't believed him . . . until she'd rocketed down her first snowy hill and nearly crashed into a tree. It had been utterly exhilarating, and they'd raced up and down the hill like children until their sleds turned to wet, destroyed mush.

After that, they'd retreated to her house for hot cocoa and a steamy makeout session.

On Wednesday, he took her out to dinner in one of the neighboring towns and insisted on paying. It had felt like a date more than a Christmas tradition, but she didn't mind. She liked dating him. Thursday, he arrived at her house with sticks, charcoal, and carrots, and they made snowmen in her backyard.

Donner, not grasping the point of snowmen, made sure to pee all over them.

Each night had ended with a passionate round of kissing and more caresses, to the point that Amy was having erotic dreams of her cowboy at night, and her body lit up the moment she saw him. She was besotted, and having so much fun that she didn't care. Had any Christmas ever been so magical?

After the snowmen, they'd ended up on the love seat and she'd straddled him and rode his thigh until she came, panting. He'd held her as she'd come down from her orgasm, his fingers trailing up and down her back with lazy touches that made her wish they had all night.

"Do you have to go soon?" she whispered.

"Soon," he agreed. "How's the new door lock working?"

"No complaints." She hadn't seen—or heard from—Greg in the last few days. He was probably avoiding her place, especially since Caleb's truck was parked directly in front of her house. She'd told Becca about Greg's intrusion and her friend had been properly outraged and reassured Amy that Greg was at heart a chicken and wouldn't come around if he thought Caleb was there.

Even so . . . she wanted her cowboy to curl up with all night. Maybe she was getting greedy, but the thought of spending the night in Caleb's arms (platonic or not) sounded like heaven. "Did you want to stay tonight?"

He stiffened under her, and she wondered if she'd moved too fast.

"It's okay," Amy said quickly. "It's not that I'm scared. I was just, you know, curious."

"I would, actually," he told her, his fingers gliding up and down her spine. "I would love to stay all night." His voice took on a husky note that made her thighs clench in response. "But I have to catch up with work, and we—me and my brothers—have to finish early. Which brings me to tomorrow night's date . . ."

"Oh?" She sat up, acutely aware that she was still straddling him like a wanton. Was he canceling on her? Right after they'd just shared some intense foreplay that led to an equally intense orgasm? Really?

He nodded, his eyes somber. "My uncle Ennis is having a Christmas party for us at the ranch. That's why we have to be done with ranch work early. I wanted to know if you'd be my date."

"Oh." Relief shot through her. "So you're not breaking up with me?"

"Breaking up with you?" His brow furrowed. "You think I'm going to let you go anywhere now that I have you?"

For some reason, that statement—maybe it was the possessiveness of it—made her bristle. She climbed off his lap. "You aren't going to 'let' me do whatever. I do what I want. You don't own me, Caleb." She marched into the kitchen, determined to compose herself.

"Amy," he said, coming into the kitchen to confront her. "I didn't mean it like that. I just . . . I have a stupid tongue."

"I like your tongue," she managed, trying to keep her voice playful. "Normally. But I don't like being told I can't do something. I don't want a controlling boyfriend."

"I understand." He was silent for a long moment, and she wished he'd say more. That he'd apologize. Tell her she could do whatever she wanted. But he said nothing at all.

She put her hands on the sink, staring out the window at the snowy backyard. The kitchen felt tense. Awkward. Did she need to say something to put him at ease? But was she just making excuses then? Was she falling back into the same patterns if she did?

Caleb cleared his throat after another tense minute passed. "You should know . . ."

Amy waited.

". . . that the moment I saw you, I told myself I was gonna marry you. But I figured that might be a bit too forward to trot out, so I say other dumb shit. I'm sorry if I hurt your feelings."

Of all the things she'd expected Caleb to say, that wasn't it.

He wanted to marry her?

She turned, gaping at the cowboy behind her. He stood there with his hat in his hands, a determined expression on his face. "Was . . . was that a marriage proposal?"

"No! Not yet, at least." He flushed bright red, the contrast stark against his dark beard. "It's just . . . sometimes I want to tell you that so you know how I feel. That hasn't changed at all. I've wanted you ever since I laid eyes on you. I don't want to own you. I don't want to smother you down or make you be something you don't want to be. I just want to be with you."

All the tension in Amy melted. She watched as he fussed with the brim of his hat, his hands clearly nervous. This was hard for him to say, she knew. It was obvious in the tight sound of his voice, the way his hands pressed and crimped the edge of his hat.

"I . . . thank you."

He nodded. "I'm just letting you know where I stand. So if I say dumb shit from time to time, remember that I'm also patient. I've waited months and months for you. I can wait longer if you need more time, but I'm right here and I'm not going anywhere. You take as long as you need to get used to the idea, but I do want to marry you." Caleb looked down at his hat, grimaced at the mess he was making of the brim, and then put it on his head. "But for now, I'd like to ask you to be my date for dinner at my uncle's party. I think it's kinda formal. He told us to dress nice and do our chores early so we could shower." He looked pained at the thought. "It's dinner and an ugly-gift exchange."

She blinked. It was a lot to take in, what he was telling her. A declaration of intentions. Not a marriage proposal, just letting her know where he stood and how he felt, because that was who Caleb was. He was steady and solid and he didn't change his mind like the wind. She knew where she stood with him . . . and it reminded her again that he was nothing like Blake. "I'd love to go to the party, but I don't have anything to bring as a gift."

"It's an ugly-gift exchange," he repeated. "The more hideous the better. You could always wrap up Humpy Santa and his wife."

"I kinda like Humpy Santa," she told him, chuckling.

That brought a smile to Caleb's face and he was so handsome he took her breath away. "I kinda do, too."

"I'll think of something," she told him quickly. "What time should I be there?"

If it was possible, his smile grew wider. "I'll check." He moved forward and put his arms around her waist, pulling her against him for another kiss. "You should know," he murmured just before he put his mouth on hers. "This is me inviting you to meet the family."

Oh shit. So it was. "You do move fast," she breathed, dazzled by his nearness.

"I just know what I want."

His confidence was impressive . . . and sexy. Now she was the one flustered and unsure. How had her tongue-tied cowboy gone from silent to seductive so quickly?

Her heart was in soooo much trouble.

* * *

If there was one thing Amy's life prior to her divorce had prepared her for, it was attending a party. She picked through her party dresses before settling on a sparkly green number with a high neck and a completely open back. Unfortunately she'd pawned a lot of her shoes at this point, so she was going to have to wear her usual nude pumps, but that was all right. Hopefully no one would be looking at her feet. She pulled her hair up into a tight bun, and for jewelry, she put on a pair of dangly plastic Santa earrings—a gift from one of her students and his parents that she'd gotten earlier that day. She didn't care if they were cheap or if they didn't match her dress—she loved them.

She studied her form in the mirror once she was dressed. Her skirt barely came to her knees, and the back was open from the neckline to the curve of her spine. Was it a little overly sexy and potentially too dressy for a small Christmas party? Yes and yes. But she wanted to see Caleb's eyes light up when he looked at her, so she wasn't changing for anything.

The last week had been magical. Each date they went on felt more comfortable than the last, and it was clear that he'd put a lot of thought into each excursion. More than the snowman making or going to dinner together, though, she loved the letters. They were rambling and funny and heartfelt. Unpolished, yes, but she vastly preferred a heartfelt message to a slick, too-clever response. She'd kept every single one of them, neatly folded in their envelopes, at her bedside, and she might have read them a half dozen times each. Maybe more.

After dithering over her appearance for a few more moments, she grabbed her purse and put on her coat—the warm, thick one that he'd given her. Amy snuggled into it for a moment, appreciating the fleece lining and the heavy bulk of it. This was a coat designed to be warm, not fashionable. It was another one of his honest, practical gifts, and she loved it.

"Come on, Donner." She grabbed the dog's leash and harness, working him into it. "You're invited to the party, too." The vet wanted her to bring the dog to "look him over" again, but she was pretty sure he just liked animals. It worked for her. Bringing Donner would be fun.

With her dog in tow, Amy took her wrapped ugly present and headed out to the car. She turned on the navigator on her phone and sang along to Christmas carols on the radio as she followed the directions to the Swinging C Ranch. This was her first time going to the ranch alone. She'd gone briefly last week to get Donner checked over, but she'd been too distracted to pay much attention, and she hadn't driven. Since she was driving herself, she was forced to pay attention, and even in the darkness, she could see just how much land the ranch itself covered. Wyoming seemed to be a mixture of snowy mountains and wide-open spaces, and it was endlessly fascinating to her.

When she pulled up to the ranch, there was a row of cars and trucks already parked up front. The ranch house itself was big and sprawling, a log cabin–like monolith that loomed over the snowy landscape. She opened the door to her car and heard the lowing of cattle in one of the nearby pastures. That got Donner's attention. His ears pricked and his tail thumped with excitement.

"We're not chasing cattle today," she told the dog as she took his leash. "Some other time."

The front door opened and light spilled out into the

darkness. It was Caleb, his big body silhouetted by the interior lights, and she could hear Christmas music coming from inside the house. He was wearing his cowboy hat, and judging by his body outline, he wasn't wearing a jacket or any sort of formal suit at all.

Okay, so she was definitely overdressed.

She juggled her wrapped present and the dog's leash as he came down the long walkway from the house to meet her. "You told me this was a party," she said by way of greeting. "So I wore a party dress."

"It is a party," he reassured her. "And I'm sure whatever you're wearing is fine."

"You say that, but you haven't seen it yet," she grumbled. Her coat hid everything.

"You're always beautiful."

"You're just saying that because it's dark," she muttered. He was always more effusive when he couldn't see her face.

He laughed. "You're not wrong."

She smiled into the darkness, waiting for him to approach. They'd come really far in the last week or so. Now when Caleb saw her, he didn't turn all silent. Oh sure, he had his moments, but for the most part, he was able to talk to her like a normal human, and she loved it. He was still boldest in the darkness, though. Maybe he always would be. She didn't mind.

Then he was right in front of her, his face hidden thanks to his hat. She could see his smile, though, and beamed one back at him. "Hi."

"Hi there. Can I kiss you?"

As if he had to ask? "Of course."

He flicked the front of his hat, tipping it back in a casual way that fascinated her every time he did it. Then he leaned in, and his lips barely brushed over hers. He smelled like aftershave and pine trees and cowboy, and she wanted to bury her face in his shirt and just breathe him in.

"It's cold out here," he murmured, taking Donner's leash from her hands. "Come on inside. You're the last one to arrive."

Amy suddenly felt nervous. His brothers were in there, and she was going to meet them. She'd met Hank a few times, of course, as he was the parent of one of her students, but she'd never really talked to him about anything other than Libby or his wife, Becca. Caleb had a younger brother, too, and he'd be at the party, as well as Caleb's uncle, the town vet. It shouldn't have been intimidating, but she wasn't at this party as Libby's schoolteacher. She was here as Caleb's girlfriend.

That made everything different.

Caleb kept a hand at her back as she headed for the house, nervously clutching the present she'd brought. It had seemed like a clever—and cheap—gift, but now she worried that no one would find it funny but her. That they'd look at her sparkly dress and think she was showing off. That they wouldn't like her. Oh god, what if Caleb's family didn't like her? She was a divorcée, after all, and some people thought that divorcées were broken, like there was something wrong with them if they weren't married any longer. What if his family judged her and found her lacking?

A week ago she wouldn't have cared. She'd have been hurt a little, but it wouldn't have mattered overall. Suddenly, everything seemed to matter. She wanted Caleb's family to like her. She wanted Caleb to be proud of her. She wanted to be a good girlfriend to him . . . even if it had only been a week.

How had it only been a week?

Caleb opened the front door and three dogs came rushing out, tails wagging. She tensed, worried for Donner, but his tail wagged with lightning speed, and for the next few moments, the dogs sniffed each other and licked by way of greeting around Caleb's legs. "That's enough," Caleb said. "Everyone inside."

The happy, wiggly flood of dogs immediately went back into the house, and Donner tried to follow. Caleb unhooked his leash and let him go, and he blended into the pack of dogs and disappeared inside. Amy watched him go, nervous. "You think he'll be okay?"

"He's fine," Caleb said, ushering her into the house. "Come on."

The interior of the house was warm and cozy. While it seemed large and imposing outside, inside it was inviting. The ceiling of the place was tall and arched, the roof peaked, and it made the house seem spacious despite the fact that the walls were thick and heavy. She could see a large fireplace in one corner of the living area, a wood stove against the opposite wall, and a large decorated tree in the center. There was a bright red rug on the floor and a TV mounted on the wall. A table had been set up with a paper holiday tablecloth and food and drink was set out atop it. The walls had wreaths and stockings interspersed with old photos of ranch life. Despite all the care taken to decorate, the living area was empty, and she could hear voices in the kitchen.

"Where is everyone?" Amy asked as Caleb took the present from her and set it down on a table near the door.

"Getting a drink, I imagine." He shrugged. "Let me help you with your coat."

She took it off and handed it to him, waiting for him to comment on her dress.

Caleb just stared, his gaze devouring her. She definitely felt overdressed, considering that Caleb was wearing dark jeans and an equally dark shirt. "Um, some of the parties I've been to in the past were a bit . . . dressier." When he remained silent, it made her nervous. "Is this okay? Should I go home and change?"

His gaze flicked to hers. "No."

"No, it's not okay?" Her heart sank.

"No, you're not changing." He rubbed his mouth with a hand. "You look . . . nice."

"Wow. You're killing me with the compliments," she teased, her feelings recovering a little. He couldn't seem to stop staring, and that was gratifying. "I wore this for you."

His gaze flicked to hers, and there was so much heat and intensity in his eyes that it made her breathless. He pulled her closer to him, leaning in to whisper. "Are you trying to make me hard in front of everyone?"

"Yes?" She fluttered her eyes innocently.

"It's working." He put a hand to her back and then pulled away as if burned. "Jesus . . . your dress . . . I don't know where to touch you."

Okay, this was definitely the reaction she'd wanted. She beamed at him. "Anywhere you like."

He turned bright red at her words, the flush creeping up his face, and that made her smile even more. "I'm gonna have to save that thought for later."

"Should I put my coat back on?" she teased, gesturing at it.

"No, but I'm tempted to give you my shirt before I introduce you to Jack," he muttered.

"Then I'm the one that's going to be all distracted," Amy whispered. "By your six-pack."

He blushed again. "It's not a six-pack."

"It's at least five."

He shot her another look. "Come on. Let's go meet the family before I find a closet and drag you in there for some kissing."

That made her all breathless. Finding a closet and doing some kissing sounded more fun than the party at the moment. "I'm game."

Caleb bit back a groan and gave her another quick, hard kiss, his tongue barely flicking against her lips before he pulled back. "You're a temptress."

She felt like one. She felt like the most beautiful woman on earth tonight, the most sexy, the most desirable. It was a heady feeling. She was a schoolteacher, and an average woman all around. Why was it that when Caleb looked at her, she felt so darn special? It was addicting, and she wasn't sure she'd ever get enough of it.

He took her hand and pulled her forward, and Amy supposed they weren't going to find a nice private closet after all. Well, darn. She let him lead her to the kitchen, where the sound of voices was, and fought back the twinge of anxiety when they stepped inside and a half dozen people turned to stare at her.

"Hey there!" Becca said, pushing her way forward from the group. She held her arms out, beaming a smile at Amy. "I'm so glad you came! Libby will be thrilled!"

She hugged Becca, feeling relieved to see a familiar face. "I think I overdressed."

"Nonsense. You look beautiful. Come and say hi to Hank. Libby's in the barn with a few of the neighbors and their kids." Becca pulled her forward, taking her hand, and Amy cast Caleb an apologetic look.

He just shook his head as if unsurprised and leaned against the counter.

Becca was a great hostess, at least. She introduced Amy to everyone, including Caleb's younger brother, Jack. Jack looked a lot like Caleb, but his features were somehow sweeter. He was definitely the prettiest of the three brothers, and judging from the look on his face, he knew it. He eyed her up and down with a slow smile until Caleb gave him a shove.

"I know she's yours. I'm just admiring the fact that you somehow managed to snare such a pretty woman. She must have a thing for silence."

Caleb elbowed him again, glaring.

"All right, stop it, the two of you." Doc Ennis—the elderly vet—stepped in between the two men and then scowled at Caleb. "Take your damned hat off, boy. Were you raised in a barn?"

"Yes," Caleb said immediately, and Jack snickered.

Then the rest of the group came back from the barn, and the kitchen was suddenly crowded with strangers. They were neighbors from the Price Ranch down the road, Becca explained. It was several families with young children, and Amy recognized Sage—the town mayor—and her husband, too. It was awfully cramped, as if no one wanted to move out of the kitchen and into the living area, and Amy was acutely aware of just how open the back of her dress was. The other women were wearing party clothes, but they were a lot more sedate than Amy's sparkling dress, and she stuck out like a sore thumb. Uncomfortable, she sidled through the crowd over to Caleb's side. He immediately put his arm around her waist and drew her against him, and she felt better.

"Sorry about this," Caleb murmured in her ear, his lips

practically brushing against her plastic earring. "Didn't know half the town would be showing up tonight."

"It's okay," she whispered back, turning to look at him. Oh. A smear of her lipstick was on his mouth from their earlier kisses and she absently ran her thumb over his lips to get rid of it.

The scorching look he gave her immediately made her breath disappear. Suddenly the kitchen felt very tight and crowded after all. There were far too many people here, and she really just wanted to be alone with Caleb. To talk to him. To hear about his day.

To kiss the hell out of him.

"You two gonna need a room?" Jack appeared suddenly, propping an elbow on Caleb's shoulder and leaning in.

"Fuck off," Caleb growled at his brother.

Jack grinned, ignoring Caleb's sour attitude. "I'm just saying that there are children present, you know. Might want to save all that touchy-feely stuff for when you're alone."

Amy blushed. All she'd done was touch Caleb's mouth. Was she that obvious? But when she looked around the room, she noticed a few people were watching them and smiling . . . so, yes, she guessed they were.

"Come on, Miss Mckinney," Libby cried out, flinging herself through the sea of adult legs before locking her arms around Amy's legs. "Come sit in the living room with us!"

How could she refuse? Laughing, she let the child lead her into the main room of the house. Caleb immediately snagged her other hand and went along with them, and Amy was glad he was sticking to her side. She normally wasn't shy around strangers, but too much of this was new to her. Plus, being a stranger in Painted Barrel was different from being a stranger in Houston. In Houston, you assumed everyone was a stranger. Here, everyone knew everyone else, so if you were an outsider, you really *were* on the outside. It was very isolating, and she'd felt so odd ever since moving here. She'd thought that going to such a small town would mean instantly being part of a warm community—like a big family. Instead, she'd felt strange and alone.

Being in a sexy, sparkly dress wasn't helping.

Folding chairs were brought into the living room, and Caleb immediately snagged one and pulled Amy into his lap. She protested, but the seating was at a premium. Caleb seemed relaxed with her in his arms, too, laughing and joking with the other cowboys. This time, it was Amy who was quiet, her arm on his shoulders while the discussion ranged from fences to this year's cattle prices to Sage's expansive ranch. It was nice to see Caleb in his element, though. He was comfortable, and if he wasn't chatty, he was at least social.

He noticed her quiet, though, and pulled her closer. "Everything all right?" he murmured against her neck.

She nodded. "Just feeling a bit weird."

"Everyone loves you," he reassured her. "It's that you're with me is the part they can't figure out."

Amy snorted. "Please. You're the best catch in town."

His eyes gleamed. "I'm not the one with multiple Secret Santas."

She had more than he thought. He didn't know about her ex sending the jewelry. Her throat got tight and she kept smiling, even though her mood plummeted just a little. Caleb didn't know. He couldn't know that she felt . . . well, like an accessory tonight. That was hard.

It reminded her too much of her past.

The chatter continued, everyone easy and casual with one another. Presents were given to the little ones from

"Uncle Ennis," and even the dogs got wrapped toys from the thoughtful vet. Amy clutched Donner's plush bone, since her dog was curled up in the kitchen with the other dogs, enjoying their company. Even her dog had abandoned her.

Why was she feeling so isolated at a Christmas party? So alone even in a room full of people?

She smiled through the ugly-gift exchange, though. The presents were tossed into a pile and people picked numbers out of a hat and grabbed gifts in order of the numbers. Amy picked number one—a fact that made her cringe, just inside, and only added to her feeling of sticking out. Her present was the ugliest carved-bear statue she'd ever seen, as big as her arm. "Thank you, I think?" she said to the laughing group.

"You're welcome," Sage's husband, Jason, said with a wink. "But I apologize in advance for the nightmares."

The rest of the gifts were obviously designed to be equally awful. Becca got a jingle-bell-covered red velvet cowboy hat. Jack got a Barbie scarf. Hank got a chicken-shaped cake pan. Caleb opened his present—a very small box—and then quickly turned bright red.

The men howled with laughter as Caleb mumbled a nonsense word.

"What is it?" Amy asked, wondering what was so funny.

He leaned in. "Horse Viagra."

Uncle Ennis winked at them. "I wouldn't advise using it on humans."

She blushed and turned red, too. "I take it that was from the vet?"

Ennis coughed. "No, actually."

Becca raised a hand, her face as red as Amy's. "It was mine." When the roar of surprised laughter died away, she spoke again. "To be fair, I thought this party would just be these yahoos." She gestured at the brothers. "Now I'm just horrified."

Amy was a little, too. But she relaxed when Ennis opened her present, a quizzical look on his face. "Is this . . . ramen noodle?" He dug into the box and pulled out package after package. "All of this? Who eats this stuff?"

"Broke schoolteachers," Amy chimed in.

Everyone laughed. Caleb's arm tightened around her waist.

CHAPTER SIXTEEN

The party ended not long after the gift exchange. The food was eaten, the gifts were unwrapped, and all the little ones needed their beds. The house began to clear out, and Amy grabbed paper plates and began to clean up. It was the least she could do to say thank you.

To her surprise, though, Caleb headed into the kitchen and handed her her coat. "Come on. We're heading out."

"Where are we going?" she asked, noticing that he had Donner's leash, too. "To my place?"

He shook his head, and his face flushed a little red again. "I thought I'd show you mine."

Oh. She hadn't once asked to see his place, but of course he lived here. A wild curiosity suddenly filled her. "I'd love to see it."

Caleb got Donner in his harness and then led the blind dog out and down the back stairs. Amy followed behind closely, noticing that there was a gravel path that forked in two different directions. In one direction was the barn, a large outdoor light illuminating rounded bales of hay stacked against the building and neat lines of fencing. Somewhere in the distance, she could hear the cattle. In the other direction, she saw two porch lights in front of tiny cabins.

"This way," Caleb said, gesturing toward the cabins.

He waited for her, offering his hand when she wobbled on the gravel path—stupid heels—and didn't rush her. When they got to his doorstep, he paused, as if drawing a steeling breath, then nodded and took her inside.

"It's not much," he confessed as she entered.

It wasn't. The cabin was about as big as a single hotel room, with a queen-size bed tucked into one corner. There was a chair and a small table near a bureau, a tiny kitchenette next to a door that most likely led to the bathroom, and a generic painting of a cowboy on horseback hung on the wall. The bed was made and the floor clean, a braided rug near the doorstep. A few pairs of boots were lined up along one wall, and a laptop was closed atop the table. The most noticeable thing was a tall, narrow bookshelf that bulged with books. She moved toward it, eyeing the spines. Some of the books were older, some newer. Almost all were nonfiction of some kind or another, from wars to farming to ancient civilizations. "You have quite a collection here."

"It was always hard to get books back home, so I tended to keep the ones I had and reread them over and over again. Once we got here, I went on a bit of a spending spree and hit every bookstore and library sale for three states over. I haven't read them all, but I'm working on it."

Amy smiled over at him. "You know what would look great here?"

"What?"

"An ugly bear statue."

He threw back his head and laughed. "If you don't want it, I'm perfectly willing to keep it. I can use it to scare off mice or something." He gestured at the one chair in the room, the one next to the laptop and table. "Have a seat."

She eyed him and then went and sat on the edge of the bed. Was it deliberate? Just a little. Did she like how he watched her move with those hungry, avid eyes? Oh yes, she absolutely did. She even crossed her legs slowly because she wanted his attention. She was being a little ridiculous, and she knew it . . . and didn't much care. "I like your place."

Caleb shrugged, pulling his hat off and tossing it perfectly so it landed on a hook on the wall, a move she suspected he'd done many, many times in the past. "When we were in Alaska, me and Hank and Jack all lived in a one-bedroom cabin with a dirt floor. So I know this doesn't look like much, but I figure a guy like me doesn't need much." He paused for a moment. "For now."

"For now?" she prompted.

He fixed those long-lashed eyes on her. "At some point a man wants to get married and start a family."

She felt herself getting warm, because he was looking at her so intently she knew he was referring to her. He was direct, Caleb Watson.

"What made you decide to move down here?"

He sat down in the chair and kicked his boots off, getting comfortable. His socks were thick wool, and she was oddly disappointed that she didn't get to see his bare feet. "Uncle Ennis said his ranch was in trouble. Needed help running things, and we'd come here several times as teenagers to spend the summer and make money. We knew how to do the basics. We were just coming off of a hard winter up north and it seemed like all our equipment broke at once—the septic pump system at the house, the solar panels, the snowmobile—and we were sick of each other and a little stir-crazy to boot. It made sense to come down here for a year, save up some cash and help Uncle Ennis, and then go back."

Go back.

Amy stiffened, disappointment crashing through her. She realized that if he came last year, he wouldn't be here much longer. "You're leaving?"

He shook his head. "That was the plan before."

"Before what?"

"Before I met you. Once I saw you, I knew I wasn't going anywhere."

Her lips parted. She gaped at him, just a little, but she could see that Caleb was utterly and completely serious. Her breath caught in her throat. "You changed your plans . . . last week?"

He shook his head. "That wasn't the first time we met."

"It wasn't?"

"The first time I saw you was this summer."

She opened her mouth to protest. She didn't remember that. Surely she would have remembered him? A big, handsome, utterly silent cowboy? But then a wisp of a memory drifted through her head. Of Hank showing up to enroll his daughter in her class and instead quizzing her about Becca. He'd had someone with him, someone she'd barely paid attention to. All she remembered was that he'd brayed with laughter every time she spoke . . . "That was you? The laugher?"

He grimaced.

"Oh my god, I didn't remember that until just now." She put a hand to her mouth, surprised. "That one meeting made you decide to stay?"

"You were the most beautiful thing I'd ever seen," Caleb told her in a somber voice. "Still are."

She melted. Utterly melted. "Oh, Caleb."

A ghost of a smile brushed over his mouth. "I'm gonna remind you of my intentions."

Marriage. Right. She smiled, deciding to tease him. "Just in case you change your mind?"

His expression remained deadly serious. "I won't ever change my mind about you."

And now she was in danger of melting through the floor. Good lord, and this man thought he had a problem with words? He was so sincere, so utterly heartfelt, that she wanted to fling her dress off and crawl into his lap. She gave him a shy smile and tried to change the subject—because what could you say to that? She liked him. A lot. But after a week she wasn't quite ready to declare never-ending love, either. That just seemed far too fast. Though if he made every day as wonderful as the last week had been, she could absolutely see falling head over heels in love with him. It was just . . . after her marriage, she was a little more cautious about happily ever after. So . . . a subject change. "I had a nice time tonight."

Caleb arched an eyebrow. "Did you? You didn't seem like you were having fun."

Was she so obvious? "I did have a good time! It was just . . . I didn't feel like I belonged. Everyone knew everyone except me."

"You knew Becca. And Hank. And Libby. And me."

"It's different, though." Amy bit her lip. "I just . . . I thought when I moved here I'd work really hard to become part of the community and get accepted, and I feel like I'm still that weird outsider. Sometimes it feels lonely."

"I'm not from here," he pointed out.

"Yes, but you already knew everyone. You have family

here. Your brothers." She shook her head. "It's different. I'm here alone."

He gave her an assessing look. "Which brings me to something I've been meaning to ask you. It's the holidays . . . where's your family?"

Ugh. That awful, anxious knot that her family always brought on was forming in the pit of her belly, just from thinking about them. But he had a right to ask. "Well," she said slowly. "They didn't approve of my divorce. They made it quite clear that when I divorced my ex, I wasn't going to be able to 'crawl back to them and expect handouts.' I think they liked him more than they liked me." She gave him a weak smile. "My father always did want a son."

Caleb frowned fiercely at that. "They took his side?"

"Oh yeah." She huffed a laugh. "They thought I was being ridiculous and hysterical. That I was making a huge mistake and that he was in the right about everything. My parents were cut from the same cloth that Blake was, you know? Took me a while to realize that what they wanted for me wasn't what I wanted."

"Blake," Caleb echoed. "That his name?"

"Yeah."

"Sounds like a jackass."

She chuckled. "He is."

"Can I ask why you got divorced? You said it wasn't cheating . . ." He trailed off, waiting to see if she'd answer.

She could push it off. Tell him she wasn't ready to talk about that sort of thing yet. But . . . wasn't she here tonight with condoms in her purse and wearing a backless cocktail dress and sitting on the edge of his bed? Because she was an adult and she could do what she wanted, and what she wanted was to hook up with this gorgeous man that made her feel so pretty and special. She supposed that if he wanted to know about her divorce, she could at least talk about it.

"Well . . ." She wet her lips, feeling incredibly nervous. It was like talking about Blake would somehow summon him to her side. "I met Blake when I was nineteen. He was the son of a golfing friend of my father's and they suggested we go out. Next thing I knew, I was being encouraged to quit college and get married to Blake. When you're pressured from all sides, it's hard to say no. My mother never understood, though. She never went to college. Just married my dad right out of high school. He was the one who worked and handled all the money. I remember my mom never even had a car. She didn't understand why she needed one. Dad would take care of everything for her." She made a face at the thought. "We had money, so I guess she never worried about that sort of thing. I didn't, either. And when I got older and Blake started to take over things for me, it just made sense that he would. He was older than I was, and very strong-willed and smart. Very willing to take risks on start-up companies, and they tended to pay off. He was good with people and knew how to work a room, and he was always dressed to the nines. I thought he was dazzling when I met him." Her mouth twisted sourly. "Looking back, I was an idiot. But I thought I was in love, so I handed over more and more of my life because I just wanted to make him happy."

"Handed over your life? How?"

Amy plucked at one of the sequins on the front of her dress. "Well, for example, I was going to college when we started dating, and then my classes started interfering with things. He wanted me with him on business trips and I couldn't go. Or he'd want to do something in the middle of the day and I had class. He pressured me so, so many times to drop everything. What did I need a degree for, right? He was going to take care of me when we got married. So I ended up dropping out with a semester left and became Mrs. Blake Todd in a wedding that filled an entire church full of people, and none of them were my friends. Blake didn't like my friends, you see. So they got slowly edged out of my life, too. I stayed at home—Blake's house, mind you— and talked to the staff, but other than that, I had nothing to do. I was expected to just sit around and be a wife. Looking back, it's very 1950s." She chuckled, trying to see the humor in the situation. "I didn't even have a checkbook. He would just give me an allowance if I needed cash. If I wanted to go somewhere, I had to make sure his driver was available. All the credit cards were in his name. Things like that. I wore the clothes that Blake liked. I had the chef make the food Blake liked. I read books that Blake approved of and listened to music that he thought was appropriate. I never cussed because Blake thought it was fucking unladylike." She couldn't resist tossing that in.

"He sounds like a real creep."

"He didn't want a wife. He wanted a Barbie doll," she agreed lightly, her fingers worrying at that stupid sequin. "Really, it was just a matter of expectations. My father had led him to think that I was going to be pliable and just so darn happy to marry him. And when I was starry-eyed in the beginning of the relationship, I thought so, too. But after we got married and I sat around a beautiful house all day with nothing to do, I was bored. I couldn't decorate because I had to run everything past Blake. I couldn't cook, because Blake had a chef that handled everything. I couldn't drive anywhere. I was just living in this little bubble and it felt smaller and smaller every day."

Even now, just thinking about it, she felt smothered. Choked. She closed her eyes, took a steeling breath.

"So after a few months of that, I started to ask for things to do. For money. For opportunities. I think I even asked him at one point to give me a job at his start-up. He was creating all kinds of apps, you see, and things were very exciting. But Blake just wanted me to stay at home." Her mouth twisted. "I would have been fine with being at home, except . . . it wasn't my home. It was his. I was just another decorative piece."

"But you got your degree," Caleb prompted after a long moment of silence.

She nodded, ripping the annoying sequin free from her dress finally. "I did. I saved my allowance for months and opened a bank account in secret. I took the classes online and did my course work on the days that he wasn't there, or I'd wake up in the middle of the night to do them. I got my degree." She cast a triumphant look in Caleb's direction. "And after that, I realized I didn't like my life. It was like I could see how it would turn out in another five years, another ten years, another fifteen . . . and the thought was horrible. So I saved more of my allowance, and when I had about five grand saved, I left in the middle of the night and filed for divorce."

"Middle of the night?" His brows went up in surprise.

"It was easiest," she agreed. "Cowardly, but easiest. Blake was really, really good at running me down and making me feel stupid. Like if bad things happened, they were somehow my fault. It was all manipulation, but that's why I left without saying a thing. I didn't want him to change my mind for me." She laughed, tugging at the thread her sequin dismemberment had left. "And I knew if I talked to him, he'd just bully me into seeing things his way. So I left and had the lawyers handle it."

"Good for you."

She laughed, wrapping that green thread around her finger. "You're the first one that's ever said that to me. I tell people about it and they always say something like, 'You left a rich, handsome man who wanted you to just stay home and look pretty? Are you stupid?' But I just . . . wasn't happy. I felt so lonely. Even when Blake was there, he never really talked to me. He didn't value my opinion. I was just . . ." She shrugged. "There. I think that's one reason that moving here appealed to me so much. I came out for the job interview and someone joked that everyone here was in everyone else's business and people grew up knowing the names of all their neighbors and I thought that sounded just lovely. Like instead of a town, you had one big happy family. But I'm here and I'm still on the outside. Maybe I always will be." She shrugged, staring down at her hands. "Anyhow, that's my loser sob story."

"You're not a loser." Caleb's voice was harsh as he got to his feet. He crossed the small cabin and sat down next to her on the bed, and she could practically feel the tension vibrating through him. He was angry on her behalf, she realized. "They just pushed you into something without ever asking how you felt. That doesn't make you a loser. It says that you trusted your parents."

"Yeah, well, Blake got them in the divorce." She shook her head. "My father was so mad at me that he screamed until his face was purple. Like I'd somehow divorced him instead of Blake. And my mother looked at me like I was crazy." Her throat got tight, still thinking of that horrible time. "I told myself I was never going to let anyone take over my life again, you know? That I was going to be independent if it killed me."

"I understand."

She managed a smile. "Everyone says that, but not many do. It's kind of sad, how much I've had to learn recently. I actually had to hire an accountant when I got here because I didn't know how to pay bills. She actually had to show me how to use a checkbook."

"Just because you didn't have the opportunity to do something doesn't mean you're the problem." His fingers brushed over hers. "I . . . missed out on some things myself."

She tilted her head back and looked at him. "Oh?"

His fingers tightened on hers, and she could have sworn an uncomfortable look crossed his face. "I don't want you to think less of me—"

"Unless you tell me to quit teaching so I can stay home and sit on your couch, I won't think less of you."

"I don't have a couch," he told her, gripping her fingers. "And let me finish. This is hard for me."

Surprised, she nodded.

He cleared his throat, and he wouldn't make eye contact with her. Instead, he gazed down at their joined hands, resting on her thigh. "I told you I grew up in Alaska. It was a real small town. Like . . . population forty or something. Foxtail, Alaska. You won't find it on any maps, but it's about an hour or two north of Fairbanks and there's nothing out there but woods and a scatter of cabins. We owned enough land that you didn't have to see neighbors for days—weeks—if you didn't want to. Sometimes we didn't see ours for months. In the winter, one of us might head into town on a snowmobile if we ran low on supplies, but the rest of the time, we were just living off the land. My dad was a big self-sufficiency guy, and after my mom passed, he made sure that we didn't need anyone." With his free hand, he rubbed at his beard. "But that meant I missed out on other stuff."

When he paused, she prompted him. "Like school? You said you missed out on school."

"On girls," he blurted. "I was never around women. Like . . . ever. It was always Hank or Jack that went to town. And me, I'd get so tongue-tied if I was around a pretty woman that I could never say anything." He swallowed hard. "You're my first relationship, and I know I'm far too old to be confessing that sort of thing, but I figured you should know."

Amy stared at him in surprise. Caleb was handsome and smart. To think that he'd never had a relationship . . . and yet she thought of the way he'd brayed with laughter that first time she'd met him. She thought of the tongue-tied, ridiculous things he'd said when they'd first met, or the way he'd gone so silent she was convinced he hated her.

Okay, yeah, she could totally believe that he'd never had a relationship. This had to be hard for him to confess, too— a grown man without a romantic past? People would think there was something wrong with him.

But there wasn't, just intense shyness.

Just like her own shortcomings didn't make her an idiot. He'd told her as much. It wasn't her fault.

"I don't know how to work the thermostat at my place," she blurted.

"Are we having a loser-off?" he asked, eyes narrowing. "You were my first kiss."

"I don't know how to drive a stick shift. Or how to read a map. Or how to do my taxes."

"I can teach you. Did you miss the part where I said you were my first kiss?" He reached up and cupped the back of her neck, his thumb grazing over her skin as their eyes met. "You're my first everything, Amy Mckinney. I'm telling you this because . . . if I'm no good at something, I want you to know why. I want you to know that it's not you, it's me."

She melted all over again. Was that why he was confessing this? So she wouldn't worry that it was a problem with her? Amy's heart swelled. She'd never met a man that was so utterly perfect in every way. A burst of enthusiasm rushed through her, and she flung her arms around his neck, kissing him fiercely and bearing them both to the mattress with Caleb under her.

His mouth devoured hers, and for long moments, it was just tongues and lips and frantic breathing. He tasted like sweets, the baked goods that had been set out at the party, and when his tongue flicked against hers, it was the best thing ever.

"What's all this?" he asked between kisses, voice husky.

"This is where you and I have sex," Amy told him, then licked his mouth.

He stiffened under her in surprise. "After all that?"

"Especially after all that." She kissed him again, then sat up and began to undo the buttons on his shirt.

"I don't have condoms—"

"I do." She gave him a little smile. "I bought some when I first moved here and was stocking up my medicine cabinet. I think I imagined a more wild and fancy-free life than I actually wanted. But I'm glad I have them." His shirt opened up and revealed bare, tanned skin and a hint of chest hair. Amy slid down on his body, her hips grazing over his as she straddled him, and buried her face in his neck, kissing and licking.

Caleb groaned, his hands sliding to her hips and clutching

her against him. His pelvis rocked against hers, thrusting between her spread thighs. "You sure you want this?"

"One hundred percent sure." Her tongue swept over his collarbone. "A thousand percent."

He groaned again, and then his hands were pulling at her short skirt, already hiked up over her thighs. He tugged it higher, until her ass was bare and her wispy, lacy thong was revealed. "You're beautiful. Look at how beautiful you are." His big hands gripped her ass and dragged her back down against the bulge in his pants, and she felt how hard and thick he was. "Let me touch you for a bit, Amy."

She sat up, nodded.

Immediately, he flipped their bodies and then suddenly she was the one on the bed on her back. He pushed her skirt higher, until it was bunched at her waist, and Amy shivered at the intent look on his face. He ran a hand over her thigh, then brushed his knuckles over her belly. "I'm taking these panties off. Not that they're not gorgeous on you, but I want what's underneath."

She shivered. Was there anything better than him declaring exactly what he wanted to do? It made her so hot with anticipation. Panting, she lifted her hips and he dragged the panties off her legs, until she was bare from the waist down underneath him. Then, he lowered his head and began to kiss up her leg.

Oh . . . they were doing that? It was on the tip of her tongue to tell him he didn't have to, that it wasn't necessary. Hadn't Blake always told her that men did it only out of necessity to get a girl in their bed? But she clamped her mouth shut as Caleb kissed higher and higher. Caleb wasn't Blake. He wasn't. And didn't she deserve just as much pleasure as he did in bed? If he wanted to give her this, she was going to let him, no matter how nervous it made her.

Caleb's mouth brushed over the juncture of her thighs, his beard tickling, and she felt the absurd urge to giggle. She bit it back, but when he nuzzled at her inner thigh again and his beard grazed her skin, it erupted from her. "Sorry," she wheezed. "Ticklish."

He chuckled and did it again, deliberately. "I like hearing you laugh."

She squirmed against him as his beard teased up and down her thigh, and then he pushed her legs further apart, exposing her to his gaze, and all the giggles died in her throat as he made a low sound of pleasure. Oh.

Then, he lowered his head, one arm wrapping around one of her thighs to keep them apart, and dragged his tongue over her folds.

She squirmed again, shuddering. Oh. Okay. That was . . . intense.

"Tell me if I do something you don't like," he murmured, and then he licked her again. And again. His tongue stroked through her folds, brushing over her most sensitive parts. When he found her clit, she sucked in a breath, arching against him. The silent encouragement told him where to focus his attention, it seemed, because then he was all over her, his mouth hungry and devouring as he worked on her clit, determined to figure out what she liked best.

Amy's hands knotted in the blankets, her legs in the air as he worked her pussy with his tongue. She was panting, making stupid-sounding noises in her throat every time he sucked on her clit, every time he did one of those little swirls, until she was practically sawing her hips against his face. Caleb didn't complain, or protest that she was moving too much. He just kept going, and going, until she was so wet that when he slid a finger inside her, she could hear it.

"Caleb," she panted. "Caleb, Caleb . . . come inside me now."

He nuzzled at her pussy again, not lifting his head. It was a silent refusal, and she suspected he wasn't going to come up for air until she came. The thought was both thrilling and a little anxiety making, because what if she couldn't come like this? Her hand went to his thick hair and she knotted her fingers there, determined to pause him for a moment.

But then he added another finger, thrusting harder deep inside her even as his mouth worked on her clit, and a hot, hard quiver worked its way up her legs. Amy moaned, jerking against his mouth as the edge of an orgasm started to shoot through her body.

It only made Caleb redouble his efforts. His mouth grew more insistent, the thrusting of his fingers harder and faster as she tensed and shuddered against him. When she came a few moments later, she realized dimly that she had a handful of his hair and was shamelessly pressing him against her instead of pulling him away . . . and that he was still giving her clit the most erotic, languid licks as she came down.

"Sorry," she breathed as her body slowly unlocked. "Did I pull your hair? I'm so sorry."

He pressed a kiss to her mound and lifted his head. His hair was a wild mess and his eyes were full of scorching heat. "You were perfect." And then he licked her again, while she was watching.

It made her entire body shiver. She felt good. Amazing, really. And he hadn't come yet. Hadn't even so much as put on a condom yet. Well, they could fix that. "Shall we undress?"

Caleb nodded and got to his feet. His face was flushed, his eyes hooded with arousal as he watched her and began to undo his belt. Then he looked over and frowned. "Mind if I put the dog in the bathroom?"

Oh god, was Donner in here? Of course he was. She sat up on her elbows in the bed, and sure enough, the dog was seated by the table, his tail wagging as he gazed in their direction, his milky gray eyes somehow *knowing*. She blushed hard. How had she forgotten all about the dog? And here she was, splayed on Caleb's bed with her dress up to her navel. "Let's make him a nest in there, shall we?" She got to her feet, tugging her dress back down over her butt, and then tiptoed into his bathroom. He was right behind her, his hand skating over her back and sending prickles up and down her spine.

"I've got towels. Let's make him a bed with those," Caleb told her, his fingertips moving lightly over her bare skin as if he couldn't stop touching her. "I'll get a bowl for some water."

A few minutes later, she had Donner set up with a cozy nest on the floor and a bowl of water nearby. She worried a little because he was blind and she didn't want him to be afraid, but he just lowered his gray muzzle and gave a little tired groan. She guessed old dogs liked a nice safe place to rest their heads, too. "I think he's good." She stroked Donner's head, rubbing his ears, and then washed her hands and left the bathroom.

The moment she did, Caleb's mouth was on hers. He'd undressed while she'd fussed over the dog, and her hands went to bare shoulders. The hot prod of his erection brushed against her hip, magnificent and obvious as hell now that he was naked, and she gasped.

His hands moved up her back, tugging at the fabric of her dress, trying to pull it upward.

"Here," she whispered between kisses. "Wait. I can get it." She let go of him for a brief moment, her hands going to the high neck of her dress, and then with a flick of her wrist, the buttons at the collar were undone and the entire thing fell forward, peeling slowly down her arms and front. Caleb reached for the material, helping it down her body, and within moments, it pooled on the ground at her feet.

He groaned, reaching up to graze her bare breast with his knuckles. "You are insanely beautiful."

Her nipple puckered harder, and she put her hand out to touch his chest, stroking her fingers against the crisp hairs that sprinkled his skin. "I could say the same for you." Her hand moved lower, and she brushed her fingers over his cock even as she leaned in to kiss him. "Let me get the condoms."

She moved to get her purse, but his hands were around her waist, pulling her back against his erection even as she fished through her wallet, looking for the strip of foil packets. He kissed her neck, his hands on her breasts, teasing them and distracting her.

"Here," she said, turning and offering him the strip.

Caleb took them from her, and as he opened one of the packets, she admired his body. She knew his shoulders were broad and his chest tanned and taut, but she'd never seen him naked. His hips had the best obliques she'd ever seen, and the bit of chest hair he had trailed down to his gorgeous, thick cock. He was pure pleasure to look at. Her hands itched to move over him again, but he was putting the condom on, trying to roll it down his thick length.

Then he cussed. Pulled it off his cock and tossed the

broken rubber on the table, along with the empty package. She'd forgotten—this was his first time. Was he nervous? Probably. Heck, she was nervous and it wasn't her first time at all . . . and she'd already come.

So she touched his hand and took the condoms from him. "I'll do it."

Caleb reached out and caressed her breast, teasing the nipple, as if touching her centered him. "If you want to."

Oh, she did. She'd take any excuse to get her hands all over him. With a seductive smile on her lips, Amy opened the packet and pulled out the condom. She set it on the head of his cock and gently rolled it down his shaft, loving the way he sucked in his breath as she touched him, as if she were caressing him instead of putting a condom on. When she was done, she lifted her arms and put them around his neck, tilting her head up for another kiss.

He grabbed her by the hips, hauling her into the air even as his mouth captured hers. The kisses between them were hard and wild, and Amy clung to him as he carried her over to the bed and then laid her on her back. He kissed her one more time and then settled his hips against hers.

Amy put her legs around his waist, her hands moving over his chest, just wanting to touch him everywhere and anywhere she could.

Caleb pressed into her, his gaze intense and holding hers. His cock felt big, stretching her with its size, and it had been a long time since Amy had had sex. It felt like the first time again in many ways, and she reached up and brushed her fingertips over his face, loving the connection between them. It didn't feel like just sex with Caleb. It felt like something else, something special. She hoped he felt it, too.

He moved slowly, pushing deep until he was fully seated in her body. She could see him straining, feel the tension in his body. "You . . . are you . . ." he gritted.

"It feels wonderful," she said in a soft voice, and arched her hips. "Touch me however you want. I'll like all of it."

He groaned, and then he was thrusting atop her, his movements graceless and fast and so rough that it began to push her across the blankets. It startled Amy at first, but she clung to his neck as he leaned in, burying his face against her throat. This was what she wanted. It was enthusiastic and real and it felt good, despite the lack of art to his movements. She tried to match his movements, but their bodies clashed, and so she just rubbed him and kissed his shoulder and murmured encouragement.

At least, she did . . . until a new orgasm started to build in her belly. It was the way he pumped into her so frenetically, all movement and action, and it was making something deep inside her wake up all over again. She gasped, her nails digging into his skin, and started to arch her hips again.

He claimed her mouth with a hot, ragged kiss, and slowed his movements, matching hers. Then they were together, moving as one, faster and faster, both of them surging toward climax. He hit his before her—she could tell by the way his body stiffened over hers and how he held his breath. How his big frame shuddered, even as he kept thrusting into her. It was those last, slow, deep thrusts that made her come, too, and the orgasm broke over her. Amy choked out his name and clung to him, letting the pleasure course through her body until she thought she would fall apart.

When the world finally righted itself, Caleb was still buried inside her, breathing hard. There was a light sheen of sweat on his tanned skin and he nuzzled against her neck, his hips jerking against hers. It was as if he couldn't seem to stop, and she didn't mind. She liked it. Each time he did, it sent little spirals of pleasure through her body, reminding her of how good she felt.

"Thank you," he murmured against her neck.

That made her chuckle. "Why are you thanking me? I did that for me."

"Dunno," he confessed after a moment and lifted his head. "Felt like I had to say something. Thank you seemed polite."

She laughed again, and then sighed as he rolled off of her and went to dispose of the condom. "That was great. I should be the one thanking you." The blankets were bunched up under her back and she tugged at them, dragging them over her naked body. It was a little chilly in his cabin, though she was just now realizing this. "I guess I should be going home soon."

He returned to her side, a frown on his face. "Why?"

Amy shrugged, snuggling down in the blankets. She needed to get up and clean up, but soon enough. For now, she was going to laze about in the afterglow for a few minutes more. "Party's over. I figured it's time for me to head out."

"It's late and it's cold," he said, sitting down on the edge of the bed and then sliding in under the covers next to her. He pulled Amy into his arms, and then her breasts were pressed to all that warm skin. "Stay tonight."

Stay? She smiled at him, snuggling close. She breathed in his scent—slightly sweaty and musky but still wonderfully Caleb. Did she have to go home tonight after all? Donner was here with her, and it was the weekend. School was out for the holidays. She had nothing she had to do in particular. "What about our date tomorrow?"

"We can start it early." He kissed the top of her head,

stroking her arm. "The big plan was to watch Christmas movies together. We can do that in bed."

"I suppose we can." She lifted her chin, gazing up at him. "It won't bother you to have me here all night?"

"I want you here all night," he told her in a husky voice. "Every night."

Such devotion made her stomach flutter with nervousness. Excitement, too. "Let's start with tonight."

CHAPTER SEVENTEEN

It was the best lazy Saturday.

They made love again, using the last of the condoms she'd brought, and after that, they just touched and kissed constantly. In the shower, she made him come with her hands, he took her back to bed and made her come with his mouth, and then they curled up in bed together, exhausted, and watched *It's a Wonderful Life, Miracle on 34th Street*, and *Love Actually*. He grabbed some leftover sweets from the main house and brought them back to his cabin, along with a full thermos of fresh coffee, and if anyone had noticed her car was still out front, she hoped they'd had the decency to say nothing.

Judging by how red Caleb's face was when he returned, though, she suspected they'd said plenty.

Even so, it was a lovely day. She curled up in one of Caleb's shirts and lingered in bed while he walked Donner for her, and they talked about movies and Christmas and nothing in particular. It was just . . . lovely to spend time with him.

She was sad when the credits on the final movie rolled and she figured she needed to get home. With a sigh, Amy put her dress on and found her shoes and tried to fix her hair back into a semblance of the tight bun it had been in last night.

"You can stay again tonight," Caleb suggested.

Amy hesitated. She wanted to. Oh, how she wanted to. Just curl up in bed with her big, sexy cowboy and let the world roll past? It was tempting. "What's the plan for tomorrow?"

He rubbed his jaw. "I do need to help with the chores around here before Jack kills me. Other than that, I figured we could wrap some presents together. I have a few things I bought for the others and I'm no good with packages." He lifted his big hands and waved them. "All thumbs."

Presents.

Oh jeez, he'd been doing an endless string of Christmas gifts for her and she had nothing for him. Nothing at all.

That clinched it. She needed to go home. If nothing else, she needed time to do some hasty online shopping so she could figure out what she could get him. "I should get home," she said firmly. "I've got a few things to take care of. Can we just meet up tomorrow?"

He nodded and kissed her, pulling her in close. "What time?"

"You want to come over after five?" she asked, doing a little mental calculation in her head. "Bring your stuff over and we can have dinner and wrap presents."

"Sounds good. I'll bring dinner, too, unless you're keen on more ramen."

Amy giggled. "Not so much."

"I'll bring a pizza, then." He kissed her again and then gazed down at her, eyes serious. "I'll miss you."

She was going to miss him, too.

Amy managed to sneak out of the cabin without running into Doc Ennis or Jack. She got to her car, settled Donner in the seat, and drove away with her face burning red. Leaving a party late the next day in her spangly green dress felt like the most obvious of obvious moves, but at least no one was there to point it out.

She drove home, her mood light. It remained light until she got to her place and noticed it was ice-cold inside. Frowning, she unhooked Donner from his leash and found the thermostat. It was set to heat. She messed with a few buttons and looked up videos online on how to work a thermostat. Hers matched the pictures, but the house was ice-cold.

Broken, then.

Figured.

Amy sighed, glaring down at her phone as she hauled a blanket around her shoulders and huddled on the couch with Donner, who cuddled close to share heat. She could always go back to Caleb's, she supposed. Send a few angry texts to Greg, demanding that he fix things, and then go to Caleb's and spend the night in his arms. It sounded like a good idea, but it niggled at her and bothered her for some reason. Did she expect Caleb to bail her out of every problem? Even the tiny ones? She knew he would—he was kind and warm and protective. He'd be here in a heartbeat to try to fix her thermostat—this after fixing her ceiling, and her faucets, and the cracks around the windowpanes, and . . .

She'd had enough.

Amy typed in "rentals near Painted Barrel" and started to browse.

Wasn't this why she'd come to Wyoming? So she could be on her own? She remembered all the times that Blake had made her feel useless and stupid. How he'd deliberately kept her name off their accounts because it made him feel big to control her money. How he told her she didn't need an education because she was with him. How he'd deliberately bought stick-shift cars because he knew she didn't know how to drive them, and it made him feel good to hold one over on her.

Never again.

There was a small apartment complex two cities over, and despite the fact that it was Saturday afternoon, the girl at the front desk answered all her questions with chirpy, happy responses. The rent was a little higher than what Amy was paying now, and it was further out, but they took dogs and maintenance was on-site. She made an appointment to view an apartment tomorrow.

Then she texted Caleb.

AMY: Slight change of plans. Can you come by tomorrow by around 3 or so instead of 5?

CALEB: Sure can. What's up?

AMY: A few things. I'm going to look at a new apartment tomorrow and thought maybe you could go with me. I'm tired of living here.

CALEB: Is that asshole bothering you again? Do I need to come over?

CALEB: I will be there ASAP.

AMY: No! It's fine. I'm just fed up, that's all. I did some searching. And can I ask for one more favor?

CALEB: Anything.

AMY: Will you teach me how to drive a stick shift?

CALEB: Of course.

AMY: Thank you. :)

She wasn't going to be the same old Amy. Never again. If life threw curveballs at her, she'd figure out how to throw them back. She wouldn't just duck and hope for someone else to take care of things. You didn't grow like that. You didn't learn. You didn't thrive.

Amy was more than ready to thrive. So she got out every blanket, layered the bed with all of them, and put on her warm clothes and snuggled down in the mountain of linens and comforters with Donner. "We're changing things up, you and I," she whispered to him. "We're going to become the best versions of ourselves." She flipped around on her phone's browser a little longer before typing in "bookstores near me" and seeing what came up.

After all, she had a few presents to buy for her cowboy.

CHAPTER EIGHTEEN

Caleb couldn't stop staring at her the next day. During the apartment walk-through, during the driving lesson afterward, he just stared at her. Just . . . stared.

After all, it was hard to look away when all your dreams were coming true.

He couldn't stop thinking about Amy. About the way she'd tasted when she'd come. The way she'd felt when he was so deep inside her. The soft sounds she made when he pushed into her. The way she'd slept, cuddled up next to him as if she'd always belonged there. He watched her like a besotted idiot as he taught her how to drive a stick shift in his truck. It didn't matter that she let the engine die at the same stop sign seven times in a row trying to figure out how to shift gears. He was endlessly patient. He could be, because he was spending time with her. Any time with Amy was good time spent.

Eventually, she managed to figure out the basics, and

with a triumphant look, she got them to her place. "I did it!" she told him, crowing just a little.

"You absolutely did," he told her, trying not to think about all the times the gears made terrible grinding noises as she figured things out. It was just a truck. Amy had done a terrific job and learned fast, a determined little scowl on her face as she shifted gears and tried to follow his instructions. "Want to order a pizza?"

"As long as we split the bill," she told him with a proud flounce of her hair as she went to her porch. She got out the keys, unlocked the door, and went inside—and immediately smothered a happily wiggling Donner with kisses. "Who's my best boy? Who is it? Is it you, old man?"

"With that kind of greeting, I was hoping it was me," Caleb teased as he stepped in behind her, the box of gifts in his grip, a massive roll of paper tucked under his arm. Her place looked good, he thought, her tree festive and lit up, and he especially liked the new shiny lock on the door.

As he stepped inside, though, he frowned to himself. "Why's it so damn cold in here?" His breath misted, and he noticed Donner was wearing a thick doggy sweater despite being in the house.

"The heat's dead," Amy told him. "Don't worry. I'm handling it."

He scowled, setting the stuff down on the table. "You're paying to live here. The heat shouldn't be dead."

"I know." She rubbed Donner's ears, oblivious to the chill. "This place is a shithole, like you said, so I'm going to move."

"Ah." So that explained the sudden apartment hunt. The place she'd looked at today wasn't great. The inside was worn and the carpet so old that it was faded at the edges.

The building was a large one and she'd be on the second floor, which meant stairs and noise, especially with a dog. Plus, she was further away from Painted Barrel, and he didn't much like that.

But it wasn't his decision. She loved the place, so she'd put in an application and had gushed to the girl in the office about how excited she was about moving. Anything had to be better than Greg's place, Caleb had to admit. "Come stay with me tonight," he told her. "It's too cold here. You and Donner can curl up at my place."

It wasn't an entirely altruistic suggestion. He wanted Amy in his bed. He wanted a repeat of last night—hopefully without him tearing condoms like a fucking schoolboy. He wanted more of his woman, and he wanted it so much that it took everything he had not to throw her over his shoulder and haul ass back to his place.

But she only gave him a stubborn look. "It was cold here last night and me and Donner got through it okay. It's fine."

So it had been out last night, too? He gritted his teeth. "I'm going to build you a fire, and then we're going to try to fix your heat."

"I'll put on some coffee. And you promised me pizza, didn't you?" She gave him a sassy wink.

Why was she in such a good mood when it was positively arctic in the house? Shouldn't she be mad at Greg? He sure as shit was. But she was in a fantastic mood, and he didn't get it. Maybe he was just sour that she was going to try to move away, as if that would somehow change things.

Building Amy a fire ended up being more time-consuming than he'd thought. She had no wood, for starters, so he went back out to the tiny grocery store in town, bought two ridiculously overpriced stacks of wood and some starter logs, and stopped by the pizza place to get them dinner. He grumbled all the way through making the fire, and grumbled even more when he tinkered with the thermostat. Amy ignored all his grouchiness, wrapping presents by the fire and offering her pizza crusts to Donner, who took them with far more politeness than he should have.

"I still want you to stay at my place tonight," Caleb told her. "Not sure if I like the idea of you having a fire going all night." In this disaster of a house, the entire thing could go up in flames. Who knew if Greg had the chimney inspected? Who knew if the fire alarms worked?

But Amy gave him another frustratingly mulish look. "I'm going to stay here. You don't have to bail me out."

Bail her out? He didn't want his damned woman to freeze. "Then I'm staying here," Caleb declared. "You and I are going to share body heat."

"Oh. Well, that sounds like fun." She wiggled her eyebrows at him.

He really, really did not understand this woman sometimes. Or any women, for that matter.

Two days later, Amy decided to deliver Christmas cookies to her friends and her coworkers. It wasn't with a completely unselfish motive, of course. She and Caleb had plans to go ice-skating, but it had snowed so heavily that they'd stayed in and made cookies instead. Now she had plate after plate of frosted red jingle bells and green holly leaves, and if she ate even one more snowman cookie, she'd be tasting powdered sugar in her sleep. So for sanity—and her waistline—she was going to give them away.

Painted Barrel's school was small, so they'd all shared

addresses and phone numbers, and Amy dropped by each teacher's house to deliver personally. It was good to see them outside the school environment, and she was welcomed with a hug and an exclamation of surprise and pleasure. Even surly Elizabeth, the school secretary and wife to the principal, invited her in for coffee. It made her feel welcome. Like part of a community after all. Sure, she was reaching out to them instead of the other way around, but it was a start.

Once she'd made all her teacher deliveries, she swung by Becca's salon. Becca was with a client, so she couldn't talk long, and Amy dropped off the cookies with a promise to text her later. After that, she just had one final delivery—to Layla.

Even though it was Christmas week, the bubbly accountant was still working in the office. Well . . . sort of working. When Amy went in, she noticed Layla had her combat boots kicked up on the desk and her crochet in her lap, her computer's screen saver dancing with Christmas trees and snowmen.

"I see that you're super busy today," Amy teased.

Layla sat up, grinning. She put her feet on the floor and her crochet away. "Family's visiting. You know how it is. My mother's determined to find me a man, so she keeps showing me pictures of her friends' sons. I told her I had to come in to work. And it's a good thing I did, since you brought sweets."

Amy sat down across from Layla's desk and put the cookies in front of her. "We made a few too many last night. Hope you're not on a diet."

"For the holidays? Girl, I know better." Layla reached over and immediately plucked a heavily frosted cookie from the tray. "So who's 'we'? The cowboy boyfriend?

Word is he's parking in front of your house practically every night."

Amy's face got hot. Okay, this was one of her first experiences with small-town gossip, and Becca had *not* lied. It absolutely did travel fast. "Not *every* night. And who told you?"

"Your neighbor brought in some receipts for tax time." Layla wiggled her eyebrows. "I'm not judging. I mean, your guy's got a tight ass. Doesn't say a thing, but I can appreciate silent and tight."

Her face was getting redder. Was that even possible? Amy cleared her throat. "He's not silent. He talks to me."

"That's good, because it'd be a bit of a weird relationship otherwise. So you two are . . . a thing? Because you seem really happy."

"I do?"

Layla nodded, munching on the cookie. "You have this glow about you. And you smile all the time." Layla winked. "And blush, too."

"He's a really good guy," Amy said softly. "I know we're moving fast, but I'm divorced, you know? I'm an adult. I can do what I want. And . . . he's just everything I ever wanted." Maybe she was just being an optimist, but she didn't see how dating Caleb could possibly be bad for her. "He makes me so happy."

"Good in bed?"

Amy blushed.

"I'm gonna take that as a yes. Stuff like that's important, you know." Layla sighed, resting her cheek on her hand. "He sounds like a paragon. I don't suppose he has a sexy single brother?"

"Actually, he does. His name is Jack."

To Amy's surprise, this time Layla blushed. "Oh. I was

just teasing. I'm not looking to date someone. Anyhow, most guys aren't all that interested in short, dumpy accountants with nerdy hobbies." She shrugged. "But, like . . . good for him on the cute brother part. Yay and all that."

Boy, Layla really had gotten uncomfortable. Amy decided to change the subject. "I'm also looking at moving."

"You are?"

Amy nodded. "There's an apartment about twenty minutes from here and it's leagues better than my current rental. I looked at it a few days ago. I'll still be in town all the time because of work—"

"And the boyfriend," Layla added.

"And the boyfriend," Amy agreed. "But I'm excited for the new apartment."

"That's awesome. I'm happy for you." Layla reached for another cookie. "So your landlord is letting you break your lease without a penalty?"

"Penalty?" Amy blinked, surprised. "Why would there be a penalty?"

Layla bit the head off the snowman cookie. "When you sign the contract, it's for a stated amount of time. Six months, a year, et cetera. If you move beforehand, you're basically depriving the landlord of his expected income, so you usually have to pay a penalty of a month's rent or something. I'm sure it's in your contract."

"Oh." Amy hadn't realized. She'd signed off merrily and hadn't given much thought to what the actual contract for the rental stated. Her head had simply been spinning with the excitement of her first place on her own. "I guess I'll take a look at it when I get home."

Layla nibbled on the snowman a moment more and then set it down. "I hate to be that friend, but as your financial adviser, too, I know you're new to this kind of stuff. I'd be a jerk if I didn't ask, but . . . the new place. You saved up for the deposit?"

Amy was starting to feel completely out of her depth and a little worried. That tense knot was returning to the pit of her belly. "What deposit?"

"Most apartments ask for a deposit." Layla gave her a sympathetic look. "You remember the deposit you paid on your current place?"

She didn't. All Amy remembered about moving in was an endless whirl of fees and the giddy feeling of being so far away from Blake that he couldn't possibly show up in her life again. Had there been a deposit? "I . . . I don't know."

"You can call them and ask. Maybe they'll waive it for you?" Layla toyed with the cookie. "If not, at least you know in advance, right?"

"Right." Amy smiled, though it felt like something inside her was slowly dying. Deposits. Money. She didn't have any money. She'd pawned the jewelry yesterday to buy presents for Caleb—a few big glossy books about war and history, and a western-themed pair of metal bookends. "I'll give them a call for sure. Speaking of, I should probably head out. I have to run a few errands before I meet Caleb tonight."

"Don't let me keep you from your hot date," Layla teased. "And thank you for the cookies! My waistline says you're a jerk, but the rest of me is happy as could be."

She smiled, made some excuse, and then left the accounting office feeling numb and hollow. Amy waited to get out to her car, drove down the street so Layla wouldn't see her call, and then phoned the apartment complex.

The answer made her want to puke.

Yes, the apartment manager told her in a chirpy voice. If her application was approved, she would need to put down two months' rent for the deposit, plus a pet deposit of four hundred dollars for her dog.

Amy felt sick, hot sweat pouring down her face. She hung up, stammering an excuse, and then stared at the dashboard of the car, limp with disappointment. How had she not known about deposits? It hadn't occurred to her that she'd have to pay Greg to leave, and pay to move somewhere else. She'd just thought she could up and do it. And pet deposits? What a rip-off.

The trapped feeling threatened to swallow her up again. It was the same feeling she'd had when she was married to Blake. It was the sensation of having no options and nowhere to turn, of being stuck in place. This time, it wasn't Blake but her finances . . . but wasn't Blake part of the problem there, too? He hadn't paid her alimony. If he had, she'd have money.

She didn't know what to do. Sweating, full of panic, she turned her car back on and slowly drove home.

When she got to her house, she thought she was having a nightmare. A stress-fueled vision of her worst nightmare come to life, because an expensive sports-car rental was parked in her driveway. She knew who that was. Dread clenched her stomach.

This wasn't real. It wasn't.

Blake was back in Houston. There was no way he'd come to the middle of nowhere, Wyoming, just to chase her down. He wouldn't . . . would he?

She parked her car in the street and squeezed her eyes shut, willing the flashy red sports car to disappear. She was just stressing, wasn't she? This was all in her head.

A hand knocked at her window.

Amy squeezed an eye open . . . and there was Blake. He loomed over her car, an immaculately groomed, handsome, utterly disapproving figure in a power suit.

"Get out of the car, Amy." She could hear his thick disapproval even through the window, and it made something within her die. That small, fragile spirit of independence just utterly disappeared. Her gut knotted, she hung her head and got out of the car.

"Where have you been?" he asked, and his tone was icy with disapproval. "I've been waiting out in your driveway for over an hour."

"Just . . . just to visit a few friends," she mumbled.

"Friends." He snorted. "I'm sure. Look at you. You're a mess." His lip curled at the sight of her heavy coat and the scarf she had wrapped around her throat. "Your hair is everywhere and you aren't even wearing makeup."

She wasn't. She'd gone out this morning not feeling the need to particularly impress anyone. She hadn't thought it would matter. Now she inwardly cringed, touching her hair. How was it that Blake could make her feel so small again so quickly? "I'm off work . . ."

"Right. At your little job. Does it feed your soul? Are you making a difference in the world with teaching nose-picking kindergartners how to say their ABCs? Real world-changing shit there, Amy. Making a real damn difference." He pointed at the door. "Come on. Let's go inside. I'm cold."

Crushed, she hopped to get her keys out, hating that she was jumping to please him even as she did it. "I like my job."

"Oh, I'm sure you do. I'm sure it's gratifying to your ego. You desperately need it stroked. You always have."

She fumbled with the keys at the lock, her mind racing.

She needed to get inside, get away from him. She needed to shut the door on her old life. Her hands trembled as she unlocked the door. Why was he here? Why wouldn't he just let her be? They were divorced. She didn't want anything to do with him. What did he want from her? She opened the door and was met immediately by a tail-wagging Donner.

"A dog, too? You don't like animals." He seemed surprised, pushing his way forward before she could stop him.

"I like this one," she whispered. "What are you doing here, Blake?"

Blake walked into her house like he owned the place, eyeing her sparse furnishings and her cluttered Christmas tree with a look of distaste. She knew what he was thinking. Back at their house, the decorator had handled all the holiday decor. The designer had put together beautiful trees to rival anything in a department store, but Amy liked her new one, made with love and a lot of laughter. She thought of the nights she and Caleb had spent laughing over the archaic, seventies-inspired garlands she'd pulled from the estate-sale box. She thought of how hard he'd worked to get her power working when the tree shorted it out.

She thought of his smile.

God, she'd give anything for Caleb to be on her doorstep instead of Blake. She stared at her ex-husband uneasily. He was handsome, perfectly so. His tan came from a tanning bed, his hair was cut by the most expensive stylist in Houston, and his clothing was tailored. He looked great, but she knew he was also an awful, awful person who made her feel bad about herself.

He slowly turned, giving her house one last lip curl of disgust, and then faced her. "I'm here because I've decided that enough is enough. This charade has gone on long enough. I hope you've gotten it all out of your system, Amy, but it's time for you to come home. Enough with this divorce and this 'independence' you think you need. If you want independence so badly, I'll give you a bigger allowance, but this is just ridiculous. You belong at my side, not wiping noses."

Clearly only one of them had realized that the divorce was supposed to be final. "I don't want to be with you." Her voice was small, timid. Uncertain. Within moments of his return she'd reverted back to her old, helpless self. Amy was filled with self-loathing.

"You don't know what you want. I thought that was obvious." He sounded utterly dismissive and so sure of himself. "Look around you. You can't possibly want to live in this hovel." Blake gestured at her house, at the furniture she'd scraped from estate sales and thrifts. "How much are they paying you at that little school?"

"Enough." It wasn't enough. She didn't want to tell him the amount because he'd laugh in her face. She knew it, too. She hadn't cared about the salary when she took the job; she was just excited to get a job so she could have experience. She knew it didn't pay well. It hadn't mattered.

She'd never anticipated having to explain herself to her ex, though.

"Don't just stand there," Blake said, shaking his head. "Pack your things. I have an important business luncheon on the twenty-sixth and need to be back in Houston before the holiday."

"I thought you were broke," Amy whispered. "You filed for bankruptcy."

He touched her shoulder in his familiar way, frowning, and she instinctively straightened like she always had.

"Businesses come and go. You know that. The important thing is to always have more opportunities coming down the pipeline. Besides, this alimony thing doesn't matter now that I'm willing to take you back."

It sank in finally what he was saying. He thought she was just going to pack up and leave with him. What she wanted didn't matter. It never mattered. "You . . . you're not listening. I don't want to go back." She gestured at her house. "I have a life here."

He put his hands on her shoulders. "You don't know what you want, Amy. You never have. This is just you crying for attention. I never thought you'd go this far, but we both know common sense isn't one of your strong suits." He chuckled as if that was funny. "But I love you and I'm willing to overlook things. Come on. Get your stuff together. The sooner we leave this hellhole, the better."

Amy cleared her throat, shrugging off his hands. "I don't want to go anywhere with you, Blake. I have a life here." She choked on the words but managed to get them out. "I have a boyfriend."

For a moment, she could have sworn his eyes blackened with anger. "You're seeing someone?"

She gulped. "I am."

Realization dawned on his face. "Ah . . . I get it. You found some other sucker to take care of you, is that it?"

Other sucker? Take care of her? She flinched, those words in particular striking home. "No. That's not how it is at all." She pointed at the door, even though her entire body was trembling. "I want you to get out, Blake."

"I know how you work," he sneered. "All of this is a game for you. You just want someone else to pick up the pieces. You're pretending to be the poor little schoolteacher until I rescue you, and since I didn't get here fast enough, you found someone else to handle things. Let me guess, he gives you money, right? Buys you things? I'm sure your sob story really does a number on him. Poor, sweet little Amy who can't afford the pretty things in life." He shook his head. "Pathetic."

"Get out!" She pointed at the door.

"You're coming home with me," he insisted. But he moved to the door. "You think on what I said. I know how to take care of you. I can give you the life you need. I know what you want. You think on it tonight and I'll be back tomorrow to pick you up." He looked her up and down, utterly confident. "And I'm going to want an apology."

The moment he stepped on the porch, she slammed the door in his face. Amy collapsed against it, panting as if she'd run a marathon. Donner immediately moved to her side, pushing his long nose under her hand until she began to pet him.

She wanted to vomit . . . except she'd have to clean it up.

Blake. That fucker had been here, in her living room. Amy sobbed out a breath, gasping for air. She felt like she was on the verge of a meltdown. He wanted her back. No, he didn't want *her*. He just wanted to win. And she'd been such a wimp when he was here, letting him into her house, letting him talk to her like she was nothing. No wonder he didn't believe her when she said she didn't want anything to do with him. She'd folded like a deck of cards the moment he even looked her way.

She clung to Donner, burying her hands in his thick fur as she listened to Blake's rental car speed away. He'd flown here from Houston to come get her. That meant he really, truly thought if he'd just showed up and acted like this was all just a spat, that she'd come running home. Did he not truly know her after all this time? It boggled the mind.

Or maybe he did know her all too well. He thought if he made her feel stupid enough, she'd cave. Give in to what he wanted. After all, she'd done that a million times before. She'd felt herself shrinking as he spoke, his words designed to make her feel like an idiot. To make her realize that her life was pathetic.

Through his eyes, it was. She was living in a dump. She was teaching for bottom-dollar wages in a small town where she was an outsider.

And she'd started dating a guy because he fixed her car.

She sucked in a horrified breath at that realization. Blake was right about her. She'd only truly seen Caleb when he showed up to bail her out. When he'd given her a ride back to town and promised to fix her car. She'd let him chauffeur her around. She'd let him fix her faucet and caulk the windows. He'd redone the ceiling in her bedroom and patched the roof, all because she'd needed it.

Oh god, she was *needy*.

Blake was right.

She'd let a stranger waltz into her life and do all kinds of work on her house because she needed it. She hadn't paid him a dime for all his time. Instead, she'd *dated* him. The sour taste of bile filled her mouth.

Here she'd come to Wyoming to be her own person and she was falling into the same patterns. After all, it was so easy to just let Caleb handle things. Caleb had handled things when her date went south. He'd handled Greg when he'd shown up again. He'd handled her house problems and her car problems. He'd even jokingly suggested that she hand out cookies to her friends today.

Amy wept, hating herself.

The worst part of all of this was that she genuinely liked Caleb. She wanted him to do these things for her. She liked having him to lean on. She liked knowing he was there to help her and she wasn't alone. Like when he'd suggested that she stay at his house because hers was freezing cold. She'd done it one night when it got too cold, another night letting him stay over because they could snuggle in bed together and stave off the worst of the chill.

He was wonderful and generous . . . and he deserved so much better than a user like her. She was going to have to break up with him, she realized. For both of their sakes.

She couldn't be the new, improved Amy if she truly was just using him, and that broke her heart.

CHAPTER NINETEEN

Caleb had spent hours decorating the barn for his date with Amy. Jack had laughed his ass off when he saw what Caleb was up to, but Jack's opinion didn't much matter. It was only Amy he wanted to impress. It was Amy whose eyes he wanted to light up with pleasure. Jack could buzz right off.

So he hung pine garlands from one end of the barn doors to the other. He hung jingle bells from the stall doors and festive wreaths from hooks, making sure that none of them were in eating reach of the horses themselves. He got on a ladder and hung strings of lights from the rafters so she'd walk into a winter wonderland when she arrived. He wove bells into bridles and braided his horse's mane with red and green ribbons.

Today, he was going to show Amy how to ride a horse. She'd confessed that she'd never even gotten near one before, and he figured it was a good skill to learn. Plus, he got to spend the afternoon with her. It was a win all around.

His letter for today was tucked into his front pocket, and he was hanging the last of the lights when he heard a car pull up.

That had to be his girl.

Grinning, Caleb closed the barn doors so he could surprise her and headed out to greet Amy.

She didn't come to meet him halfway. In fact, she got out of her car, leaned against the door, and huddled into her light jacket as if it were freezing outside. Why was she wearing that damn thing again? The one he'd gotten for her was much warmer, and today was a snowy, blustery day. She looked miserable, too. "You okay, Amy?"

"We need to talk," she told him in a wobbling voice.

His senses went on alert. "Talk. About . . . ?"

"I can't do this," she practically whispered even as he came close enough to see that her face was deathly pale, her eyes strangely hollow.

"Our date this afternoon?" She didn't look like she was feeling well. "No worries about that. It can wait." She didn't know it was horseback riding, and he sure wasn't taking her out when she was this wretched-looking. "You feeling all right?"

She shook her head. "I'm not talking about our date today. I'm talking about all of this. You and me. I can't do this." Her voice rose in a hysterical note. "I can't do you and me, Caleb."

For a brief moment, it felt as if the ground dropped away from him. As if the world was ending. She'd been with him and found him lacking . . . somehow? But that didn't make sense. He'd spent the night at her house last night, had woken up to her kissing his chest, her cold toes pressed between his legs. She'd initiated sex that morning, and he'd left her side with a smile on his face.

Something had happened. "I don't understand what you're saying. What's changed?"

"Me," she told him, wild eyed. She slammed her hand to her chest. "I'm the one that's changing. I'm the one who needs to change, Caleb. You're fine. You're great." Her face crumpled. "You're perfect, okay?"

Now he was really damn confused. "You want to sit down and talk somewhere, Amy?"

"No." She shook her head. "I'm tired of people talking to me and telling me what I should think. I thought about this on my own, and I realized that this isn't right for me. You're wonderful, Caleb, and I really do mean that." Her voice broke. "But this can't work between us. I can't do a relationship right now."

He didn't think she was serious. Not when she looked so very distraught. "Amy, love, we need to—"

"No," she said again, louder. "No. Just . . . no, okay, Caleb? Please believe me when I say no. I think you're amazing but I can't do this right now. Any of this." She shook her head frantically and then fumbled back toward her car.

He wanted to chase after her, but she was acting erratic. The last thing he wanted was for her to peel out of the gravel parking lot so fast she lost control. He was forced to watch her back her car up and head back out, leaving him behind.

Caleb didn't understand what had just happened.

She'd broken up with him. Obviously. That part stung. It stung his pride and it made his chest ache, because he wanted her desperately. Every moment that he spent with her just reinforced how much he loved her, how she'd always been the right one for him. He'd known it the moment he saw her.

He'd thought she was falling for him, too. She'd never seemed unhappy on their dates. She'd been delighted with every letter he'd given her, confessing his feelings one piece at a time. She'd smiled and laughed when he woke her up in bed.

They'd made love last night staring into each other's eyes and she told him she'd come so hard she'd seen stars. He'd kissed her and gone down on her again just to make sure she saw those stars twice.

For it to all change now, this afternoon, hours after he'd been at her side?

Something had happened.

Bewildered, he watched her car head down the road and disappear. He wanted to text her . . . but she was driving. Hell, he wanted to get into his damn truck and follow behind her. Just show up at her house and demand answers. Grab her and kiss her until she relented and decided they'd be together again.

He didn't understand what had just happened . . . at all.

Caleb watched the long driveway for a while, just in case she turned around and declared that she'd changed her mind. He hoped she'd show up and tell him what was bothering her, so he could help her figure it out. But the road remained empty, and his chest ached with a strange hollowness.

Maybe she'd meant it after all.

He wandered back toward the main house, feeling that hollowness spreading through his body. With Amy, he'd found joy in the smallest of things. He liked everything about spending time with her, but now days—weeks, months, years—without her stretched in front of him like slow torture. If it really was over between them . . . what did he have to look forward to? Why was he even here in Painted

Barrel? Just to be near her? Even if she didn't want him around?

He'd do it. On the off chance she needed him, he'd always be there for her. It didn't matter that she didn't want him. He'd always, always want her. Amy was it for him.

When he went inside, Uncle Ennis was sitting at the dining room table across from Jack, doing crossword puzzles and drinking coffee. "Thought I saw your girl's car pull up," his elderly uncle commented.

"You okay?" Jack asked Caleb, frowning at him. "You look . . . strange."

Caleb ran a hand down his face. "I think Amy just broke up with me."

"You think?" Jack echoed.

Caleb shrugged, unable to find the words. When they continued to stare at him, he let out a frustrated breath. "I don't know. She just came here, all frantic. Said it wasn't me but we couldn't be together."

"It might be you," Jack said. "She might just be saying that."

Caleb thumped down into an empty chair, drained. He couldn't process it. No Amy? Never again? It didn't seem possible. "I don't understand."

His uncle peered at him over his bifocals. "What exactly did she say, again?"

Caleb had to think about it. "She was crying. Said I was perfect . . . and then said she couldn't do a relationship right now."

"Ah." Uncle Ennis gave him a knowing look. "It's not you, then." He tapped his pencil on the crossword puzzle. "What's a three-letter word for 'to obfuscate'?"

"I don't even know what obfuscate means," Jack replied.

"It means . . . well . . . it means when you . . . obfuscate something. You know. You hide it or something." His uncle paused. "I think."

Caleb resisted the urge to snatch the crossword puzzle from his uncle's hands. "Can we talk about my problems, here?"

Uncle Ennis looked over at him again. "It's not you. I said that. Take heart."

"It could be him," Jack teased, obviously unaware of how close Caleb was to snapping. "I mean, if you had to date Caleb, you'd probably lose your shit at some point, too."

Caleb glared at his younger brother, then turned back to his uncle. "If it's not me, what is it?"

For a moment, Uncle Ennis continued to study his half-completed crossword. Then he glanced over at Caleb. "Put yourself in her place. She's divorced, right? New to this town. Lonely. The look on her face sometimes reminds me of one of the dogs I rescued back in the day. It was abandoned on the side of the road and I think it broke a little piece of his spirit. Every time I left, he howled at the door for hours. Every time I came back, I could have sworn there was this look of surprise on his face, like he didn't expect me to return. And when I did, instead of being happy to see me, he'd bite me." The old man chuckled.

This . . . was a nonsense story. What did this have to do with his woman? "Amy's not a dog."

"I didn't say she was. The mentality is similar, though. Something's hurt her badly in the past and she's in defense mode. She's lashing out because she doesn't want to get hurt again. She's trying to protect herself before you hurt her."

His Amy . . . hurt. It was like something clicked into place. The wild look in her eyes. The tears and frustration.

Her constant need to be independent despite her aching loneliness. She was hurt, all right. Was that what was happening, then? Was she pushing Caleb away because she was afraid he'd break her like her ex had?

He'd never hurt her. All he wanted was to love her. To be at her side and see her smile. To wake up in the morning with her in his arms, and to go to bed at night knowing she was right there next to him. Caleb loved her with all his heart. Had since the first moment he saw her.

If she was hurting, he wanted to fix it. And she was giving up on him because . . . what? Because something in their relationship had scared her? He needed to see her. To reassure her that he was never going anywhere. That he'd be there for her, always, in whatever way she needed.

He got to his feet.

"Going somewhere?" Jack asked.

"Need to think about how I'm going to fix this," Caleb said. "And what Amy needs from me."

"Attaboy," Uncle Ennis said. "Before you go . . ."

Caleb turned to him. "What?"

"Three-letter word for obfuscate?"

Caleb sighed. "Haven't the foggiest."

Jack snapped his fingers. "Fog!"

"It is fog," Uncle Ennis said. "Good call, boy."

If only everything in Caleb's life were that easy. He left the kitchen and went back to the barn, thinking hard. He leaned against the barn door, eyeing the decorations. Amy would have loved them, he knew. She was so thrilled about everything he did for her, as if she never expected such kindness. That broke his damn heart all over again.

His uncle was right. Something had spooked her, and she was running before she could get hurt again. The question was, how did he fix it?

* * *

The answer to his problem came to him in the middle of the night. A fresh snow fell on the ground, thick and white, leaving the world blanketed in silence. It reminded him of Alaska on nights like this, and for some reason, it cleared his mind. Helped him think.

He couldn't "fix" Amy.

There was nothing wrong with her. Was she terrified of being hurt again? Probably. Did she truly want to break up with him or was she just saving herself? He didn't know the truth to that one. But he knew what he could do—the same thing he'd always done. He could be there for her. He could quietly support her and let her figure out her own way, all the while taking care of her. He could show her he wasn't going anywhere. That whatever she needed, he'd provide.

And maybe she'd learn to trust him.

Didn't matter if it took a long time. He wasn't going anywhere. That was the best way to prove himself to her, Caleb realized. Not with fancy gifts or big productions. Just quietly being there for her.

So he got up that morning before dawn, gazed out at the thick blanket of snow, and dressed. He tossed the snow shovel into the back of his truck and headed into town, parked in front of her house, and then cleared the driveway. He cleared the sidewalks, too, because he wanted it to be safe for her to walk. She was from the South, and all this snow was new to her. She slid all over the icy walkways because she hadn't quite figured out how to get her feet in the winter yet, so he was going to quietly help out. He scraped the porch clear of snow, too, as silently as he could. She probably needed a good night's sleep after yesterday's turmoil, and he didn't want to wake her.

Even so, the light went on in the living room, and a few moments later, the front door opened. Amy stood there, shivering in her thin robe, her arms crossed over her chest. Her normally smooth dark hair was an utter mess, and her eyes were red and swollen from crying, the tip of her nose pink.

Despite this, she was the most beautiful thing he'd ever seen.

"What are you doing here?" Amy whispered, looking at him. There was longing in her eyes, and hurt, he realized, and his uncle was absolutely right. Whatever it was that was driving Amy right now, she still cared about him. It was a relief to see.

He wanted to grab her and pull her to his chest. To hug the hell out of her and let her know that everything was going to be all right. There was a wariness to her posture, though, that told him it wouldn't be permitted. So he just leaned on the shovel and tried to shrug, casually. "I'm shoveling snow."

"But why?" Her eyes watered and she swiped at her cheeks. "Why are you here?" There was a broken little catch in her voice that tore at him. "I told you we were done."

"I know." Caleb forced himself to sound casual. Unaffected. It was harder than he thought, especially with those tears rolling down her cheeks. He wanted to brush them away and kiss her so hard that she was never sad again. Instead, he kept leaning against that damn shovel. "I wanted to do this anyhow."

"I didn't ask you to," she told him, accusing. "I didn't ask you to do any of this. Anything! I can shovel my own walkway!"

Her outburst was surprising. "I know you can. I just did it because I wanted to. Because I love you."

She looked up at him with eyes shining with tears. Her face crumpled, and then a ragged sob tore from her throat. "Caleb—"

"I know. It's okay." He caressed her cheek, reaching out to touch her. "I promise it's okay."

Amy sobbed harder, her shoulders shaking with her sadness. She looked so ready to collapse that he couldn't stand on the porch any longer and just do nothing. Fuck doing nothing. He tossed the shovel aside and picked her up instead, carrying her into the house. She cried against his neck, burrowing against him as he carried her to her room and gently laid her on the bed. Donner was still in the blankets, his tail thumping cautiously as he sniffed the air. Caleb touched him, too, gave him a quick pet to reassure him, and then his attention was back on his Amy. His beautiful, sad, lovely woman.

"Tell me what's wrong so I can help you, baby." It was the first time he'd called her something like that, and it felt good. Felt right.

She cried harder, reaching for him. "I'm such a mess."

"You're not a mess." He sat down on the edge of the bed and pulled her into his arms, her legs crosswise over his lap. She clung to his neck, wetting his coat with her tears, and he stroked her hair and her arm, just touching her. Comforting her.

"I am a mess," she insisted, sniffling. "I wanted to be so independent, and I'm terrible at it. I can't do anything. I'm broke and alone and I'm using you and I'm just . . . miserable." A fresh round of tears erupted. "I wanted to be my own person and here I am, doing the same stupid shit.

I'm falling into the same old traps and I'm dragging you down with me."

"You're not dragging me anywhere I don't want to go," Caleb reassured her, stroking her back.

"Yes, I am. You fixed my ceiling, and my roof, and my window, and my sink . . ." She hiccuped. "And my car! You did all kinds of things for me. You drove me for days. You bought me a coffee maker. And I let you do all of it because I'm a user. I'm the *worst*."

"You're not using me—"

"Yes, I am!"

He tried to follow her logic. "So, what—you let me fix up your house, and then to repay me you . . . slept with me?"

She gasped and slapped his shoulder. "No!"

"Then why do you think you're using me?"

"Because I should be independent—"

"I think you're mistaking independent for stubborn," he muttered.

She smacked his shoulder again. "I'm serious!"

"I am, too." Caleb held her closer, selfishly enjoying the feel of her in his arms, of her legs across his lap, the way she fit just perfectly against him. He wanted to bury his face against her neck and just breathe in her scent, breathe in *her*. Amy. The woman he loved, whose sadness was a palpable thing between them. "You never asked me to do any of those things, Amy. I did them because it didn't feel right to me to see the problems and ignore them."

"That's just it," Amy said miserably. "I didn't ask you, but I didn't have to. I just acted helpless and you swept in and I let you."

"My side wasn't completely innocent, either. I got something out of it, too, you know. I got to be around you. I actually took more time fixing things just so I could be around you, remember?" When she looked up at him, he gently touched her cheek, brushing away some of the tears. "There's nothing wrong with asking for help or leaning on someone, baby. I helped you because I wanted you to have a sink that didn't drip. Nothing more."

Her eyes filled with fresh tears. "I didn't want to use you, Caleb. I never wanted that."

"You never have. I don't know where you got it in your head that you did."

She shook her head, sad.

"Just because I support you doesn't mean that I'm being used. I help you because I like you, as a person. I help you because I'm a decent human, unlike that shithead Greg. I help you because I want to build you up, not tear you down or use it against you. That's the difference."

Amy gazed up at him with such sad, sad hope in her eyes. "I'm sorry."

"Don't be sorry." He took her hand in his, kissed the palm. "Even if you don't want to be with me, I'm still going to look out for you. Not because I want to push you back into my arms, but because I love you and care about you. If you don't want me right now, it hurts me to my soul, but I understand. You do what you have to do, baby. I'll support you all the way."

She flung her arms around his neck and squeezed, tight, her face against his neck. "You're the best man ever."

"No, I'm not. I'm a shy cowpoke who never spoke a lick to any woman until you came along. Being with you makes me better, though. I bet in another year or two, I'll be able to say hello to the cashier at the grocery store."

He liked that she let out a tiny giggle. Just a tiny one. It was a start. "What do you want?" he asked her.

"You," she said softly. "I want you, Caleb."

"I love you," he told her again. "Nothing about that has changed. If you need time, I'll give you time. But I'm still going to shovel your walkways because I don't want you slipping and falling."

Her lower lip quivered. "I love you, too," she whispered. "I don't care that it's only been a few weeks. You're the best thing that's ever happened to me."

His heart soared. He brushed away more tears. "Then what do you want to do?"

She thought for a long moment, her fingers curling against his jacket. "I want you . . . and I don't want us to break up."

"Then we don't break up." Caleb wanted to shout with joy, but he somehow managed to keep his voice calm.

"But I don't want to use you. I want to be independent."

He nodded. "I am absolutely fine with that. Like I said, all you need to do is point the way and I'll be right at your side."

She straightened a little. "I think . . . I want my apartment."

"Then get that apartment."

Her expression fell. "I can't. I don't have the money. I'm all out of clothes and jewelry."

He frowned. "You've been selling your clothes?"

Amy managed a small smile through her sniffles. "Oh yeah. Everything was designer and high-end. It was the only stuff I really got out of the divorce, other than the promise of alimony. So I've been selling my shoes and my handbags and anything I could to make ends meet while I waited for checks to come in." A little sigh escaped her. "Money that's never going to come in, now. My ex filed for bankruptcy just to screw me out of my alimony payments."

Hearing that made him irrationally angry. What kind of asshole let his woman suffer because she wanted to spread her wings? "I'll give you that money," he growled. "You tell me how much you need."

"No!" she said quickly. "I don't want your money. I don't want to use you, Caleb."

"You never have. I don't know where you got it in your head that you . . ." Where was this coming from? He suddenly had an idea. His eyes narrowed. "You said your ex made you feel small. That he made you feel useless. Did he call you? Fill your head with this shit?"

"He didn't call me." She smoothed her fingers over the front of his coat.

Caleb sighed with relief.

"He showed up on my doorstep."

Just like that, every muscle in his body went on high alert. The need to protect her—to shelter her—roared through him. "He *what*?"

"He's here in town," she said in a small voice. "He showed up yesterday and tried to get me to go home with him."

Everything in him was screaming to find the bastard. His jaw clenched, and he could feel muscles twitching in his effort to remain calm. "What did you tell him?"

"At first, I just . . . let him talk. I just shut down." She buried her face against his neck again, quivering. "I hated that about myself. It only took moments for him to tear me down again."

"But you're here," he managed to say calmly. "You didn't go with him."

"I told him I had a boyfriend," Amy confessed. "And that I didn't want to go with him."

Fierce joy rocked him. She'd stood up to the bastard.

She'd stood up to the man who'd tried to make her so damn small and told him she had someone new. She had Caleb. He was so damn proud of her. Even more than that, everything was clicking into place. "Did he show up before or after you came to tell me we were done?"

"Before," she admitted, shamefaced. "He made me feel . . ."

"I know." Caleb could very well guess how her shitty, controlling, terrible ex-husband made her feel. "It doesn't matter. I'm proud of you for standing up to him."

She sighed. "Don't be too proud. He didn't believe me. Or maybe he thought if he just kept talking like I was a babbling idiot that I'd believe him and cave. Either way, he said he'd be back today and that I had to be packed." Her mouth twisted. "I'm not packed. I'm not going anywhere with him."

"Good." He rubbed her back again. "That's step one. You realize that you are an independent person and you don't need his shit. Even if you and I don't work out, you need to remember that you are an amazing, kind, thoughtful, generous person, Amy Mckinney, and anyone that tells you otherwise is a jackass and a fool."

Her eyes met his. "I want us to work out."

"I want that, too." Caleb was determined to make the two of them work. He was willing to be as patient as he needed to be, as long as the end result was Amy in his arms. "And you want your apartment."

"I can't afford it."

"Then you figure out a way to get the money, baby. If you want it, go after it." He tilted his head, studying her. "Can I loan you the money?"

A stubborn look crossed her face. "No."

Caleb grinned, because he'd known that answer before he even asked. "Then you figure out another way. You get a second job. Or you get a loan from the bank. You'll figure something out. You're smart."

Her eyes lit up. "A loan from the bank. I tried to get one when I first got divorced, but they said I didn't have enough credit established. I've had a credit card for months now, though . . ." Amy beamed at him. "That's a wonderful idea. Let's go to the bank right now."

"Right now?"

"What's wrong with right now?"

"It's almost Christmas. Even if they're open, they're probably going to be swamped." It was still early, the pale winter sunlight barely peeking through the gray clouds. "But I'm happy to go stand in line with you all morning if that's what it takes."

She chewed on her lip, thinking. "I guess it can wait until tomorrow. Or, no, the day after tomorrow." Her gaze focused on his face again and she studied him, eyes flicking up and down. "Are you . . . are you busy today?"

Any plans he'd had went out the window the moment Amy had tried to break up with him yesterday. She was his priority. "I thought I'd spend today with the woman I love . . . but only if she wanted me there."

Her smile grew wider. "She does."

"Then I'm sure we can think of a few things to do today." He leaned in and lightly kissed the tip of her nose.

Amy lifted her head, raising her mouth for a kiss. "I have a few ideas."

"Just a few?" he murmured, lips brushing over hers.

"They're all basically the same idea," she confessed. "And they all involve me getting you undressed."

"Funny, I was going to say the same thing."

She laughed and then quickly sobered, her gaze serious. "I'm so sorry, Caleb. I didn't mean to hurt you. I just panicked."

"No need to apologize, baby." It felt good to call her that. So good. Caleb kissed her again, his lips playing lightly over hers. Sweet, gentle caresses were what he wanted to give her right now. They'd made love passionately before. They'd made love with enthusiasm, and they'd been frisky and played and teased as much as they'd kissed. But right now, he wanted to be tender with her. To make her realize just how very loved she was. So he pressed another kiss to her mouth, and then began to kiss lightly along her jaw. "Never apologize. Just let me be here to support you."

"If we're together," she told him in a trembling voice, "I'm going to need my own place. Not this one, but someplace where I can be independent."

Did she think that was a deal breaker for him? He didn't mind. "At some point I'm going to want to marry you and move in together. But I'm happy to wait for as long as you need."

"At some point I'm going to want that, too. Just . . . not yet." Her fingers curled in his hair, holding him as he went to her ear and nipped. A little sigh of pleasure escaped her when he took her earlobe and began to gently suck on it. "I want to keep my job, too."

"Fine with me."

"I'm just telling you this because I want you to know where I stand," she explained, breathless. "It doesn't mean I don't need you in other ways." Amy sounded uncertain once more, as if she were afraid he was going to lash out at her.

He simply kissed her earlobe again, then traced the outline of it with his tongue. "All I ever wanted was to be at your side, Amy. I don't need to own you. Be as independent as you like. I'm your partner, not your owner."

"That's the difference, isn't it?" Her voice was soft.

"It's everything."

"Caleb," she whispered, his name reverent on her tongue. "I missed you. I thought about you all night and cried. I wanted you so badly but I didn't trust myself not to use you. Not to fall into the same trap I did before."

"I won't let that happen," he promised her. "I like the way you are now." He hesitated, lifting his head. "Though I would prefer for you to stay someplace that has heat." She must have had a fire going last night, he figured, because her bedroom was only frigid instead of ice-cold.

"I'd like that, too," she told him. "For now, can we just share body heat?"

He thought she'd never ask. Caleb kissed her on the mouth again, slow, tender, and thorough. When she was breathless and squirming in his lap, he gently set her down on the bed and peeled his coat off.

Donner immediately moved to her side and began to lick her face.

Amy sputtered, laughing, and hugged the dog around his neck. "Perhaps we should put you in your warm bed in the *other* room, hmm, my old man?"

"I'm in favor of that," Caleb agreed.

"Come on, Donner," she said, scooting out of the bed. "Let's get you the peanut-butter jar and you can lick it while your dad licks other things." She tossed a saucy wink at Caleb, shaking her hips as she headed out of the bedroom and into the living room.

Damn, but he loved that woman. His heart felt like bursting from pride at her stubbornness, and at the sheer joy of being with her. No matter what came up, they'd solve it together. They just had to communicate. He pulled off layers of clothing, removing his shirt and pants, his socks and his boots, while she murmured and baby-talked to the dog in the other room. By the time he was down to his boxers, she'd returned, and her gaze devoured him. She had such hungry eyes, his Amy, as she moved toward him. She extended a hand, touching his stomach and tracing down his abdomen before moving to cup his cock. "I love the way you look," she confessed to him. "I could look at you all day long and not get tired."

"Funny, I feel the same way about you." He put his hand to the tie of her robe and undid it. The flannel material fell open, and he'd never thought red-and-green-checkered plaid was so damned sexy. On her, anything would be sexy, though. It wasn't just her body, but the way she looked at him, the way she smelled, the way she moved, the way she made those soft noises of need. Everything that Amy was turned him on. It was just another reason she was utterly perfect for him, in every way.

Underneath the robe, she wore his T-shirt. He hadn't even realized she'd stolen it from him that night of the Christmas party, but it made him even harder just seeing her wearing it. He loved it, loved the sight of her long legs peeking out from underneath the hem, the shift of her loose breasts against the fabric. He pushed the robe off her shoulders and then pulled her against him for another kiss, his hands sliding to her hips and then hiking the shirt higher.

She wasn't wearing panties underneath.

Caleb groaned against her mouth. It was like she'd instinctively known just how much he needed her. How badly he wanted to touch her. He pulled the shirt over her head, revealing her beautiful body to him, and laid her gently on the bed. He devoured her with another kiss, his hand on one perfect breast, his beard scraping the lower half of her face pink. Over the last while, the sight of that flush of pink had started to become intensely erotic to him. Now he wanted to see it on her pretty breasts, on her belly . . . on the insides of her thighs.

He moved lower, taking her nipple into his mouth and sucking lightly.

She moaned, arching against his mouth as he made love to her breast, teasing the tip with his tongue as his hand teased her other nipple, making sure both peaks were hard and taut with arousal. He loved her breasts, loved how sensitive they were, and within moments, her nipples were a rosy red, one wet from his tongue, and the beard flush had scraped over the curve of her breast, turning it pink. He moved to the other breast, giving it equal attention while she panted and squirmed under him, her hands in his hair.

"Caleb," she begged. "Oh, that feels so good, Caleb. Your mouth . . ."

He flicked his tongue over her nipple. "Do you like it?"

"God, yes."

"Good." He gave her breast one final nip and then moved lower, scraping his beard along the gentle swell of her belly, until she was undulating under him, little whimpers escaping her throat. He pushed her thighs apart, and she was hot and wet and so, so ready for him. He loved how wet she got, how slick her folds became when he touched her. It made him feel like a fucking king. He dragged his tongue up and down her sweet pussy, tasting her, before settling in against her clit and beginning the steady teasing that she loved so much. She always seemed surprised when he went down on her, as if he was giving her a gift instead of the other way around. He loved the taste of her, but even more than that, he loved her reactions. It was worth everything to feel her thighs flex against his ears, to feel her body quiver as she came. He held tight to her hips, his mouth on her clit as he flicked and teased, and she bucked against his mouth, gasping his name.

Caleb was going to stay there, too, until she came. But she reached for him, brushing her fingers against his face as he nuzzled her folds. "I want you inside me, Caleb. Please. I want to come with you inside me."

That was a plea he couldn't refuse. With another kiss to her sweetness, he lifted his head. "I'll get a condom."

The birth control had been in her bathroom, in a cabinet, but since he'd started staying over, they'd moved it to her bedside drawer. He found the strip, tore one off with movements that were more confident and more practiced by the day, and rolled it on quickly. Every moment that he wasn't touching her was a wasted moment, and he wanted to touch her again, to feel her skin against his. He moved back to her and kissed her once more, hot and conquering. With his tongue, he stroked deep into the well of her mouth in a silent promise. *This is mine,* he silently told her.

She met him with her tongue, the kiss deep and slick, and he moved over her, settling his hips against hers. Amy's thighs were wide, and when he pressed the head of his cock against her entrance, he felt her quiver with need.

He sank into her, burying himself to the hilt, even as he kissed her.

This is mine, he repeated silently as he began to stroke. *This is mine. This is mine. You're mine.* He silently chanted it over and over again as he thrust into her, working her body to a fever pitch. It rang in his head as her nails dug into his skin and she began to arch, her movements erratic as her orgasm built. It reverberated through every cell of his body as she came, her walls squeezing him so hard that his own release roared through him, and he came, pumping into her with firm, fierce strokes.

Amy was his, now and forever. It didn't matter if she was in an apartment, or if she was a teacher, or anything else. All he'd ever wanted was her, her smiles, her laughter, her happiness. As long as he had that, nothing else mattered.

CHAPTER TWENTY

Amy curled up against Caleb, wriggling at the feel of his cock still buried inside her. They'd made love three times in a row, pausing between frantic rounds to catch their breath, only to get another burst of need and tackle each other. She was sweaty, her hair a mess, and she'd never been so happy. His big body spooned hers from behind, his hand on her breast, his breath on her neck.

"Merry Christmas Eve," he mumbled as she twitched against him.

For some reason, that struck her as absurdly funny, and she giggled. "Merry Christmas Eve to you, too. Is it officially Christmas Eve? I don't think the sun has gone down yet." They'd spent all morning in bed, and possibly part of the afternoon.

So far, this was turning into her favorite day ever.

She felt him shrug. "Time doesn't matter, as long as I'm with you." He pressed a kiss to her neck, then her shoulder. "Your present is in my car. Should I go get it?"

A little flutter sparked in her belly. "You brought my present?"

"Yeah. I figured I'd give it to you anyhow, even if you and I didn't work out." He kissed her shoulder again. "Gotta say, I'm glad we did, though."

She was, too. "Yours are under the tree." They'd been just another thing she'd cried over last night, along with his shirt, his favorite mug, and the scent of him on her pillow. It had been a really teary night. It had felt wrong to push him away, but she hadn't trusted herself.

Talking to Caleb had made it all come into perspective. He didn't want to own her. He just wanted to be with her. That was the difference, wasn't it? It had been Blake who'd constantly made her feel like she wasn't good enough. Blake who had wanted to know where she was at all times, what she was doing, what she was spending. Caleb just wanted her to smile.

She relaxed, snuggling down against him. "But we have to get out of bed to get the presents."

He nipped at her shoulder with his teeth, sending a ripple of pleasure through her body and making her acutely aware of his cock still deep inside her. "I guess I'll sacrifice myself and get dressed. I should toss this condom, anyhow. You stay there."

She let out a little sigh when he moved away from her, his body leaving hers. It was immediately cold in the bedroom without his warmth, and so she pulled the sex-scented blankets around her like a cocoon. "Check on Donner, too, will you? Make sure he's not in a peanut-butter coma?" The jar had been nearly empty when she'd given it to him. She'd almost tossed it last night, and then had kept it to keep him distracted. He did love peanut butter so much. He got it all over his gray muzzle and it was the cutest thing.

Smiling, she turned in bed and watched Caleb as he emerged from the bathroom, cleaned himself up, and pulled on his jeans and boots. "Be right back," he promised, kissing her before leaving the bedroom.

She closed her eyes and snuggled under the blankets, wondering how many condoms they had left. She wanted to lie in Caleb's arms all day, but she knew they'd been steadily working through her supply. Maybe she'd call the doctor when she got paid again, get on the pill. She could take control of that situation, she decided, and it was an idea she liked. She wondered what it would feel like to have sex with Caleb without the condom, and daydreamed about that for a brief moment.

The doorbell rang.

That was weird. Amy sat up in bed, frowning. Why would Caleb ring her doorbell if he was going outside . . .

She gasped, surging out of bed. Oh no. Oh god, no. She knew who that was. She knew who would ring her doorbell today.

Blake. Fucking Blake.

Amy dragged her shirt on—well, Caleb's shirt—and finger-combed her hair. She dragged her robe over her body, but the tie was nowhere to be seen. Shit. She wrapped the robe tight around her waist and then, holding it closed, left the bedroom.

Caleb stood at the front door, and she saw Blake was facing off against him on the other side of the threshold. Both were scowling at one another, and she saw Blake was wearing another tailored suit . . . while Caleb wasn't even wearing a shirt. His tanned chest and tousled hair made it obvious what they were doing.

She ran a hand through her hair again and tried to find

her courage. "Go away, Blake." God, did her voice have to choose that moment to squeak?

"I told you I would be back, Amy," Blake said in his most patient and dismissive voice. "You were going to pack your things so we could leave, remember?" His lip curled as he studied Caleb. "Clearly there was a misunderstanding."

Caleb looked over at her, and she mentally cringed. *Please don't hate me. Please don't hate me.*

But his eyes were calm as he gazed at her. "You want to handle this, baby, or do you want me to?"

It felt like all the breath she'd been holding suddenly left her.

He was going to let her figure this out. Let her choose. For some reason, she smiled. Amy felt stronger. Prouder. She stood a little taller as she hugged her robe closed, and surprisingly, she didn't feel a bit of shame—not anymore—at her ex-husband catching them undressed. "I've got it. Thank you, Caleb." She turned to Blake, taking a few steps forward until she stood in front of the door—and in front of her lover. She faced down her controlling ex-husband with a calm expression, even though her heart was pounding. "There's no misunderstanding. I never said I would go anywhere with you. You said that. I never agreed."

His jaw tensed, like it always did when he was about to snap. It used to fill her with terror, knowing that she was going to get an earful of berating. "You're being irrational, Amy," he warned.

"I'm not," Amy said, and her voice was stronger this time. "You're the one that's not grasping the fact that we got divorced. I have court documents that say we're done, Blake. I left the state to get away from you. What part of this can't you seem to understand?"

"You don't know what you want," he said, dismissive. His gaze flicked to Caleb and his lip curled, but she noticed he made no move to come into the house.

Good. "I do know what I want, Blake. It's not you. Go away."

"Amy, be reasonable."

She thought she was being perfectly reasonable; she really was. "I don't want you in my life, Blake. I thought that the divorce made that pretty obvious."

"You're making a mistake."

"No, I'm not."

The tone of his voice changed, going from dismissive to persuasive. "Please, Amy. I . . . miss you. I want you back. I didn't realize how much I needed you until you were gone."

Once upon a time, she would have melted over this. Felt like she was making the right decision to stay at his side, even knowing there would be more inevitable negative comments, more backhanded attacks that would make her hate herself. Now that she was gone, though, she didn't miss him at all. She was able to see how he'd worked her to get what he wanted. He'd say anything in the moment, as long as it got him results. The words meant nothing to him.

She was never going back. "You can't miss me, because you never had me, Blake. You just want a puppet to dance to your little games. I'm not doing that anymore." Amy straightened, tall and proud, and gestured at his sports car. "Also, if you can afford to rent that, you can afford to pay me alimony. I'm talking to a lawyer in the New Year, so be ready for that. I want the money I'm owed, and I'm staying here. We're done. There is no 'us' anymore. We're divorced. I have a life, and you need to get one."

Caleb huffed a quiet sound of approval, his hand going to the small of her back in silent support.

The support made Amy happy. Even so, what made her happier was that she realized she didn't need his touch to be strong and brave. Just having him at her side, reassuring her with his quiet presence that he had her back, had given her the courage she needed to stand up to her asshole ex. It was like Caleb had said—they were better together. They were stronger together, as partners in life instead of one leading and the other following.

Funny how things all made sense with a bit of perspective.

"This is your last chance," Blake said, crossing his arms over his chest. "I'm not going to ask again, Amy. You should be thrilled I'm even here to try and rescue you."

Rescue her? From what? Freedom? Independence? A man that loved her and a job that made her happy? "This is *your* last chance," she retorted. "If you don't get off my porch, I'm going to call the sheriff and file a restraining order on you. I'm sure that'll look great in front of the judge when I file against you for unpaid alimony. You're going to look like a crazy stalker who can't take no for an answer." She made her expression pitying, just because she knew that would drive him crazy. "It's not a good look for you, Blake."

Blake's jaw clenched. "Last chance . . ."

How many times did she have to say no? Jesus.

Caleb cleared his throat and put his hand on her shoulder. "Have you said what you need to, baby?"

She nodded. "Yeah. I have. Just shut the door and let's go back to bed." She tossed that in deliberately.

"I'll do you one better," Caleb said. He surged forward, grabbing Blake by the lapels of his tailored coat, and flung her ex off her porch with an easy motion, tossing him as if he were a bale of hay. "Get out of here," Caleb called out to him as he sprawled in the snow. "You're trespassing."

And then he slammed the door shut behind him.

Amy sagged, all of the bristling energy escaping her. Oh god. Had she really done that? Had she stood up to Blake and refused to let him run her down? It made her so happy . . . but it was also exhausting. She felt drained as Caleb approached her.

He put his hands on her shoulders and looked her square in the eye. "You did fantastic, baby."

Hearing his pride made her feel better. "Thank you." She paused, fighting the urge to rush to the window to see if Blake was returning. "Is he . . . gone?"

"We'll know in a minute."

Amy remained tense until she heard the sound of his car start up. She moved to the window and peeked out the blinds, and sure enough, he was driving away.

He was gone. She'd made it clear that she was done with him, and he was leaving. She'd won.

She felt like celebrating. How long had she wanted to stand up for herself? How long had she dreamed of putting him in his place like he did to her all the time? Even when she'd divorced him, she'd snuck out and left, because it was too hard to confront him and stand up for herself. But she had today. She felt like a new person.

She turned to Caleb, smiling. "He left."

He rubbed his jaw, scratching at his beard, and for a moment, he looked uncomfortable. "Was that okay?" he asked. "What I did?"

"Tossing him off the porch?" Amy asked. When he nodded, she chuckled. "It was perfect. We make a great team."

Caleb grinned. "That we do."

* * *

Hours later, they emerged from the bedroom and curled up in front of the fire to snuggle in blankets and exchange Christmas presents. She moved Donner's bed next to the fireplace to share in the warmth, and the old dog was currently snoring, sprawled and content.

Even though it had happened earlier that day, Amy was still giddy with the knowledge that she'd handled Blake. She'd taken care of things. She hadn't let him bully her into submission. And she'd thrown in that line about the lawyer to make him sweat. She had no doubt that he was deliberately maneuvering not to pay her the money she was owed, all to make her desperate. Maybe she'd lawyer up in the New Year—surely someone would take her on—or maybe she wouldn't. The important thing was that Blake was going to sweat about it, and that was enough of a Christmas present for her.

Caleb sank down to the floor with two mugs of hot cocoa, topped with thick whipped cream, leftovers from one of their baking dates. She took her mug from him and sighed with contentment. "This might be my favorite Christmas ever."

"Really? You haven't even opened your presents yet." He smiled at her over his mug, so handsome it made her heart squeeze.

"It's not about presents," she confessed. "It's about being happy. I don't think I've ever been happier." She looked around her small house, at the ramshackle furniture and the cold-frosted windows. Was it a little run-down? Sure. But it was her place. She could decorate however she wanted. She could pull out every bit of furniture and replace it all with yoga mats. She could hang beads from the ceiling and paint the walls a ridiculous shade of medicinal pink, all because she simply wanted to. It was her life.

The possibilities felt endless.

Not that she'd do any of those things, of course. But the knowledge that she could do whatever she wanted, dress however she wanted, and act however she wanted? It was thrilling. That was the best present, she realized. It wasn't anything that came wrapped in a gift box, but a sense of independence. It was knowing that you could make your choices and the person at your side would support you and want the best for you.

Looking at Caleb, she knew he was that person. He'd support her dreams. If she wanted to give up teaching and make soaps in the basement, he'd support that. If she wanted to teach for the next fifty years, he'd support that, too, because he just wanted her to be happy and fulfilled. The thought made her giddy with joy.

"If it's not about presents, then I guess we don't need to open them . . . ?" He pointed at the box under the tree with her name on it.

"Well, maybe it's about presents a *little*," Amy teased back. There were four gifts with his name on them under her tree, too—three books and the bookends. She hoped it was enough. Money was tight—money was always tight.

Caleb picked up the large box with her name on it and handed it over to her.

A curious smile spread across her face and she took the present from him, then began to unwrap it. An all-too-familiar label stared back at her from the front of the box. "Louboutins? You got me a pair of Louboutins?"

He shrugged. "A place a few cities over had some in, and I recognized the red sole. You're always wearing fancy shoes, so I thought I'd get you a pair."

A horrified giggle escaped her throat, and she pulled the familiar black sparkly shoes out. She'd put them on consignment a few weeks ago . . . These were her old shoes. "I'm always wearing them because it's all I have. I . . . think these were mine."

"The ones you sold?" Caleb looked crestfallen. "I had no idea."

The giggles wouldn't stop coming. She kept laughing, clutching the present to her chest. He thought she loved the expensive shoes so much that she chose to wear them exclusively? They pinched her feet and were incredibly impractical for a schoolteacher. But she wore them because it meant one less thing to have to buy at the store. Here she'd sold off most of her high-end shoes . . . and he'd bought some back for her. It was so funny to her, though, that Caleb genuinely thought she loved high heels, so she laughed and laughed, until he began to laugh with her.

"I'm officially the worst boyfriend ever, aren't I?" He gave her a rueful smile. "Giving you back a pair of shoes you sold?"

That sobered her up. "You're the best. Don't ever believe otherwise." She clutched the shoebox to her chest tighter. "I love it, because it was thoughtful. Thank you, Caleb."

"That's not the only thing I got you—thank goodness." He pulled out a small envelope from the tree skirt and held it out to her.

"My letter?" Her eyes lit up.

"Actually . . . no." Caleb raked a hand through his messy hair. "It's not a letter because I was too rattled after our breakup to write one. I'm sorry."

"It's all right," she said quietly. "I'm sorry, too. I shouldn't have done it. I thought I was doing the right thing for both of us, but I overreacted."

He shrugged and reached for her hand, pulling it to his lap. "We're together now. That's all that matters."

They were. Amy smiled at him, then opened the envelope. Even before she could pull out the piece of paper and read it, he was explaining.

"It's not what it looks like," he began.

"It looks like a gym membership." She arched an eyebrow at him.

He rubbed his hand down his face, awkward. "I promise it's not. I just know you were talking about how it was hard for you to make friends here because you felt like an outsider, and I know you live alone, and while I want to be at your side every day, I also don't want you to feel like I have to be. So I got you a gift certificate to join the self-defense classes they have at the gym. They're on Wednesday nights, and Becca said she was signing up, so I figured you'd know someone."

He got her classes so she could make friends and protect herself? Her eyes grew misty and she clutched the paper to her chest. "Oh Caleb. I love it."

"Are you sure? Maybe I should have gotten jewelry after all."

"God no," she breathed. "These are honestly the most thoughtful gifts I've ever received. I don't want jewelry. I want someone to think about me . . . and you did. I love them both, and I love you." In a strange way, she loved that he gave her high heels, because it meant he paid attention to her.

That was everything.

He gave her a sheepish smile and leaned in. "Merry Christmas, baby."

She kissed him, putting her heart and soul into the kiss, and when they pulled away, she couldn't stop smiling. Self-defense classes. What a clever, thoughtful thing. It was perfect. It was perfect. She folded the certificate up and tucked it under her leg. "Open yours?"

Caleb unwrapped his presents, exclaiming over each of the books and handling them with careful, reverent fingers. She could see the pleasure on his face, and his grin grew even wider when he unwrapped the bookends. "This is all perfect. Thank you so much."

It really was a superb Christmas.

CHAPTER TWENTY-ONE

The day after Christmas, Caleb sat in his truck and tried to be patient. He was in the parking lot across from Painted Barrel's little bank. Amy had gone in alone—insisted on it—to talk to them about getting a loan for the apartment she wanted to move into. He'd floated the idea of her moving in with him, but even before he'd suggested it, he knew she wouldn't take him up on it. She'd refused, politely. It didn't hurt his feelings. He understood that Amy needed her own place for a while. She needed to feel comfortable with having her own space before she could share his.

And Caleb was content to wait.

At least, when it came to that. Waiting for her outside the bank was slight torture, though. He could see her through the windows, talking animatedly with the bank associate as she sat at a desk and filled out paperwork. He drummed his fingers on the steering wheel as she handed the papers over, and he watched as she pressed her fingers to her mouth, waiting as the banker typed things into his computer and talked. He couldn't guess what they were saying. Was he letting her down easily? Breaking it gently to Amy that she wouldn't qualify? Caleb didn't know. If she didn't qualify he'd . . . well, he'd help her think of something. He wanted to give her the money in his savings account. He wanted to just hand it to her, no strings attached, but he knew Amy well enough that he knew she wouldn't take it.

She needed to do this her way, and he understood.

Didn't mean he wasn't chafing to jump in there and help.

After what seemed like a hundred years, Amy got to her feet. She shook the hand of the man behind the desk, her expression unreadable. The banker handed her a folder of paperwork—a good sign, Caleb hoped—and then she left the bank.

Caleb held his breath, waiting as Amy came out of the building. He got out and opened the door on the passenger side for her, waiting for her to speak up, to tell him how it went. She said nothing, just climbed into the truck with a serene expression on her face.

Uh-oh. Was the silence hiding her disappointment? Caleb closed the door and went back to his side of the truck, the wheels in his head turning. If she didn't get the loan, they'd figure something out. Maybe they could sell things online. Run errands. Heck, maybe she could do Uber or Lyft for the locals. Maybe his Uncle Ennis would need an assistant for a brief while. Maybe—

Amy squealed and threw her arms around his neck, her grip chokingly tight.

Caleb patted her back, letting her squeeze. "That's good, I take it?" he managed.

"I got it!" she told him excitedly, releasing his neck. Her

hands slid to his chest and she beamed at him as if she'd won the lottery. "He said my credit rating was practically nonexistent so I couldn't get a loan."

He frowned. "That's . . . bad, then?"

"But!" She pulled the paperwork out and showed him. "The bank is doing a program where you can get a credit card and pull money from it like cash. The interest rate is horrific and it's going to take me years to pay it back." But she smiled so broadly that he knew she didn't care. "The bottom line is, I have the ability to move whenever I want."

"And do you want to? I'll support you no matter what you decide."

"I know you will." She reached over and squeezed his hand. "I love the new apartment, though. It's not perfect, but I think it'll be wonderful. So I do want to break my lease and move. It'll mean a bit more of a drive in to work, but on the plus side, it'll also mean Greg can't wander into my bedroom."

"That's a big damn plus."

She laughed, the sound so light and happy that it filled him with joy. "It is."

He smiled at her, his beautiful, sweet Amy. He loved that she was so happy. So in control of what she wanted. She wasn't going to let anything stop her. It didn't matter that the bank's loan had awful interest rates. To her, it represented freedom, and she was willing to pay extra for that. "So, what now? Do we show up at Greg's place and give him hell?"

She squeezed his hand, then dragged it onto her thigh as if it belonged there. "Actually, no. I don't want to deal with him today. Tomorrow, maybe. Or after the paperwork is signed at the other apartment. It doesn't all have to be done at once, you know? Today, I think I'd just like to hang out together."

"In that case, you want your final day of presents?"

Amy looked over at him in surprise. "Final day?"

"Yeah, I had a big production set up for you the other day, when we broke up."

"You did?" Her eyes got wide. "What is it?"

He buckled his seat belt and backed the truck out of the parking space in front of the bank, turning and heading toward the edge of town, toward the distant hills where the Swinging C Ranch was nestled. "Horseback-riding lessons. Figured my independent woman would want to learn everything she could, including how to saddle and ride a horse."

Amy's newest squeal of delight and hug nearly ran him off the road.

EPILOGUE

One Year Later

It was the night of the Christmas Carnival, and Santa was nowhere to be found.

Amy had promised to meet Caleb at the school in costume. He was Santa again this year, but they hadn't ridden together to the carnival. He had to help with some broken equipment over at the ranch, but he promised to meet her at the school. He'd *promised*. It wasn't like Caleb to be late for something, but he'd been awfully distracted earlier that morning.

She wasn't entirely sure why. The upcoming holiday? They'd finished their Christmas shopping early, and dozens of wrapped gifts sat under the tree at Amy's apartment, waiting for Christmas Day. She'd even managed to sneak a couple extra gifts in there for Caleb to unwrap, even though they'd sworn they weren't getting each other anything for Christmas.

To heck with that. She'd gotten him a digital tablet so he could read books electronically, and a few gift cards for online book purchases. It had cost her a pretty penny, but that was what credit cards were for. Hers were manageable now, thanks to the alimony payments that now came on time. She'd hired a lawyer in the New Year, just as promised, and all it had taken was the threat of legal pursuit and Blake had caved. He'd sent the missing payments and hadn't missed one since. Last she heard, he was dating some eighteen-year-old.

She didn't care. That wasn't part of her life anymore.

The payments were going to end soon, though. Alimony didn't last forever, just long enough to help her get on her feet. And that was fine, too. Amy had used the payments to get her new apartment and some decent furniture, but now that she was caught up on her bills, she found she didn't need the money as much as she'd thought. Amy had been saving most of it for the next place to live.

She wanted a house.

More than that, she wanted a house with Caleb.

They'd been dating for more than a year now, and she'd never been happier. Amy adjusted her itchy, curly, white Mrs. Claus wig on her head as she peered down the decorated hall, looking for her man. She loved Caleb more with every day that passed. He'd never made her feel trapped or worthless. He'd just quietly supported her, and even when they argued—usually over stupid, small things—he never attacked. He just disagreed. Even arguments with Caleb weren't all that bad.

He really was the perfect man, and she adored him. He'd been careful to give her her space, helping her move into her apartment and not complaining even when it was a longer drive to visit her. He still came by almost every single day, and most nights he stayed at her place, or she stayed at his.

Amy liked her independence, but she liked being with Caleb more, and when it came time for him to leave at night, she was the one demanding that he stay.

Now she wished she'd fought harder to get him to go to the school with her. Amy checked her phone. Ten minutes before Santa's Workshop was scheduled to open, and the children were already lining up. The halls of the school were crowded, and she waved at familiar faces and parents even as she tried to look past them, searching for a familiar bearded face.

"You look cute," a voice to her side said. "Maybe we should try some silver dye the next time you come in to get your hair cut."

Amy adjusted the wire-rimmed costume glasses on her face and beamed at Becca. "Is it a good look?"

"The best," Becca swore, huffing to her side. Her friend was very, very pregnant and her hands were supporting her rounded belly as she waddled forward. Hank had his hand on his wife's shoulder protectively. He wasn't smiling, but she knew enough about the Watson brothers now that it didn't bother Amy. They were just a gruff type.

Amy smiled at him anyhow. "Have you seen your brother? Caleb's supposed to be here for you know what." She tilted her head in the direction of Santa's chair.

He shook his head.

"Boy, this carnival sure is growing, isn't it?" Becca said. "I just saw Cass and Annie heading for the Cake Walk. And Sage is handing out tickets at the pie-throwing booth. I have to admit, I was tempted to throw a pie at Jason, but then I keep thinking of all the laundry poor Sage would have to do."

"The carnival is growing," Amy agreed absently, trying not to look too distracted. "My class is almost twice the size it was last year."

"And yoga class is full," Becca agreed.

Amy nodded. She and Layla and Becca took yoga together—or they used to. Now Becca didn't do much and it was just Layla and Amy, but they had other friends in class. It was always a fun time. Amy wasn't even mad that Becca had bailed on the classes—she was too envious of Becca's pregnancy. Her friend had gained weight with the baby, but oh man, was she glowing. And her husband positively hovered over her, as if she were made of fragile glass.

Amy's biological clock had definitely started ticking. She pictured herself with a baby in her arms, Caleb hovering protectively over her, and sighed. That was further out in the future. She'd fought so hard for her "freedom" that she suspected Caleb didn't even have marriage on his radar. Not that she was dying to get married again. It was just . . . she knew it'd be okay if it was with Caleb.

He was her happily ever after, ring or not.

A big, heavy arm slung over her shoulder. "I didn't know you and my brother were into role-play. That's kinky."

Amy squirmed out from under Jack's heavy arm and poked him in the side. "Can you keep it down? There are children here!"

"Sorry." Jack's grin told her he wasn't all that sorry. Incorrigible brat of a man that he was, Amy couldn't help but smile back. "Where's Santa?"

"That's the question, isn't it?" Amy crossed her arms over her chest, shifting against the uncomfortable duct-taped bra that kept her breasts from being too prominent in the costume. "He's supposed to meet me here."

Hank coughed. His face turned red, and he pounded on his chest.

Becca turned and gave him a little push. "Why don't you

go give Libby some more tickets? You know she's probably already gone through the ones she has."

He nodded, disappearing into the crowd.

Becca just shook her head, smiling. "Libby swore she's going to win the biggest prize the games give away."

"If anyone can, it's her," Amy replied, watching as Jack wove away into the crowd as well, disappearing once more. With his hat on and from a distance, he looked heartbreakingly like her Caleb. But . . . Caleb wouldn't be here in jeans and plaid and wearing a cowboy hat. He was supposed to be here as Santa. She bit her lip and looked at her phone again. No texts. No calls. No word at all. "I'm worried, Becca. I haven't seen or heard from Caleb all afternoon."

"Oh, honey. I'm sure he's on his way." Becca rubbed her belly absently. "Maybe go look for him? He might not have realized where Santa's Workshop was being held at. Maybe he took a wrong turn when he got to the carnival."

"But it's in the same place that we were at last year," Amy said, bewildered. "He knows where this is. Why would he get lost?"

"You know men." Becca shrugged. "I'm gonna go find myself a seat."

Amy anxiously looked at the forming line, at Miss Lindsey, the new fourth-grade teacher, who was manning the camera. She didn't look worried at all—in fact, she looked excited for some reason. Didn't she realize they had no Santa? "I'm going to go look around real quick," she told Miss Lindsey. "I'll be right back."

"Go on," Miss Lindsey said. "I'm just going to fiddle with my camera." And she giggled.

Perhaps Miss Lindsey had been hitting some holiday

punch too hard, Amy thought sourly as she headed down one of the crowded halls. It was filled with parents and teachers and children of all ages, and Christmas decorations dripped from every surface possible. "White Christmas" played over the loudspeakers, and in the distance, "The Bunny Hop" began to play, a sign that the Cake Walk was in full swing. Gosh, where was Caleb? She was getting so worried. It wasn't like him to just not call.

Her heart hammered. There was fresh snow on the ground. Surely he hadn't gotten into an accident, had he?

Jack passed by again, talking to her friend Layla. Amy grabbed his arm and pulled him aside. "Jack, I'm worried. Caleb hasn't called and he's about to be late."

"Huh." He scratched at his short beard. "I thought I saw him go in your classroom."

"He did? Why?"

Jack shrugged. "I dunno. That's where I saw him last."

Okay, that was strange. Maybe he'd gone in there to change? Amy murmured an apology at Jack and hurried toward her classroom. Thank goodness she'd gotten new boots for the costume. They weren't as fancy as the others—just plain black—but at least she could walk quickly and not murder her feet. She headed into her silent classroom, opening the door. The lights were out, the room just as empty as she'd suspected. "Caleb?"

To her surprise, the closet door opened a touch. "In here."

Relief flooded her . . . followed by bewilderment. "Caleb, what the heck are you doing? Are you changing?"

"Not exactly." His voice sounded muffled.

She opened the closet door, surprised to see that the lights were off inside—and let out a yelp of surprise when he pulled her into his lap. "Caleb! What the heck?" She flipped the light on and gasped at his appearance. "Why are you so sweaty? Are you sick?"

Her handsome boyfriend was wearing most of his Santa costume. He had the stuffed belly and overcoat on, and the pants, but the beard and hat were nowhere to be found. Instead, Caleb's dark hair was touched with sweat and his face was flushed. Worried, Amy put her hand to his forehead. He felt a little hot, but how hot did people normally feel?

"I'm just . . . having a hard time." He tugged her closer and buried his face against her chest, then lifted his head. "Why are your breasts so hard?"

She laughed, her hands going to his shoulders. "I told you I had to tape my boobs down. Remember?"

"It's a crime against humanity," he muttered, holding her tightly.

"Why are you having a hard time?" She ran her fingers through his hair, not caring that it was sweaty and damp. This was her Caleb. She loved everything about him. "Are you nervous, babe? You were awesome last year. It's little kids. You know you'll kill it the moment you put that beard on." It was still fascinating to her that someone so utterly confident could have moments of sheer panic. It usually happened around strangers, and she always knew when Caleb was uncomfortable because he'd clam up and say nothing . . . or start mixing his words up. It was charmingly endearing, but it also made her ache for him.

"Not worried about the kids," he said, resting his head against her flattened breasts. "Just . . . I've been thinking."

She froze. "Thinking about what?" Her voice came out strained despite her effort to make it light and carefree.

"This." He pulled a small box out of his pocket and held it up to her.

Amy sucked in a breath. It was a small velvet box, the size that would hold a ring. Oh god. Was this . . . ? A brilliant smile crossed her face. He was proposing? Joy rushed through her.

She opened the box . . . and burst into laughter at the sight of the house key pillowed where a ring should have been. "A key, huh?"

"A key to my heart?" he teased, giving her an awkward smile.

She slid her arm around his neck, settling into his lap. "I'm not sure why that makes you so nervous, babe. We've been together for a year now. In all that time I don't think you've slept alone in your bed for more than a week. Aren't we past getting nervous over keys?"

"Does that mean you say yes?" He tilted his head, looking up at her.

Amy chuckled. "You know I'd say yes to you for everything. I love you, Caleb."

He gazed up at her solemnly. "You would, huh?"

"I would."

"In that case . . ." He pulled a second box out of his pocket and held it out to her. "Will you marry me?"

She held her breath, not entirely sure this wasn't another joke. It wasn't like Caleb to be cruel, though. With trembling hands, she took the box from him and opened it. This time, there was a ring inside. It was beautiful, a golden band twining about a small teardrop-shaped diamond. She didn't care that it wasn't enormous or ungodly expensive like the one Blake had gotten her. This was from Caleb—her Caleb—and that was all that mattered. "Oh," she breathed out, finally.

"I know it's early," he told her solemnly. "I know you want your freedom, and I would never hold you down or make you do something you didn't want to do. I just want you to know that I've loved you from the moment I first saw you, Amy Mckinney, and I'll hold that ring for as long as I need to. You don't have to take it right now—"

"Yes," she interrupted, excited. "Yes. Yes!"

A bright smile broke across his face. "You're sure? I don't want to rush you—"

"Yes!" she said again, flinging her arms around his neck and hugging him. "It's not too early at all. It's perfect, Caleb. I love you!"

"I love you, too, baby," he murmured, then kissed her long and hard. After a moment, he broke away and grinned. Then he bellowed, "She said yes!"

A cheer erupted outside the coat closet door.

Amy's jaw dropped. "You . . . didn't."

"I might have." He got to his feet, slid her off his lap. "Shall we go say hello?"

They opened the closet door together, and immediately a camera went off. Amy blinked at the flash, and then she saw Miss Lindsey, grinning and clearly in on things. Behind her were dozens of people—from Jack and Layla to Sage and her husband Jason. There was the yoga instructor, her fellow teachers, and Becca and Hank. Uncle Ennis stood in the back, along with others she knew from around town. People she'd gotten to know. People she'd gotten to love.

All of them were in on this. All of them knew exactly why Caleb—her wonderful, sweet Caleb—had been late to his Santa appointment.

He was busy setting all this up. He'd planned all of it. He knew how much community meant to Amy, and he'd made sure that everyone she knew and loved was here to see their moment.

"Merry Christmas, love," Caleb whispered in her ear.

Truly, he'd given her the world.

Keep reading for a sneak peek
at the next Wyoming Cowboys romance

THE BACHELOR
COWBOY

Coming January 2021 from Jove!

W ell, ain't you the prettiest sight," Hank drawled as Jack showed up at the barn that morning. The oldest Watson brother pulled a dollar out of his pocket and held it up. "Can I bid on you, Prince Charming?"

At his side with a pitchfork, Caleb snickered.

"Shut the hell up, both of you," Jack grumbled. He rubbed a hand over his jaw, feeling a little self-conscious. "I just came to tell you two that I'm heading out and I'll be back later."

"Did you shave for us?" Caleb teased. "You shouldn't have. I like my men hairy."

"I'll be sure and tell Amy that," Jack shot back. In fact, he had shaved. Was feeling a little foolish about it, too. It was just . . . he knew he had a pretty face, and in the last while, he'd let his beard get bushy. He figured if he was going to be in a bachelor auction, he'd let his vanity take over.

Jack Watson was gonna be the best-damn-looking Valentine's charity bachelor Painted Barrel had ever seen.

So yeah, he'd shaved his face clean of the big, hairy winter beard even though it was still cold out. He'd put on his favorite black cowboy hat. Put on a tighter-fitting black button-up and some tight jeans that hugged his ass. Boots. The works. Was it a little vain? Sure.

Did he look amazing and ready to break some elderly hearts? Absolutely.

"You're just jealous that you don't look as good as me," Jack teased his brothers, tipping his hat back. "Besides, I have to look like I'm worth at least a couple hundred bucks to the ladies that are showing up at this thing. I can't have Clyde beat me in the bachelor auction."

Hank stared at him. "Old Clyde? From Price Ranch?"

"Yeah."

His big, bearded older brother stared at him. His mouth twitched, and then he snickered. "I can't believe Clyde's your competition."

"Oh, believe it." Jack shrugged. "Word is that Hannah's bringing her wallet and she's gonna spend a fortune on him."

"And you're dressing up for this?" Caleb asked, a dubious look on his face.

"Well, yeah. Amy and Becca asked me to do this. I might as well go all out." He pointed at his brothers. "And you two owe me big."

Hank scowled in his direction. "Why the heck would we owe you anything?"

"Because it's your damn girlfriend"—he pointed at Caleb—"and your wife"—he pointed at Hank—"that are running this ridiculous show. They're the ones that guilted me into doing this instead of helping out around here."

"Maybe you'll get lucky," Caleb offered. "Maybe some local angel with nice boobs will bid on you."

Hank just looked as if he was trying not to laugh.

Jack was pretty sure that the odds of any local angel showing up to this Valentine's auction were pretty slim. Or his angel would be gray-haired and old enough to be his nana, not his date.

Now that he was thinking about it, maybe he shouldn't have shaved. Jack rubbed his naked jaw again. *Charity,* he reminded himself. *This is for charity and for your sister-in-law and for Amy. You aren't doing it because you're expecting to score.*

It's charity. Nothing more.

I can't believe you brought your crochet to the auction," Amy hissed at Layla as they sat at the numbered table.

"Believe it, sister." Layla hooked another loop in the scarf she was making and shrugged. "Mrs. Kilpatrick brought hers."

"She's ninety."

"So? She's still here to buy a bachelor. Like me."

"Yes, but . . ." Amy protested, and then sighed. "It just seems weird, that's all."

"The weirder it is, the more I like it." Layla did a few more loops, concentrating on her project. In a way, it helped her calm down. She was incredibly nervous—and sweaty—at the thought of having to bid on a guy at the auction today. She knew she was the backup plan and hopefully it wouldn't be necessary. Maybe several ladies looking for love would show up with fat wallets and make this charity shindig a success.

Layla had her suspicions, though.

For one, the room wasn't more than half full. The Painted Barrel Animal Helpers Committee had decorated the gymnasium at the high school in all manner of construction paper hearts and pink garlands. There were pink and red flowers at every round table, and white tablecloths to add a touch of romance. There was a volunteer DJ (who looked like he was fourteen) putting on romantic music, and pink balloons filled the room. Each table had cute stationery and glitter stamps so you could write a love note for your valentine. There were heart-shaped cookies with bright red frosting and Layla had already eaten two of them. It was all really cute.

Problem was, no one was there.

Oh sure, the elderly bingo-hall folks had shown up, but they hadn't quite come in the numbers that Amy and Becca had expected. Maybe word hadn't gotten out. Maybe there was a football game on. Maybe people were wanting to do other things with their Valentine's Day than bid on a bachelor, but whatever the reason, the situation was looking pretty grim.

Layla hooked faster, her hands sweaty and nervous. "So how many bachelors did you end up with?"

Amy looked miserable. "Eleven. We had another last-minute drop. Turned out his girlfriend lost her dentures and didn't want to come out in public without them. Not that I blame her, but it just means less money for the charity." She twisted her hands in her lap.

"We could both buy a bachelor," Layla suggested. "I can spot you the money."

"I think we have bidders for the others," Amy said, her gaze roaming the curtained stage like the most impatient stage mom ever. "But if we don't hit our goal, I might have to take you up on that."

Layla glanced around. "Where's Becca?"

"She's coordinating props and making sure they're all fed."

Do . . . what? Layla wasn't entirely sure she'd heard that right and meant to ask, but a woman with a steely gray beehive and an absolutely glittering dress pushed her walker up to their table and sat down. She smiled at them. "Hello, girls."

"Oh man, I love your dress," Layla told her sincerely. "Were we supposed to dress up?" She glanced down at her worn black cardigan over a gaming T-shirt and jeans. Her hair was in her usual bun and she wasn't wearing makeup other than a slick of tinted lip gloss. Maybe she should have dressed up, but she was trying to throw a vibe into the universe: if she didn't look like a hot piece, she wouldn't need to win a man at auction.

"Honey, when you're my age, you take any excuse to put on fancy clothes." The woman chuckled. "I'm Cora."

"Layla," she said, offering her hand. "This is Amy."

Amy beamed at her. "Thank you for coming, Cora. Do you have your eye on anyone in particular?"

"All of them," Cora said with a sassy wink, and Layla decided she wanted to be Cora when she grew up. She patted her little spangly coin purse. "I'm going to bid on all of the bachelors because no one should go home alone."

"That's amazing." Amy clutched at her chest.

"Total baller cougar move," Layla agreed, and Cora just chuckled and waved a hand in the air.

The lights flashed and went down and the music stopped. A microphone clicked on and when the lights flicked back up, Sage Cooper-Clements came out on stage. She was wearing a bright red sweater dress and beamed at everyone. "Thank you so much for coming out to support the Painted Barrel Animal Helpers Committee. This committee was founded in order to provide our town with a place for stray animals to stay in safety. As you all know, since we're on the small side"—she paused for the inevitable chuckles—"we don't have very many municipal buildings. Our library is in the water department, as is city hall and my office and . . . well, pretty much every city job imaginable." She grinned, dimpling. "But if we raise enough money today, we're going to add on to the municipal building and make a place for our furry friends. To show you just who we're building this addition for, each of our bachelors is going to come out with a dog that is currently being housed with volunteers until we can find him or her the perfect forever home. So you can not only bid on a bachelor today, but you can bid on a dog, too."

Polite applause filled the room.

"But I don't want to stand up here and talk to you all day. We're here for the men, right?"

More polite applause.

Oh god, Layla was secondhand embarrassed for poor Sage, having to try to pep up this mostly empty room. Seriously, why were there so many tables? Painted Barrel wasn't a huge town, and if half of it had shown up, Layla wasn't sure if the gym would be full then. This seemed like a lot for just eleven bachelors to be auctioned.

As if she could read Layla's mind, Amy leaned over, a worried look on her face. "We were supposed to team up with another town to do this but they fell through on us." She bit her lip. "I can't believe it's been so hard to pull a charity together."

"I know, you'd think people would want the tax deductions, am I right?" Layla joked.

Amy batted at her arm. "Very funny."

Well, to Layla it was.

"We'll start the bidding at five dollars for each guy," Sage said. "And we'll go in increments of fives until there's a winner. You're bidding on each gentleman and his particular skill set. The person that wins their bachelor will coordinate with him for the 'date' of their choosing. Good luck to all the ladies out there." The music started again and Sage exited off the stage and went to a podium just at the edge. "We'll start with bachelor number one . . . Garvis Newsome!"

The music from *Magic Mike* started playing—"Pony" by Ginuwine.

Layla groaned and picked up her crochet again. "I am *sweating*, Amy. This is so mortifying for these men."

Garvis strutted out onto the stage. He had the skinny, bowed legs of a man that had spent most of his life in the saddle, and a weathered face with a white handlebar mustache that Layla had only seen in memes. She knew a lot of people in Painted Barrel, but Garvis was not one of them. He tipped his cowboy hat back and then started to do a little dance. She wasn't sure if it was the Cabbage Patch or a dab, but it was making her incredibly uncomfortable. As he strutted forward in his red-and-black-plaid shirt and leather vest, he carried the leash of a very confused copper dachshund. The wiener dog gamely trotted after the cowboy, and sat the moment they hit the middle of the stage and scratched at his ear.

"Garvis is a much-in-demand farrier," Sage called out in a chirpy voice. "Do your horses need a little TLC? Do you need a little TLC yourself? Then take a good look at Garvis! He's our first bachelor for the day. Let's start the bidding, shall we?"

"One dollar!" Cora called out in a reedy voice.

There was a ripple of laughter. Sage smiled, and then

leaned into her microphone. "The bids start at five dollars, everyone."

"Two dollars!" Cora yelled.

Layla leaned over to Amy. "I am totally nervous-sweating right now."

"Oh god, I am, too," Amy whispered back. She clutched at Layla's hand, making it impossible for Layla to do more crochet. Not that she could, anyhow—her hands were so clammy from secondhand embarrassment that the yarn was losing all tension. She set it down on the table for now and let Amy squeeze her hand in support.

"Five dollars," someone called out.

Garvis clapped his hands with delight, startling the dog at his side. It barked at him, and the crowd laughed once more.

Amy buried her face in her hands.

"Surely someone can bid more than five dollars?" Sage asked, a worried smile on her face as she gazed out at the crowd.

"Two dollars," Cora called again. No one laughed this time.

Oh god. Here was where Layla took one for the team. She squeezed Amy's hand and then raised her free one into the air. "Two hundred dollars," Layla called.

The room erupted with noise. Layla thought Sage was going to come over the podium and kiss her with gratitude.

"All right," the mayor called happily. "We have a bid for two hundred dollars! Sounds like someone needs a big, handsome farrier to come over for an afternoon!"

Onstage, Garvis flexed.

"Two hundred fifty," called another voice, and Layla breathed a sigh of relief. She wasn't even sure what a farrier was, but if it had something to do with horses, he was out of luck. Layla had a house cat and that was it.

Luckily, the bidding started to rise in earnest, and there was a lot of laughter and good spirits as the money slowly escalated. When it hit seven hundred fifty, the bidding came to a standstill, and an elderly woman jumped up with glee when she was announced the winner. The people at her table cheered, and even Garvis looked thrilled. Layla remembered that Amy had mentioned something about most of the bachelors being "bought" by their girlfriends anyhow. Even so, it looked like everyone was having fun. Garvis bounded off the stage and handed off the wiener dog's leash, exchanging it for a bouquet of bright red roses, which he presented to his new date.

That was a little disappointing. Layla had kinda been rooting for the wiener dog. He looked so small and confused up on the stage next to the cavorting cowboy.

"Okay," Amy breathed. "Seven hundred fifty isn't bad. That's not bad at all. If they all go for that much, we just might hit our goal."

Layla leaned over, the accountant in her taking over. "Actually, you'd still be seventeen hundred and fifty dollars short—uh, never mind." She bit off her own words at Amy's frustrated glare. Boy, nobody had a sense of humor when it came to this auction.

At the other side of the table, poor Cora looked depressed and Layla felt so bad for her. Maybe she hadn't heard the rules and that was why she'd bid so low. Layla reached out and touched the other woman's arm. "Don't you worry, Miss Cora. We'll get you a bachelor today, I promise."

Cora giggled. "I was bidding on the dog."

A woman after Layla's own heart.

* * *

The auction rolled a little more smoothly after that. The next few bachelors all sold for several hundred dollars each, though not as much as Garvis. Each man came out with a cute dog, strolled around the stage while Sage extolled their virtues, and then the auction would begin in earnest. Cora bid a dollar each time, and Layla wasn't sure if Cora was just the world's oldest troll and having fun at their expense, or if she genuinely thought her dollar bid was legit.

Layla bid two more times herself, when no one was quick to bid right out of the gates. The first time, it was for Mr. Johnson, who she always ran into at the grocery store. And then she bid for old Mr. Hill, who mowed lawns, because he got peed on by the puppy he was holding, and because, well, Layla's lawn could use a little work. And it was all for charity anyhow.

She figured if she was having to buy her love, she might as well get some weeding out of it. But she was quickly outbid on him, and really, that was fine.

Cora turned and looked at Layla with a pitiful expression. "You and I aren't having much luck today, are we?"

"It's okay," Layla told her reassuringly. "We're bound to get lucky at some point. Did you have your eye on someone in particular?"

"Well," Cora thought, and sighed. "I still keep thinking about the fat wiener from before."

Layla blinked.

"The dog," Amy whispered behind her hand, trying to hold her smile.

Oh riiight. The wording was just too perfect. Layla bit back a snicker and cleared her throat. "You know, Miss Cora, we can check in after the auction and see if the dog is available to adopt. That's supposed to be the point of this whole thing—to find homes for stray animals that need some love."

Cora brightened. "Do you think so, dear? I've been saving all month and I'd love a companion." She fingered her two wrinkled dollars that she kept bidding over and over again.

Layla's heart broke a little. Was that all that Cora had as her savings or was this just more of her confusion? Or her trolling? Either way, she vowed that she would make sure that Cora had a dog in her arms by the time she left, even if Layla had to pay for it. She glanced over at Amy, but Amy was chewing on her lip, writing numbers down on a napkin and desperately trying to do the math as the next bachelor came out onstage. Layla had done the numbers in her head, and they were still close to three thousand dollars short of the goal. That had to be disappointing for her friends, who'd worked so hard to pull this together. There were still two bachelors left, with the second to last being bid on right now. He had a pit bull puppy in his arms and his girlfriend was bidding on him . . . but it wouldn't be enough money. Even if Layla bought the last bachelor due to lack of bids (which didn't look as if it'd be the case given how the other auctions had gone), it wouldn't be enough. Maybe Layla could do some research, look up some tax incentives for the city that might make up the difference—

Amy grabbed her arm as the bidding continued. "Don't look now," she hissed. "But your mother is here."

Every bit of Layla went cold. Janet Schmidt was here? At the auction? This day was going from bad to much, much worse. "Please tell me you're joking."

"She's near the door. Looking for you." Amy patted her arm. "I'd tell you to hide in the bathroom but we both know she'd probably find you."

She would. Janet had been known to peek under stall doors looking for Layla in the past. "She thinks I'm here to bid on a boyfriend," Layla whispered as her mother caught sight of her and waved.

"Lucky for you Jack is up next," Amy said, patting her hand.

Oh lord. And all the "bachelors" so far were more Janet's age than Layla's. Her mother would sense a plot for sure, and then she'd get bombarded with all kinds of nagging and guilt and her weekend would be ruined. Layla glanced over and Janet raised a hand, waving.

"Are you bidding, ma'am?" Sage asked from the podium.

"I'm just here to see my daughter. She's going to bid on a man," Janet called out loudly, trotting over to Layla's table in ridiculously high heels.

Cringe. Cringe twice. Layla kept smiling even though the urge to flee was running rampant through her system. Why did Janet always do this to her? Janet was the mom that showed up in the low-cut bandage dress at Layla's school dances. She was the mom that flirted with the teachers. The mom that always made sure the attention was on Janet and not Layla.

Of course she'd show up to a bachelor auction to try and nose in and see what her daughter was up to. Part of it was Janet being an overbearing mom. Part of it was Janet being bored. And part of it was Janet wanting a slice of the action. Her mom would absolutely not be above flirting with a guy that Layla was interested in. She'd done it in the past. Was it shitty? Yes. Was it something Layla expected at this point? Also yes.

So she shouldn't have been surprised to see her mother. Yet somehow, Layla always was. She always expected Janet to be a bit more . . . mom-like. Never happened.

"There you are," Janet cooed. She thumped into the empty chair next to Layla and set her Chanel bag on the table, blocking Layla's view of Cora entirely. "How goes the bachelor hunting, Layla-belle?"

"It's just fine, Mom. What are you doing here?" God, even her tone sounded sulky and petulant, like she was fourteen again.

Janet licked her thumb and tsked, reaching forward and smoothing a flyaway hair at Layla's temples. "Honey, did you even fix your hair this morning? I thought you were trying to get a man."

"It's fine, Mom."

"Is it?" Janet gave her a wintry little smile that said she didn't agree. She glanced over at Amy and cooed at her. "Hello, sweetheart. Are you bidding on a man, too?"

Amy just chuckled. "No, my boyfriend's working today."

"Look at that," Janet said in a low voice, leaning in toward Layla. "She's got a boyfriend *and* her hair looks fantastic. What a coincidence?"

"Ugh, Mom. Please. Just stop it."

Janet raised a be-ringed hand in the air. "I'm just saying, Layla-belle. You know I just want you to be happy."

"Do we have any more bids?" Sage called. When no one else answered, she banged her gavel on the podium. "Sold, for five hundred thirty dollars. Congratulations, you two!"

Everyone at the table clapped politely. Layla noticed that Amy added that to the math on her napkin, but it wasn't enough. Unless the final bachelor pulled in twenty-five hundred dollars, it wouldn't be what the city needed to make the project a success. And no one had gone for more than seven hundred fifty that day.

Janet leaned over to Layla, still clapping. "That last one was a bit gray. Are they all older?" She gave her daughter an interested look. "Should I find myself a sugar daddy? Are any of them rich?"

"Mom," Layla groaned.

Amy just laughed. "I don't think any of them are exactly wealthy, Mrs. Schmidt. Everyone's bidding on the total package—the dogs, the skills the bachelor can provide, and for charity."

"Well, that's disappointing," Janet said brightly, then leaned over to her daughter. "Besides, I already have a sugar daddy."

Layla groaned again and buried her face in her hands.

"Oh, stop being such a baby," Janet said. "I'm allowed to have needs."

"It doesn't mean I want to hear about them."

"Well, who else am I going to tell?" She sat on the edge of her chair, peering at the stage. "So where is your man? Which one is he?"

Amy shot Layla a curious look.

Right. She'd told her mother she was going to be bidding on a guy she liked here. Looked like she was going to have to bid on Jack Watson either way. With luck, someone would outbid her quickly and she could feign disappointment and then this whole sordid mess would be over. She'd take out her feelings on some pastries and an evening of cross-stitching pithy sayings about narcissists and feel better by morning. "He's coming up soon."

"Well, while we're waiting, I brought you something." Janet tossed her bright red hair and reached into her purse. She pulled out a folder of papers and slid it toward Layla, then offered her a pen. "You said you'd notarize these for me, right? I thought I'd bring them over."

"I didn't say I'd notarize anything, Mom." Janet was a master at the art of pushiness. She pretended like you'd already agreed to something, hoping you'd forget and cave. "What is this?"

"Just those documents that we talked about. For the property."

Layla flipped open the folder. There were maps, weather charts, and discussions about flooding. Pictures of the land. A long, detailed letter explaining that to the party's best knowledge, no flooding had occurred since ownership had transferred to Janet Schmidt's hands. Well, that was a flat-out lie. Rather than create a scene, Layla closed the folder again. "I'll look at it later."

"Just do it fast," Janet said brightly. "I want to get that property on the market quick. If I sell by summer, I'm going to take a European cruise."

She opened her mouth to protest, but the microphone whined with feedback, gathering everyone's attention. A dog howled somewhere offstage.

"Sorry about that," Sage chirped into the mic. "Are we ready for our final bachelor? He's a good one!"

Amy grabbed Layla's arm in silent terror.

Right. This was the moment she'd promised she'd bid if no one else did. Janet grabbed Layla's other arm, no doubt thrilled to get a good look at her daughter's "man." Layla felt a little like she was trapped between two opposing forces.

The music started and the lights flickered. This time, the song was "Where Have All the Cowboys Gone" and a tall man strolled onto the stage with the same dachshund from before.

"One dollar!" Cora bellowed.

"Oh my," Janet murmured as Jack Watson swaggered onto the stage. Layla didn't say anything. Her tongue was glued to the roof of her mouth.

Because Jack Watson was an utterly gorgeous dream of

a man. It had been months since she'd seen him, and so
Layla had forgotten just how intimidatingly perfect he was.
He was tall, with broad shoulders, and seemed to take up
half the stage with his sheer presence. His cowboy hat and
clothing were entirely black, giving him a sinister, sexy
vibe. He had the wiener dog tucked under his arm like a
football, and scratched at the floppy copper ears with a big,
work-hardened hand.

He'd shaved, too. Layla had remembered a scruffy
beard—so incongruous with a man as gorgeous as him—
but it was gone now. Instead, she could see his chiseled jaw,
the full lips, the perfect nose that led up to thick, equally
perfect brows, and gorgeous dark eyes. He grinned out into
the crowd, and his teeth were as perfect as the rest of him.

"I'll bid on his package," Janet murmured, fanning herself.

"Mr. Watson is a ranch hand at the Swinging C," the
mayor called out, as if reading a bio. "He's a Virgo and a bit
of a romantic. Want to ride horseback into the mountains
for your date? This is your man. He's also good at helping
repair fences and working in the barn if that's more your
thing. Bid on him and you can discover what you've been
missing in your life without a big, strong cowboy."

"I know what I've been missing," Janet commented.

"Mom!"

"What are we bidding for our cowboy?" Sage asked.
"Shall we start?"

"ONE DOLLAR," Cora bellowed, disgruntled from her
tone of voice.

This would be so funny to Layla if she didn't have to be
part of it. As it was, the room got quiet, and her stomach
dropped. She remembered that Jack was a last-minute volunteer and had no significant other lined up to start the

bidding on him. Surely that was criminal. A man that perfect should have legions of women lined up to bid on him. As it was, she sucked in a deep breath and raised her hand.

"Five hundred dollars," Janet cried, bidding before Layla could get the chance.

What the hell?